SPICE
TRADE

SPICE TRADE

ERIK MAURITZSON

THE PERMANENT PRESS
Sag Harbor, NY 11963

For information, address:
The Permanent Press
4170 Noyac Road
Sag Harbor, NY 11963
www.thepermanentpress.com

Library of Congress Cataloging-in-Publication Data

Mauritzson, Erik, author.
  Spice trade / Erik Mauritzson.
  Sag Harbor, NY : The Permanent Press, [2017]
  ISBN 978-1-57962-496-5
    1. Detectives—Sweden—Fiction. 2. Mystery fiction.

PS3613.A88315 S65 2017
813'.6—dc23   2017008731

Printed in the United States of America

For Suzanne

1

Falling Girl

Weltenborg, Sweden

Friday, January 20, 8:12 p.m. She crawled along near the edge of the steep roof, the sharp-cornered, icy tiles cutting into her hands and knees, a biting wind laced with cold rain catching at her thin cotton slip. Gashes in her arms and legs bled from struggling through the broken attic window. The cold, and overwhelming fear, distracted her from the pain.

She tried not to look four stories below where rain-coated pedestrians hurried along the brightly lit, traffic-filled street as a fierce wind tried to pull umbrellas from their hands. She yelled to them, but her parched throat only produced a few throttled sounds.

Through squinting, tear-filled eyes, she could just make out the large chimney at the end of the roof. Braced against it she prayed she might somehow be able to attract attention. The girl crept slowly forward, her knees and palms slick with blood.

Her right hand slipped on the icy surface. Panicking, she tried to recover, fingers frantically scrabbling for a hold as her legs slid out from under her and over the roof edge, pulling her body along.

No one heard her strangled cry as she fell.

Directly across the street, Le Gourmand was crowded despite the rain beating down on the city. Loud voices and abrupt bursts of raucous laughter rang out from a group celebrating Friday at the long, dark mahogany bar.

Rudi, the owner and a friend, had found a window table for Walther Ekman and his wife, Ingbritt, in the quieter, elegant little dining room with its white damask, flowers, and candlelight.

Although it had now become a habit, their monthly night out had not started that way. It had been a conscious effort to break the daily routine long-married couples often fall into.

"This wine smells really good," Ekman said, as he inhaled and then raised his glass to Ingbritt.

Taking a sip from her glass, she said with a smile, "And tastes good too. You picked the right one, Walther."

Absorbed in their dinner, at first they'd seen nothing beyond the thick glass, but turning in her chair, Ingbritt noticed a crowd gathered across the street.

"I wonder what that's about," she said, staring out the window.

Looking outside, Ekman said, "Whatever it is someone will deal with it." It was the end of a stressful week and he was tired. He wanted to ignore whatever was going on, but as police chief superintendent he was never really off duty, much as he would have liked to be.

They saw Rudi heading for the door, curious to find out what was happening. A few minutes later he was back, and hurried to their table.

"I hate to interrupt your dinner, but I thought you'd want to know, Walther. A woman has fallen from a building across the way. An ambulance and the police are coming."

"I'd better take a look," Ekman said, frowning as he got up. He reached over to the coatrack with a resigned look at his wife. Ingbritt just nodded. Over thirty-five years together she'd seldom reproached Ekman for his work's frequent, unexpected interruptions. It was one of the reasons he loved her.

The steady rain had already slowed the heavy traffic, which now crawled as drivers peered curiously at the growing crowd on the sidewalk. Starting across the road, Ekman cautiously threaded a path between vehicles.

Using his six foot five, 270 pounds, he bulled through the outer ring of people around the girl's body, their necks craning to see over the heads of those closer to her.

"Stand back," he barked. "I'm a police officer. Stand back." Slowly, grudgingly, the throng parted, until he could make out the slender form sprawled on the wet pavement.

Shoving through the last circle of gawkers, Ekman knelt by her, ignoring the damp seeping into his trousers, and placed two thick fingers on her throat searching for the carotid artery. There was no pulse. She was young, probably early twenties, and had been pretty before her head smashed against the cement.

Ekman was surprised to see that she was naked under a sodden cotton slip bunched around her waist. Reaching over, his first impulse was to pull it down and cover her, but he stopped himself; he couldn't disturb the body before the forensic team arrived. He stood up and, looking over the crowd, saw two police officers running toward the scene.

People parted for the uniforms. When the officers saw Ekman standing beside the body they looked surprised and saluted.

"How did you get here so fast, Chief?" said the older of the two, a woman. "We just got the word a few minutes ago."

"I was across the street." He gestured toward the restaurant's brightly lit windows. "Move everyone back. And call for more officers to set up a perimeter."

They heard the wailing of a Klaxon and saw an ambulance coming toward them, its glaring strobe lights flashing, slowly advancing between vehicles that had begun to move aside.

As the officers urged the onlookers back, Ekman moved away and looked up at the building the girl had fallen from. A few faces had gathered at windows, peering down at the scene. We'll have to question everyone with a window facing this way, he thought, including those across the street.

None of the windows were open and the roof was steeply pitched. From where he was standing, he could see no way to get onto it. Where had she fallen from?

It was a puzzle, but one he didn't have to solve now. He took out his mobile and called his deputy, Chief Inspector Rapp, the duty officer that evening.

"Alrik, it's Walther. There's been a death, a young woman, fallen from a building at," he searched for the house number, "375 Vallgraven. Yes, I just happened to be having dinner across the street. This may be an accident or something worse. Two uniforms are on the scene and more are coming. We'll have to cordon off about half the block.

"We need a pathologist and crime scene officers out here now. You'd better alert public relations too. The press and TV will be here sooner than we want. And I'd like to have an inspector in charge, with at least two detectives. Is Gerdi Vinter working? Good. She'd be the right one to handle this. I'll be in Saturday. Have her brief me in the morning. Thanks."

Ekman walked back to the restaurant, and hanging up his dripping coat and hat, found that Ingbritt had already eaten most of her dinner.

"I didn't know how long you'd be, so I just went ahead," she said apologetically. "They're keeping the rest of your food warm for you in the kitchen." Their night out had become just one more evening lost to his work.

He sat down heavily. The sight of the girl's broken body had wiped away his appetite.

"How bad is it, Walther?"

"She's dead. We should know more tomorrow about how it happened and why."

"How old was she?"

"Young, somewhere in her early twenties, I'd say."

"What a terrible waste."

"Yes," he said, and left it at that. Young or old, a violent death was always a waste, but the younger the person, the more poignant it felt. Senseless deaths weighed heavier on him than ever. In thirty-one years on the force he'd become more, rather than less, affected by their visceral impact. If he ever became so hardened that he didn't react emotionally, he thought it would be past time to retire.

2

THE KEEPER

January 20, 9:50 p.m. The Keeper's assistant was worried. More than that, he was frightened.

He stood on the outer fringe of the crowd kept well back from the scene by the blue-and-white tape police barrier. A large, brightly lit tent now shielded the girl's body and glaring klieg lights illuminated the area. Technicians in white head-to-foot protective suits, glistening from the still falling rain, were moving from the tent to their evidence van and back again.

An ambulance sat at the curb and two attendants stood near it, waiting for the pathologist and forensic specialists to finish their work so they could move the body. A television mobile unit with large antennae on the roof was parked just behind the ambulance, and a reporter was talking with a woman who appeared to be in charge of the scene. She periodically interrupted his questions to direct the other officers.

Tired of stale sandwiches and pizza, the assistant had broken the rules and left to get a real meal in a Lebanese restaurant on the corner. He knew something was wrong just after he'd gotten back and heard the ambulance siren. Checking the closed-circuit TV and not seeing her, he unbolted the bedroom door.

The smashed chair, and the leg used to break the small window, were lying on the floor. He could see blood on the jagged edges of the remaining glass where she'd somehow managed to wriggle out onto the steeply pitched roof.

He hesitated at first, then called the Keeper; he didn't want to hear what the other man would say.

"I'd gone out for only a little while. I know I shouldn't have, but I'd just looked at the TV screen and she seemed to be sound asleep. She must have been faking and heard the door close. What should I do?"

Instructions were given in a curt voice. He would have to leave. There was no time to thoroughly sanitize the place before police, questioning tenants, knocked at the door.

He put the CCTV screen and video recorder in a cheap, battered suitcase, along with his spare shirt and a sports magazine. Going to the hall closet, he hurriedly got her clothes and shoes, and shoved them in the case.

In the bedroom, he untied the leather restraining straps at each corner of the bed and packed them inside. Then, lifting a picture on the wall, he took down a wireless, pinhole TV camera that he stowed with the other things. Looking in the adjoining bathroom, he grabbed her few toiletries. He glanced quickly around the apartment for anything he might have overlooked and then went out, locking the door.

Watching the busy technicians, he started when he felt a hand on his shoulder, and turned to see the handsome face of the Keeper.

"Come away, Ahmed. You don't want to be seen standing in the rain staring at them."

The two, Ahmed, stocky and dark, carrying a suitcase, the other, tall and blond, walked without speaking down the street and around the corner to a black Land Rover.

"We need to get to the farm and figure out what to do," the Keeper said as he started the engine, glancing over at the younger man.

"I screwed up," said Ahmed, looking down at his hands, as he twisted them nervously in his lap. "I'm really sorry."

"Don't worry about it. These things happen. We'll deal with it."

For the next two hours, they drove in silence broken occasionally by the Keeper's questions and Ahmed's mumbled replies. Accompanied by the swishing of wipers clearing lingering rain, they headed along increasingly narrow roads into the countryside north of Weltenborg and southwest of Stockholm.

Turning left onto a barely visible, muddy track, they slowed and continued on for another five minutes. Ahead of them, looming abruptly out of the darkness was a large barn, and a little distance away, a ramshackle, two-story wooden farmhouse with yellow light streaming from downstairs windows. Pulling into a side yard, they parked next to a panel truck, and walked around to the porch.

Going up creaking steps, the Keeper knocked on the door, which was unlocked and opened by a large, slab-faced, completely bald man who stepped aside to let them in.

"Is everything quiet, Gotz?" asked the Keeper.

"Yes," he replied. Looking over at Ahmed, he said, "How did it happen?"

Ahmed shrugged, dropping the suitcase by the door as he entered.

The Keeper said, "Let's have some coffee." He went through to the kitchen, and sat down at a table in the middle of the room. He gestured for Ahmed to join him as Gotz put two full mugs on the table, and then leaned against the rear wall, looking down at them.

As they sipped the steaming black coffee, the Keeper said, "What do you think our options are, Ahmed?"

"I don't know."

"They'll find out that you rented the apartment. And your fingerprints and DNA are all over it, right?"

"Yes," he replied in a subdued voice.

"Then they'll soon identify you, begin a search, and your name and picture will be in the papers and on TV. Isn't that so?"

"I guess."

"No guessing about it. It's inevitable. So what should we do?" the Keeper asked, his pale blond eyebrows raised inquiringly. "We can't let them get you." He leaned back in his chair.

"Maybe I should leave the country," Ahmed said, his eyes on the floor.

"That's a possibility. But when they can't find you in Sweden, they'll look elsewhere. These days, Europol and Interpol are all connected with local police. So this wouldn't go away; it would continue to be a major problem."

"I could hide here," he said, his eyes wandering around the room.

"For how long, Ahmed? Years? I don't think that's really feasible, do you?"

Ahmed shifted in his chair, glancing nervously first at the table and then the walls.

"Then what should I do?"

"It's not what you should do, it's what we must do to keep you safe from the police." Looking up at Gotz, who'd moved behind Ahmed, he nodded slightly.

Gotz whipped a thin, steel wire loop over Ahmed's head and around his neck, pulling hard on the wooden handles at each end. Ahmed half rose from his chair, grabbing frantically at the wire cutting deeply into his throat, his legs kicking wildly, knocking over his chair as he tried to breathe, then collapsed across the table, spilling the coffee mug. The dark liquid pooled on the table, dripping onto the cracked, white linoleum.

"It wouldn't have been worth the risk trying to get him out of the country. If he'd been caught, he'd have given them everything in a minute," said the Keeper as he stood, looking down at Ahmed. "It may create problems with his people in Marrakech, but we had no choice."

"None at all," said Gotz, bending down to pull out the garrote deeply embedded in Ahmed's neck. He took it over to the sink and carefully washed it and then his hands. Wiping the garrote with a kitchen towel, he folded it and shoved it into a pants pocket.

"You'll be able to take care of him?" the Keeper asked.

"I'll manage, although the ground's almost frozen. Probably out back, behind the barn."

"No, not here. At sea, would be better. From your boat near Halmstad."

"All right. It's late, but I'll do it tonight."

"Good. Drop him as far out as possible."

Wearing work gloves, they first took the CCTV equipment out of Ahmed's suitcase. Then Gotz removed Ahmed's clothing and pulled a paint-stained canvas tarp around the naked body. After tying rope tightly around and attaching the suitcase now filled with riprap from the ditch out front, they carried the heavy bundle between them to the panel truck. Gotz reached over and opened the rear doors and they shoved it in.

The Keeper glanced at his watch. It was almost midnight.

He stared at the other man. "We need to keep this between just the two of us."

"Of course," said Gotz, his face expressionless. He turned, climbed into the truck, and backed it out.

The Keeper put Ahmed's clothes in a paper bag; he'd burn them later in the trash barrel behind the house. Then he wiped down the kitchen table and floor, and set up the CCTV screen and recorder to see what had happened.

The girl lay face down, spread-eagled on the bed, naked under her partially pulled-up slip. She was gagged to stifle screams, her hands and feet bound tightly by straps to each corner of the bed. Pillows under her stomach pushed her buttocks up. The onscreen clock showed 7:18 p.m. The Keeper fast forwarded.

At seven thirty, the client came in and took his clothes off, folding them carefully over the chair, and neatly aligning his shoes and socks under it. Then getting on the bed, he climbed on top of her, and began slowly caressing her body. He pulled her slip all the way up and started to spank her, first lightly then harder, hearing her muffled groans as her buttocks became bright red. He turned her face toward him and saw sheer terror written on it at what was to come. He smiled.

The Keeper fast forwarded again.

He didn't care to watch; sex with women didn't interest him. He believed the client had insisted on a short, slender girl because he couldn't admit to himself that he really wanted a boy. The Keeper had no problem with his own orientation and would have been happy to provide a young male if that's what was wanted.

Their clients had wide-ranging tastes: some, like this one, wanted boy substitutes; a few, real teenage boys; others, the majority, wanted women of assorted sizes, shapes, and ages. Over the three years of their operation, they'd found what they needed primarily in Eastern Europe. They seldom used a Swede or any woman from Scandinavia. Too many unexplained missing persons from a small country with mostly unbribable police would have soon become a problem.

Despite diverse tastes, none of their clients were interested in willing whores of either sex. They were all alike in their need for a very special kind of excitement. Only real fear and total domination, not playacting, could provide the strong arousal they needed. Knowing the huge risks they were taking amplified the illicit thrill.

The Keeper's services were unique, and correspondingly costly.

It was thirty minutes later by the on-screen clock when he saw that the client had finished. Sated, he'd wiped himself with a towel, put on his clothes, and walked out of the room.

A few minutes later, Ahmed came in, released the bindings, and removed the gag. The girl got up slowly and turned around, sitting on the edge of the bed with her head hanging down facing his crotch. Ahmed opened his pants and took out his already hard penis. Putting his hands behind her head he forced her mouth toward him. Her face was a blank mask as he used her; then she fell back exhausted. Ahmed straightened his pants and left.

The Keeper wasn't upset by what Ahmed had done: the girl was an expected perk. But he was an imbecile not drugging her and tying her up again before he went out. It was just as well they'd gotten rid of him. He was a walking liability; besides, he'd never liked him. Now the police would be pushing their investigation into her very public death. All because of that stupid, stupid fool. They couldn't afford any more mistakes.

What a waste. It wasn't only current revenue, it was lost future profit from reselling her through Marrakech to their less particular Middle Eastern customers. Nordic girls like her were rare, especially thoroughly broken-in and tractable ones, and fetched a huge premium. The Keeper had been planning to ship her to Marrakech after this client grew tired of her, as he'd become bored with her predecessors when they'd become apathetic and weren't so obviously terrified.

She'd been exactly what the customer had ordered. He didn't want to travel to the farm like everyone else. He was so taken with her that he'd paid triple to have her brought to town where she'd be more accessible. He'd be upset now. We'll have to find him a replacement.

The Keeper smiled. With the videos we have, he'll be paying us forever no matter who we give him. But we don't want to push him, not yet; he's promised us more customers.

3

GERDI VINTER

Saturday, January 21, 8 a.m. It had been a long night and Gerdi Vinter's face was pale with fatigue. She sat in Ekman's office sipping her fourth coffee that morning as she summarized the night's investigation. They'd spoken to people on the street, in the building the girl had fallen from, and in the apartment houses across the way. No one had seen her until she fell.

Ekman stood at the windows while he listened, gazing out on Stortorget, the city's main square, its cobblestones gleaming from last night's freezing rain. He was wearing his usual somber office outfit: starched white shirt, vested black suit, and tie.

It was his silent memorial to Bernt Osterling, his longtime partner, murdered during a robbery twenty years before, while Ekman was on leave. He knew it was pointless, but somehow dressing this way on duty helped ease the still-lingering guilt at not having been there for Bernt.

"Preliminary examination showed she died on impact. We should know more by Monday after the autopsy. She narrowly missed a couple of people. It's a miracle no one else was hurt."

"Did you find where she fell from?"

"Yes. Scanning the building with binoculars, we located a small, broken window in an attic apartment on the fourth floor. Cuts on her shoulders and elsewhere showed she'd somehow squeezed through it onto the roof. At the apartment, no one responded to our knock, so thinking someone inside might be injured and couldn't answer, we broke in."

That was her excuse for not getting a warrant. Ekman had no problem with it. Trained as an attorney he knew what the law required, but wasn't perturbed when his detectives ignored legal niceties if it led to speedier justice for victims.

"There was no one there. Forensics spent the night going over the place and we should have their report soon."

Ekman turned to face her. "What was your impression?"

"There was very little furniture and no personal items. It looked like someone had hurriedly cleared out. The most interesting things were a bedroom door that could be bolted from the outside and a chair leg used on the window."

"Conclusion?"

"The woman was a prisoner and desperate. She got out by breaking the window. It was a tight squeeze even though she was very slender, with narrow shoulders and hips. The glass cut her as she struggled through. She only had a slip on, it was freezing, and she could see the roof was slippery and steep. What she was escaping from must have been much worse. Probably sexual abuse."

Ekman sat down heavily in his battered swivel chair. This could be a solitary rape, but it might be something more. He knew sexual abuse of women was widespread and human trafficking a growing cancer. Ekman had dealt with these cases before, but they turned his stomach. He despised the people who did this. To him, they were humanity's dregs, devoid of any redeeming empathy for their victims that he'd sometimes found in other criminals.

"What are your next steps?"

"Besides missing persons, we'll check fingerprint and DNA data bases and see if the autopsy and forensic reports help identify her. And we'll try to find out who rented the apartment. If he showed ID, there may be a copy in the rental agent's file. If not, we'll ask whoever dealt with him to sit down with our sketch artist."

"You're assuming it was a man?"

"Maybe I shouldn't, but that seems likely."

"I agree. Once you have a picture, see if anyone in the building, or adjoining buildings, recognizes him. Check local stores, bars, and garages. Maybe someone will know him.

"But first, Gerdi, go home and get some sleep so you can function. Tell Enar I want him to work with you on this and keep things going while you rest," he said, naming his assistant, Inspector Enar Holm. He knew that Gerdi and Enar already were more than a work team: they were living together.

Vinter stood up. She was shaky from exhaustion. "Thanks, Chief. I'll fill him in and then crash." Ekman looked after her retreating back. She and Enar were favorites of his.

Standing over the kitchen range, Enar was scrambling eggs in a pan while Gerdi sat at the table, sipping orange juice.

"You can brief me while you eat, and then it's off to bed," he said, putting a plate of eggs and buttered toast in front of her.

As she ate, Gerdi summarized what she'd told Ekman. They needed the pathology and forensics reports, but those probably wouldn't be ready until Monday at the earliest. In the meantime, Ekman wanted them to pursue the investigation as best they could.

"Okay," Enar said. "I'll pick it up while you rest and when you feel ready, you can join me. I guess he expects us to work through the weekend."

"What else?" said Gerdi. Ekman was famous for pushing death investigations especially hard.

Holm had gotten hold of the rental agent and asked her to open her office. Now he waited patiently while the dumpy, sixty-year-old woman looked through a filing cabinet behind her desk.

"This is terrible," she said, as she fingered her way through the packed cabinet. "That poor girl. Nothing like this has ever happened in the building." Finally she located the file and put it on her desk in front of him.

"Please look for yourself."

He flipped open the folder and found the rental application with a photo of a driver's license. They'd hit it lucky.

The furnished apartment had been rented two weeks ago for six months by Ahmed Chafik. He'd paid cash.

"We need all of this," he said. "I'll give you a receipt."

She hesitated for a moment, then agreed.

"We'll have to canvass the building, and then stores in the area, to see if anyone was friendly with him," Holm said, handing copies of the enlarged driver's license photo to the two detectives working with him.

Inspector Rosengren, a short man with thinning red hair, pursed his lips. "The guy's really ugly," he said, looking at Chafik's small, close-set eyes, low forehead, and heavily pock-marked face. "People should remember him."

Rosengren's partner, Alenius, thin, tall, and usually silent, just nodded.

Holm was discussing the case with them, when Vinter came into the detectives' brightly lit bull pen with its ten sets of paired metal desks facing each other.

"You're supposed to be getting some rest," Holm protested, as Rosengren smirked. Everyone knew they were a couple. Alenius listened without expression.

"I slept for a couple of hours and then got restless. I thought I'd come in and see what you guys were up to," Vinter said, looking at the three men. "Just to make sure you stayed on the right track."

Holm laughed and summarized what they had so far. She was impressed.

"Okay, it looks like somehow, even without me, you've made a little progress. Where do we go from here?"

"We need to check out the address on his driver's license," Holm said.

"Okay," said Vinter. "Let's do it."

4

THE COLLECTOR

Friday, November 11, 9:30 p.m. He'd spotted her from across the room. She was very pretty, with short blonde hair, and the right size: small and boyishly slender. Perfect. Just as she'd been described to him. The bar was crowded. He'd had to maneuver through the packed bodies to get next to her.

Now they were pressed shoulder to shoulder. Even so, he had to bend down toward her and raise his voice to be heard over the loud talk and throbbing electronic techno music blaring from huge speakers.

"That's a lovely necklace," he said, looking at her amethyst and silver pendant.

"Thanks," she said, startled that this muscular man, in his midthirties, with two days' stubble on his handsome, boyish face, would notice.

He saw her surprise and grinned. "No, I'm not gay. I used to be in the jewelry business."

She would never have taken him for a jeweler. She looked him over skeptically.

"That's an interesting pickup line," she said, grinning back.

"It's not a line. I was a jeweler until two years ago when I sold my store."

"Here in Weltenborg?" she asked. "What was it called?"

"It was in Malmö. The Silver Whale." He extended his hand. "My name's Tomas, by the way."

"What do you do now, Tomas?"

"I look after my investments. I know it sounds lazy, but it's actually challenging work."

"You're lucky." She paused. "I'm Lynni."

"Pleased to meet you, Lynni. Are you with someone?"

"Not tonight." He was really in luck.

"Can I get you a fresh drink?" he asked, looking at her empty wine glass.

"Sure, chardonnay, please."

He pushed through the packed crowd around the bar and ordered. When the wine arrived he reached into his pants pocket for a small vial, and with his hand over the glass concealing it, flipped the lid open with his thumb and squeezed a few drops of Rohypnol into the wine. Putting the container back in his pocket, he swirled the glass, making sure the drug was thoroughly mixed, and made his way to her.

He handed her the drink. "Skål," he said.

"Aren't you having anything?"

"I've already had more than I should," he said.

They chatted for the next ten minutes, obviously interested in each other. Lynni told him she was a dental hygienist, originally from Uppsala, and worked in Weltenborg. She shared an apartment with two other women. The others had gone out dancing tonight with their boyfriends.

"And how come a girl like you," he said, looking at her with obvious admiration, "doesn't have a boyfriend to go dancing with?"

"I'm sort of between boyfriends now," she said.

"Maybe I can help you with that."

"You certainly are a fast worker," she said.

Suddenly she leaned against him.

"Are you all right?" he asked.

"I'm feeling dizzy, light-headed."

"It's too hot and crowded in here. Let's get some fresh air. It'll help you feel better," he said, shouldering people aside as he guided her toward the exit. He got their coats from the check-room, draping hers around her shoulders.

Outside she had trouble walking and had begun to stagger.

"You need to sit down. My car is just down the street," he said. Putting his arm around her waist, he slowly walked her to a blue Mercedes 550SL coupe. Opening the passenger door, he eased her in.

Her eyes were closing.

"Just sit back and relax," he said. "I'll be right here," going around to the driver's side and getting in.

When her eyes had been shut for a few minutes and he was sure she'd fallen into a deep sleep, he started the car and pulled quickly away from the curb.

5

THE TEAM

Sunday, January 22, 8 a.m. The five members of the team Ekman had assembled had just settled in their seats when he came in and took his usual place at the head of the conference room table.

Vinter and Holm were on his right, facing Rosengren and Alenius. The four had worked through the weekend and their faces showed their fatigue. Alrik Rapp, bullet-headed and bulky, sat facing Ekman at the opposite end of the table.

Ekman turned to Holm, "Enar, what do you have?"

He summarized what he'd discovered about the apartment rental and handed Ekman and Rapp enlarged copies of Chafik's driver's license photo.

"I checked our data bases; he has no criminal record. He's twenty-six and came to Sweden from Morocco a year ago to work at a company in Stockholm. His work permit required fingerprints, so I got them and passed them on to forensics to match against those in the apartment. Alrik has their report."

Vinter continued. "Enar and I went to the address he gave on his driving license. It's on the second floor of an upscale building at 708 Dorisgatan. He wasn't in. The manager told us he lives alone. We leaned on him to let us look around, but we didn't see anything unusual. Chafik's car, a new Volvo S40, was still parked in a garage behind the building. He's also got a computer." She looked at Ekman. "We'll need warrants to do a thorough search of the apartment and car, and take that computer."

"Get me affidavits and I'll speak with Prosecutor Kallenberg. You'll have them today."

"Rosengren?" Ekman said to the red-haired detective on his left.

"Alenius and I showed his photo in some Muslim stores and to people who live near his apartment, mostly around Axgatan where a lot of those people live. The guy's so ugly we figured he'd be remembered. But if they knew him, no one was talking. You know how these damn Muslims hang together," he said, looking around at the others for agreement.

"Let's get something straight right now," said Ekman, his face tight. "This case involves a Muslim. Don't forget that some immigrants are naturalized Swedish citizens. Everyone, I repeat, everyone, whether or not they are citizens, will be treated with respect. There will be no further remarks or knowing looks. Is that understood?"

"Sorry, Chief. I didn't mean anything," Rosengren said, but they all knew he had.

"Alrik, you've been looking impatient and from your expression you've got something important to tell us."

"It's good news, Chief. We've matched the woman to a missing person in our data base. She's Lynni Dahlin, twenty-two, a dental assistant, reported missing on November 15. Her brother, Nils Dahlin, lives in the city and formally identified her. He was really broken up. We'll be interviewing him later about her friends.

"The autopsy showed the fall was the cause of death: severe skull damage and a broken neck, as well as other injuries. Death was instantaneous. The time, as we know, was last Friday night, at eight fifteen. Her body had numerous cuts from broken glass, and other cuts were on her hands and knees, probably from the roof tiles. Dark bruises on her wrists and ankles indicated she'd been tied up.

"Forensics found her fingerprints and DNA in the apartment's bedroom and the adjoining bathroom. Chafik's fingerprints were all over. There were also some unidentified fingerprints and DNA in the bedroom. Hair and fiber were collected. From a half-bath in the hall, they found hairs with follicles attached, so DNA was extracted. The working assumption is that the hair is Chafik's.

"Just before death she'd been raped. Traces of semen were in her mouth. But Rapid DNA analysis confirmed that a second man was also involved: unidentified semen was found in her anus. Her vagina and anus were heavily bruised. Those bastards really did a number on her," he concluded, looking grim. He had a teenage daughter.

"Good work, Alrik. You've given us a lot to go on," said Ekman. "What we know is that she was raped and Chafik was one of the men involved. I'll ask Kallenberg for an arrest warrant, in addition to the search warrants. We need to find out everything we can about him and any associates, and see if we can identify the other man. Gerdi and Enar will execute the warrants for Chafik's car and apartment. After forensics has gone over his place and car they'll need to bring the computer in for the techs. When Dahlin escaped and fell, Chafik must have panicked. He's not going back to his place.

"Alrik, put out an APB for him. You've all seen the reports on TV, the Net, and the newspapers," Ekman said, holding up the front page of Saturday's *Sydsvenska Nyheter*, which featured a picture of the police at the scene of Friday night's fall. "So let's give the media his photo and Dahlin's, and a hotline number. Rosengren and Alenius, you'll be screening the calls." Seeing their downcast expressions, he said, "I'm counting on your experience to sort out the cranks from the likely tips.

"This is a high-profile case. We've made good progress thanks to your hard work. But we'll be under increasing pressure to produce more results. Any comments or suggestions?"

Vinter said, "Chief, why don't we also start looking at known sexual predators to see if any of them might have a Muslim connection?"

"Good idea. You can pursue that after you search Chafik's apartment. While Gerdi's doing that, Enar, talk with leaders of mosques to get them involved. It's in the interest of their community to have this resolved quickly.

"Anything else? Then we'll meet again on Wednesday at eight. Good hunting."

6

MEMORIES

Sunday, January 22, 7:10 p.m. Ingbritt was just taking a roast chicken from the oven when she heard the garage door open. A few moments later Ekman hung his things in the hall closet and came into the cheerful, white-curtained kitchen.

"That smells wonderful," he said. "Is there anything I can do?"

"Everything's ready. Just open a bottle of wine. It's in the refrigerator," she replied with a smile.

Over dinner she asked about the case and Ekman summarized what they knew.

"That's horrible, Walther." Ingbritt became very silent. She's obviously upset, Ekman thought. I shouldn't have told her the details.

"It's the world we live in now," he replied. But he knew this wasn't accurate. The world had always been like this. Sexual assault was an unspeakable, commonplace experience many women everywhere shared.

In the past, he'd discussed similar cases with his friend Jarl Karlsson, a psychiatrist. Jarl had said these assaults were committed primarily by psychologically weak men who only felt powerful and sexually excited when raping or brutalizing and humiliating women. It was this feeling of control that most excited them. They became fully aroused by dehumanizing their victims, turning them into objects to be used for their pleasure.

It basically had to do with how they'd related to their mothers, Jarl said. Ekman had just nodded: more Freudian psychobabble. None of it made any difference to him. He understood these men very well, but nothing could mitigate what they did. He felt as little compassion for them as they felt for their victims.

INGBRITT PICKED at her chicken, her thoughts moving against her will to the mental door she'd closed and locked years ago, before she'd met and married Ekman at eighteen.

She'd been fifteen and her parents had gone out that evening to dinner. She was alone with her mother's older brother, the always joking, jowly Olander, who had gotten her tipsy on two bottles of wine. She'd become disoriented by the unaccustomed alcohol, and he'd been solicitous, suggesting she'd feel better resting in her bedroom.

At first, they'd sat side by side on her bed talking quietly. Suddenly he'd begun stroking her hair and trying to kiss her, and when she pulled away, ran his hand roughly up her skirt. Then, using his weight, he'd forced her back on the bed, and ripped off her underwear. She just lay there, too stunned to scream or push him away.

Ingbritt still recalled, as though it had happened yesterday, the feeling of his sweat dripping on her and the grunting noises he made as he raped her. Afterward when he'd finally gotten off her and left without a word, she'd cried, it seemed to her, for hours.

She'd put her torn panties and the blood-spattered bed sheet in a trash bag and the next day tossed it in a dumpster behind a restaurant. Ingbritt had been too distraught and ashamed to tell her mother, let alone her father. But she made sure whenever Olander visited that she was never alone with him. He always spoke to her with a smile, as though nothing had happened.

When Olander'd died three years ago at seventy-eight, Ekman had acted surprised that she wasn't interested in going to his funeral. She'd made the excuse that she had to finish proofing her latest children's book.

Ingbritt had become unusually quiet, her eyes focused on her plate. Ekman kicked himself again for having upset her.

"I shouldn't have talked about the girl. I'm sorry," he said.

She lifted her head. "It's all right, Walther. I was just thinking of something else."

"It can't have been a very happy thought. Care to share it?"

"It's best forgotten," she said, and changed the subject. "We have apple pie for dessert." She forced a bright smile as she stood up to get it.

7

THE FARM

Saturday, November 12, 7:50 a.m. She woke in a large double bed, the crisp white sheets soft against her body, and suddenly realized she was naked. Lynni sat up, still a little groggy, not understanding where she was at first as she pulled the duvet against her and looked bewilderedly around the cheerful, rose-colored room. There were two doors; a table stood against the front wall with two chairs. Sunlight streamed through a barred window behind her to her right.

She was overcome by panic. How had she gotten here? And where was she? She froze for several minutes as she sat in bed, her mind racing around and around. She couldn't remember what had happened last night.

Finally, cautiously, she got up. She felt the urgent need to relieve herself. On bare feet she went to the open door on the left which led to a small bathroom. After using the toilet, she splashed cold water on her face trying to become fully awake. Her mouth tasted foul. Opening a packaged toothbrush beside the sink, she cleaned her teeth with the new tube of toothpaste there, and took a long, thirsty drink from a large bottle of mineral water that had been placed nearby.

Looking in the mirror, she put her hand to her throat, suddenly realizing that her necklace, a birthday present from her brother, was gone. Behind her a white cotton slip hung on a hook next to the door. She put it on, glad to be wearing something, even if it was too large.

Coming out, she went to the window and peered through the bars. The sun had just come up. She saw that she was somewhere in the countryside, on an upper floor of what seemed a large building. To the left she could make out a brown, stubble field and nearby, an old farmhouse.

Going to the heavy door facing the bed, she turned the knob. It was locked. She pulled at it, but it wouldn't budge.

Lynni again tried frantically to remember how she'd gotten here. Memory returned gradually. She recalled stumbling out of a bar with a man. At first she couldn't think of his name, then it all slowly came to her. He was Tomas, the handsome jeweler. She'd been feeling ill and he'd helped her to his car. Everything after that was blank.

Was this his place? And why was she locked in? Someone . . . Tomas? . . . had undressed her and put her to bed. Had they made love? She didn't know.

She banged on the closed door, calling out loudly, "Hello! Is anyone there?" over and over. She finally gave up, sat back down on the bed, her panic returning, and then got up and started banging again. After a while, she heard footsteps on stairs. They stopped outside the door, and a moment later she could hear a bolt being slid aside. She backed away as the door swung open.

A tall, heavyset woman in her midforties, with doughy features and mannishly cut dirty blonde hair, stood facing her. She was dressed in something resembling a nurse's old-fashioned, starched grey uniform. The woman bent down and picked up the tray that she'd placed on a stand outside the door.

"*Good morning, Lynni. I've brought you some breakfast,*" *she said in a cheerful voice, coming into the room and putting the tray on the table. She closed the door and pulled back a chair. With a wave of her hand she motioned for Lynni to sit down.* "*Please help yourself.*"

Lynni ignored her gesture. "*Who are you and why am I here? And where is this place?*" *she asked, her voice quivering.*

"*My name doesn't matter, dear, but you can call me Matron,*" *the woman replied.* "*As for this place, we call it the farm. And why you're here? Lucky you, you've been chosen for an exciting new life. I'll explain everything, but first have something to eat before the bacon and eggs get cold. Here's some coffee,*" *she went on, pouring two cups from the carafe on the tray.* "*I'll join you.*"

The smell of the food made Lynni realize she was ravenous. Looking at the woman through narrowed eyes, she slowly sat down and taking up a fork, began eating quickly. Matron sat opposite her, watching and sipping her coffee.

In a few minutes, Lynni had wolfed down everything and drunk all her coffee. The woman poured her another cup.

"*I see you're a purist like myself when it comes to coffee: just black,*" *Matron said.*

The food and the woman's low-key manner had somewhat eased the tension Lynni felt in this bizarre situation, and she attempted a slight smile.

"*Okay, now tell me what this is all about.*"

"*Are you adventurous?*" *Matron asked.*

"*No more than the next person.*"

"*But don't you find life as a dental assistant boring?*"

Lynni was taken aback. How did she know that? Then she remembered mentioning it to Tomas. He'd apparently spoken with this woman about her, including her name and occupation. What was going on? What did they want from her?

"*Only a little,*" *she replied.* "*Mostly it's fine.*"

"I know you're bewildered and rather frightened by this situation, but we find it's important there be a break in ordinary life to prepare you for a new and different one," Matron said in a soothing tone and, reaching over, patted her hand.

"But I don't want a new life. I'm happy with the one I have," Lynni protested, pulling her hand away.

"That's only because you haven't experienced all that life has to offer, dear," Matron said in a patronizing voice.

"I want to call my brother. Now," Lynni demanded. She was fed up with this weirdness and had decided she didn't trust this woman, with her phony sympathy. "And why was the door locked? You can't keep me here," she said, her voice rising as she stood up. "This has gone far enough. I want my clothes, purse, jewelry, and phone, and a ride to my apartment."

Matron had also gotten up and suddenly leaned over the table and slapped Lynni hard across the face. Her head rocked back from the blow.

"I try to be kind, but you don't appreciate it, do you, you ungrateful little bitch?"

Lynni stood frozen, petrified by the totally unexpected attack. Tears ran down her face as she held a hand to her reddening cheek. Matron, looming over her, noticed that Lynni was shaking.

"No more making nice. Instead we'll teach you what it means to be afraid," she said, her face contorted with a mix of anger and perverse pleasure. "So you want a ride? We'll give you one you'll never forget."

Turning toward the door, she pulled it open and called in a loud voice, "Gotz, come up here and help me open our little present."

8

KALLENBERG

Monday, January 23, 1:30 p.m. Ekman was hungry and looking forward to lunch at his favorite Chinese restaurant a few blocks from headquarters. He had more than an hour before his appointment with Arvid Kallenberg, the prosecutor who'd taken Malin Edvardsson's place when she was promoted to Malmö.

"I'm sorry to be leaving, Walther," the bird-like, slightly hunchbacked woman had said to him almost a year ago in her courthouse office when he'd come to say good-bye.

"I'll miss you, Malin," he'd replied and meant it. She'd been personally as well as professionally supportive during the traumatic Grendel case last year, the most horrendous in his long career.

"Please come to see me, when you're next in Malmö."

"Actually Ingbritt and I will be up your way next month to visit our daughter, Carla, and grandson, Johan. I'll give you a call before then."

"Wonderful. I'd like to invite you to my new home."

"We'll look forward to it," he'd said. Then she'd surprised him by reaching up and giving him a hug.

"Take care of yourself, Walther," she'd said as he left. Like Ingbritt, she was concerned about her friend's frequent bouts of depression, and his increasing girth.

He fought off the depression as best he could with Ingbritt's help, but although he wanted to lose weight, did nothing about it.

LEAVING HEADQUARTERS Ekman looked up before he crossed Stortorget Square, jammed with pedestrians and traffic, and saw that the chill grey sky and scudding clouds promised rain, or if the temperature dropped a little, snow. He turned on busy Brannkyrkagatan toward the Chinese restaurant in the middle of the block.

The obsequious host smiled when he saw Ekman.

"Right this way, Chief Superintendent. I have a nice, quiet table for you," he said, leading him to one in the back corner of the crowded room.

Ekman wasn't sure when he'd first become so well-known. Over thirty years on the force his major cases had sometimes brought him unwanted attention. But it was probably his picture plastered across the papers and TV screens throughout Sweden during last year's hunt for Grendel, a mass murderer maniac, that had made him more famous than he'd ever wanted to be. He'd always preferred to work anonymously. Now he had to grudgingly accept that it was no longer possible; much against his will, he'd become a celebrity.

His disgruntlement didn't stop him from enjoying his favorite dish. He chewed contentedly on the Peking duck slices and scallions he'd rolled in thin crepes slathered with sweet hoisin sauce.

Looking at his watch, he turned down the waitress's offer of dessert, paid the check, and picking up his briefcase, headed for the nineteenth-century stone courthouse three blocks away.

After tipping a half salute to the guard who knew him, he boarded an ornate, creaking elevator that brought him up to the familiar, white marble floored hall leading to the prosecutor's office.

At Ekman's knock, Arvid Kallenberg raised his head from the court papers he was reading and stood up.

"Come in," he said.

Kallenberg was in his early fifties and had been a prosecutor his entire career. Almost as tall as Ekman, but much thinner, he was impeccably dressed in a dark grey suit and wore conservative rimless glasses.

Ekman missed Malin, but had found Kallenberg fairly easy to work with, although he could be a stickler for observing every legal nicety.

Kallenberg led Ekman to a comfortable couch, taking the facing armchair. Like Edvardsson, he preferred to do things informally instead of remaining behind his large mahogany desk with the gilt-framed photo of his sister's family.

"What's this new case like?" Kallenberg asked sitting back, one sharply creased pants leg crossed over the other.

Ekman described what they had so far on the dead girl and what they would be doing next. Reaching into his briefcase, he handed Kallenberg the affidavits for the arrest warrant for Chafik and the search warrant for his apartment.

He knew the prosecutor could take over the investigation at any time, but didn't think it would happen at this early stage. He hoped Kallenberg would just leave them alone to develop the case without interfering.

"It sounds like you have things well in hand," Kallenberg said, after taking a few moments to scan the affidavits. "I'll speak with the district judge right away and the warrants will be sent over later this afternoon."

"Thanks. There's a long way to go yet, but I think we're making good progress and the apartment search could move things along even more quickly."

"I agree. Just keep me posted with written reports, okay?"

"You'll get them every day."

"Sounds good," said Kallenberg, getting up and walking Ekman to the door.

Back at his desk, Kallenberg unlocked a drawer, took out a mobile phone, and placed a call. He pulled off his glasses and smoothed his blond hair as he spoke, leaning back in his tall swivel chair.

"I'm handling it. You don't have to do anything. It's being taken care of, so for God's sake, stop worrying," he concluded, ending the call.

Some people, he thought, appear outwardly strong, but prove totally spineless under pressure. It was a problem he'd have to deal with. He sighed, put his glasses back on, and turned his attention to the papers he'd been reading before Ekman arrived.

9

HAAKE

Monday, January 23, 3:15 p.m. A short, grey-haired man in his sixties, Fredrik Haake had just put his phone in his pants pocket when his wife came into the room. She saw that he hadn't shaved and was dressed in wrinkled tan slacks and an old brown sweater.

"You haven't forgotten about the cocktail party this evening, have you?" Kajsa Haake said, coming across his study's plush, forest-green carpet and brushing her lips against his cheek. A thin, forty-two-year-old blonde with surgically tightened features, she already was wearing a black, knee-length silk dress with a round, glittering diamond brooch at her shoulder.

"No, of course not. I'm looking forward to it," he lied. He hated these chattering functions that gave her so much pleasure. She relished showing off the expensive modern art collection that filled their huge house overlooking a lake in the exclusive Arboga district outside Weltenborg.

Most of their guests used the excuse of admiring the art in order to get themselves photographed for the society page of the newspaper that covered these parties. It was this publicity, and even more, the chance to ingratiate themselves with the Sodra Sverige Bank's chairman and his wife, that brought them out.

Haake intensely disliked having to make small talk with these fawning sycophants. But he needed to keep his wife content. It was important for several reasons to maintain the façade of a happily married couple. He went upstairs to get ready.

He'd married her for her family's financial connections. Their sex life had never been more than perfunctory, and had diminished until now they hadn't slept together in years. He knew she had lovers, but was very discreet; he didn't care, as long as there was no scandal and she remained friendly.

The short, slim-hipped, thirty-year-old blonde in a low-cut purple dress stood in a corner of the two-story great room. As she laughed with the three men who surrounded her, she sipped a second glass of champagne she'd just taken from the tray of fresh drinks a waiter had brought.

Haake watched her from across the room. This pretty woman seemed to him an older version of the girl who'd died a few days ago. What was her name? The newspapers had mentioned it, but he had trouble recalling: Lynni Dahlin, that was it. Her name sounded vaguely familiar, but he couldn't place it.

Apparently he'd made more of an impression on Lynni than he'd intended. He smiled to himself at his choice of words.

He regretted her death: it was a considerable inconvenience. Haake remembered his sessions with her gave intense pleasure. Lynni had obviously been so frightened it had always gotten him hard, unlike the prostitutes and useless pills he'd previously tried.

Should he approach this woman? He was frustrated that a replacement for the girl would probably take awhile. The only sexual release he now had was masturbating as he thought about her.

With this woman, the risk was unlikely to be worth it. Watching her interaction with the men, he thought she'd probably be only too willing and he wouldn't be able to get it up. Haake shrugged to himself and went over to the lavish smörgåsbord on a side table for a plate of shrimp.

10

MALMER

Tuesday, January 24, 9:10 a.m. Ekman's back was already beginning to ache as his large rear perched precariously on one of the small, hard wooden chairs facing Deputy Commissioner Olav Malmer's huge walnut desk.

His shaven skull gleaming in the overhead light, Malmer sat rigidly upright in the high, red-leather desk chair, adjusted to make him look taller than his five foot five. He was a small man in more than height, and couldn't tolerate someone like Ekman who towered over him. More than that, he was basically an amateur police officer, a political appointee who hated having to rely on Ekman's expertise.

He listened, his face impatient, as Ekman briefed him on where they stood with the Dahlin case.

"You've made some progress, but the media are always breathing down my neck. You haven't given me enough to satisfy them, Walther." As usual his greatest concern was possible adverse publicity.

"I thought with Chafik's and Dahlin's photos we'd fed them some raw meat."

"Yes, but now they expect to be fed every day," replied Malmer.

"It may be your job, but it's not mine," Ekman said flatly, looking right into Malmer's light blue eyes. He usually accommodated him just to make life a little easier, but there was only so much bullshit he could tolerate. He and Malmer both knew he couldn't be disciplined, let alone dismissed for insubordination: he was far too senior and too famous; besides, he had several friends on the National Police Board.

Malmer didn't respond immediately, just pressed his lips into a tight line.

Then with a forced smile, he said, "Well, Walther, I suppose that's right. I handle our relations with the outside world and you do the investigations. But I want you to take this case on personally and not just direct the work. It's become a media magnet and the commissioner and I expect a quick resolution. Can I assume you're in favor of that?"

Ekman ignored the sarcasm. He had several priority cases going at the same time, but his intuition told him this one was particularly important.

"Like you, I want this one solved as fast as possible. If you think it will speed things up, I'll get directly involved."

"Good. I expect daily reports," Malmer said, and turning away, began going through some paperwork on his desk as though Ekman wasn't there.

Ekman slowly got up and left the room, closing the door quietly behind him. The bastard thinks he has me doing what he wants, but actually he's handed me the excuse I was hoping for, he thought. Lynni Dahlin's death, and what had led to it, were constantly on his mind.

11

THE BROTHER

Tuesday, January 24, 3 p.m. Nils Dahlin, a burly man of
thirty with thinning, sandy hair, who worked as a piano tuner,
sat facing Ekman and Rapp in the interview room, talking
about his sister.

He'd formally identified her broken body the day before.
Standing beside Rapp in the corridor outside the room where
she lay, he'd suddenly begun to cry uncontrollably, the tears
streaming down his cheeks. It had taken him many minutes
to regain his composure.

Dahlin turned to Ekman, "We were the only ones left in
the family. Our parents were killed in a car crash three years
ago. There aren't even cousins. She was all I had."

"That must make it especially hard," said Ekman. He
knew only too well what deep personal loss felt like.

"We'll try to be as brief as possible, but we need all the
information you can give us about your sister, what she was
like, her friends, relationships with men, and anything else
you think might help," said Rapp.

"We're particularly interested in the days immediately
before she went missing," added Ekman.

"Lynni was a good person," Dahlin said, looking up at a corner of the room, remembering. "She was warm and cheerful, and had a great sense of humor. Everyone liked her. I can't understand how this could have happened." He paused. "I miss her a lot. She meant everything to me."

"We know she shared an apartment," Rapp said, consulting his notebook, "at 538 Hornsgatan, with two other women. How long had she lived there?"

"About six months. She moved in first and advertised for two women to share the apartment, then the others joined her."

"And what can you tell us about her flat mates?" asked Ekman.

"Not much. I don't know them very well. I just met them a couple of times when I went to pick up Lynni for dinner or a movie. They seemed nice enough."

"How about Lynni's boyfriends? Do you know who they were?" Rapp said.

"She'd just broken up with a guy, Kalle Jakobsson, the week before she vanished. They'd been dating for almost a year."

"Who broke it off?" asked Ekman.

"Lynni did."

"Why was that?"

"She'd discovered he'd gotten into drugs. He'd changed a lot and she decided she couldn't deal with it."

"Do you know where he lives?"

"No, just somewhere here in Weltenborg."

"Did you notice anything different in Lynni's behavior immediately before she went missing? Or did anything out of the ordinary happen?" asked Rapp.

"Not really. Everything was as usual, except she seemed more relaxed not seeing Kalle."

"Is there anything else you can think of that might help us?" Ekman asked.

"I wish I could, but there's nothing else."

"We have your home and work numbers, Herr Dahlin, and we'll contact you when we know more. We appreciate your help. The officer in the hall will show you out," said Ekman, standing.

Dahlin shook hands with each of them before leaving.

"What do you think?" Ekman asked Rapp.

"He seemed really attached to her and genuinely upset."

"I agree. But we still need to run a background check on him. Also, let's find out the terms of Lynni's will, if she had one, and the size of her estate, since he's the likely beneficiary. There also could be an insurance policy."

"You really believe he had something to do with her death?" asked Rapp, his face showing his surprise.

"Probably not. I just want to make sure we cover all the bases."

"Okay, we'll do that, then take a look at her flat mates and that ex-boyfriend."

12

BREAK-IN

Wednesday, January 25, 8 a.m. The five other team members were standing around in his conference room talking when he came in.

Ekman took his place at the head of the table as the others sat down.

"Okay, let's get started." Ekman turned to Vinter who was seated on his left. "What do you have for us?"

"Not good news, Chief. Enar and I went to Chafik's apartment yesterday with a forensics team to execute the warrants. When we got there, the seal we'd put on the door was broken and it was unlocked. Either Chafik somehow evaded the surveillance car we had out front or someone else broke in. We think it wasn't him because the place was a mess, papers scattered everywhere, drawers dumped out. Chafik would have known what he was looking for. Worst of all, the computer we saw was gone." She turned to Holm.

"Forensics went over the place and his car very carefully," he said, "and the only prints were Chafik's. Whoever broke into the apartment must have been wearing gloves. He obviously didn't care if we knew the place had been tossed. We don't know if he got what he was looking for, but we did a thorough search to see if we could find anything he missed. The papers on the floor were just old bills and ads, but we discovered one personal letter stuck in a magazine."

Vinter continued, "It was from Morocco, postmarked two months ago, addressed to Chafik in English, but the letter was in Arabic. We had it translated. Because of the way it referred to family members we figured out that it's from an uncle and mostly about family news. But at the end, it says . . ." She took out a paper and read, ". . . 'I trust the job I arranged for you will continue to go well, *insh'Allah*. May the Prophet Muhammad (peace be upon Him) watch over you.' "

"Having sex isn't a bad job," said Rosengren. He fell silent as Ekman glared at him.

Ekman was getting very tired of these snide remarks. If Rosengren weren't such a good detective, he would have taken him off the team before this. One more out-of-line comment and he'd be gone.

"Gerdi, I'll need the letter writer's name. We have to find out more about this Moroccan connection. I'm going to ask Garth Rystrom to put me in touch with Interpol," Ekman said, naming his friend, a superintendent at the National Criminal Investigation Department in Stockholm.

"If we could just get a look at Chafik's bank records, we could find where his money was coming from," suggested Rapp.

"You're right, Alrik. But do we know what bank he used?"

"We didn't find any bank statements, Chief," said Holm. "Maybe the thief took them. However, Chafik could have just banked online. Without his computer, we don't know where to look."

"For now, I guess that's a dead end," Rapp said.

"Not necessarily," said Ekman, looking up thoughtfully at the ceiling. "Gerdi, why don't you get in touch with the companies that sent Chafik the bills you found and find out how they were paid. He probably used a credit card online or a check by mail. If we follow the number to a bank, we can get a warrant for the account statements."

Rapp's expression brightened.

"Gerdi, you were going to check out sex offenders with a Muslim background," Ekman said.

"I found two recent guys in Weltenborg, Chief. One has been in prison for the last year for sexual assault. The other one, a Hassan Nassoor, was picked up just a week ago for groping a woman in a downtown store. He agreed to be fined by the prosecutor and that was the end of the matter. Nassoor has no priors. I'm still going back five years looking for others."

"Alenius, what about phone tips?" Ekman asked, turning to Rosengren's silent partner. Rosengren was usually the spokesman for the duo, but Ekman was still irritated and had decided by ignoring him for now to let him know it.

"A lot of calls, Chief, but after we questioned them closely, nothing that seemed solid enough for a follow-up."

"Enar, any luck in the Muslim community?"

"I spoke with imams at the two local mosques and they didn't remember seeing him at services. They didn't think he was observant. I stressed how important cooperation with us was because Chafik's involvement in Dahlin's death was public knowledge and a lot of people will think it reflects badly on local Muslims generally. They're very sensitive to that. I don't think they're concealing anything. They want him caught and off the front pages and TV as quickly as possible."

"Okay then. Enar, go back to the Muslim shops and restaurants and see if anything about Chafik has surfaced now.

Gerdi, you pursue the bank angle. Let me know if you need a warrant. Alenius and Rosengren, keep on with the phone tips. Yes, I know it's tedious, but persistence can pay off when you least expect it. Alrik and I will be talking with Dahlin's flat mates and her former boyfriend. Let's plan on meeting again on Friday," Ekman concluded.

13

A THEORY

Wednesday, January 25, 1 p.m. The restaurant Ekman liked was diagonally across Stortorget Square from police headquarters and he and Rapp headed there for lunch, two more pedestrians among the bustling crowd. Ekman usually ate alone. It gave him time to relax and sort through the morning's events, but today he'd felt the need for company and asked Alrik to join him.

The sky was a brilliant blue, unusual for this time of year, with white clouds moving quickly under a brisk wind. Looking back over his shoulder, Ekman saw for the hundredth time how incongruous the five-story, ultramodern, white police headquarters was, looming over the cobblestoned plaza ringed with Renaissance buildings and centered on a bronze fountain. It was two years since they had relocated there, but he still wasn't used to it and probably never would be. It was too glaring an anomaly, and much too sterile for his taste.

Ekman often frequented the small restaurant. It had decent food and he could get a drink. Rapp usually went to the police cafeteria with its reasonable, if pedestrian, fare; he

didn't really care what he ate, food for him was just suste-
nance. He knew that for his boss it was one of life's great
pleasures. Ekman's waistline was evidence of how often he sur-
rendered to temptation.

"What looks good to you, Alrik? I talked you into coming,
so it's my treat," he said, peering with interest at the day's
menu that filled the chalkboard hanging on the brick wall to
their right.

Turning to look it over, Alrik said, "Thanks, Walther. I
guess I'll have the special, the smoked salmon on rye."

"And something to drink?" urged Ekman.

"Okay, if you insist," he said, smiling. "A Dugges ale
sounds good."

Ekman was relieved; he wanted a drink, but didn't want
to be the only one indulging.

A young woman came over to take their orders. Ekman
chose pea soup, followed by a plate of pork with rutabaga,
and a bottle of the ale.

"I must be hungrier than I'd realized," he said, with an
embarassed grin.

Ekman wanted to hear Alrik's take on the case. He understood that Rapp often didn't speak out at meetings because he
deferred to Ekman to summarize where they were and how
they should proceed. He'd recommended Rapp's promotion to
chief inspector a year ago because he knew Alrik was more
than just a brawny cop: he had a sharp eye for details and
good instincts about people.

"So, Alrik, what does the case look like to you?"

Rapp was silent for a moment, gathering his thoughts. "It
feels like there may be more to it than a simple rape."

"What makes you say that?" Alrik was echoing Ekman's
own take on things and he wanted to find out if they saw the
case the same way.

"It's the Dahlin girl. She had to know she was risking her life getting out on the roof, especially in that weather. She did it because she had no choice. It must have been the only chance she had to escape. We know she'd been a prisoner for almost two months because of the date she went missing. She'd only been kept at that apartment, possibly drugged to keep her quiet, for two weeks at most before she fell, so she had to have been held elsewhere.

"Wherever she was, she'd probably also been tied up and raped there, and not just the night she escaped. We know from DNA that another man besides Chafik raped her. It could have been just these two scumbags, but I can't help wondering if others weren't involved. Maybe they'd argued with Chafik and his buddy and forced them to move her. But what's really puzzling is why those two decided to bring her to an apartment in the center of town. It was a dumb choice, much too conspicuous. If we can figure out why they did it, we'll be closer to solving this.

"Of course, there's no evidence of anyone besides the two we know about, but I think we should consider the possibility of a sex-trafficking ring. I could be wrong of course. It's just how I feel."

"I don't think you're wrong. It's what I feel too."

"So how do we follow up?"

"Let's go ahead with the interviews we planned. We'll keep them open-ended, not just about Chafik, and see what surfaces."

Their lunches arrived, and they ate in silence. Ekman glanced out the window at the passing crowd. Maybe among them was the other man who'd raped Dahlin, or perhaps one of the unknown men he and Alrik guessed might be out there. What makes them different from the rest of us is believing they have the right to ignore the rules that make the thin veneer of civilization possible.

He looked across at Alrik. It doesn't matter to us why they're like that, we just try to stop them before they can inflict more damage. He'd spent most of his life doing just that. It was a never-ending, largely thankless task. His father, Gustaf, appalled when he'd left the family's dull corporate law practice to join the police, had warned him it would be like this. Since then he'd often thought Gustaf had been exactly right.

14

THE LAME MAN

Wednesday, January 25, 10 a.m. *The black Mercedes sedan that had brought him pulled slowly away. He stood at the curb watching it leave, an overcoat over one arm, his other hand on the raised handle of the small aluminum suitcase the driver had taken from the trunk and placed beside him. Then he turned, trailing his wheeled case, and limped under the huge, lattice-shaped, white concrete canopy. Although today was a cool fourteen degrees Celsius, the entrance to ancient Marrakech's starkly modern Menara Airport was designed to offer travelers some shade from the blistering heat of Morocco's fierce summer sun.*

The Norwegian Air Shuttle's nonstop flight to Stockholm's Arlanda airport left an hour later. In five and a half hours he'd be in Sweden, one of the few European countries he hadn't been to. Closing his eyes, he reclined in the soft leather of the wide business-class seat, sipping the orange juice he'd requested, brought to him as soon as he was seated by a striking, thirty-something female flight attendant. He went over yesterday's interview and considered how he would go about the task ahead of him.

The afternoon before he'd been invited for tea at the ancient house in the crowded medina, the old quarter.

He walked briskly through the huge Jemaa el-Fnaa market square, filled with canvas-covered stalls selling every fruit, vegetable, and spice imaginable, food vendors with fragrant smoke rising from charcoal grills, snake charmers, fire eaters, acrobats, pickpockets, and dumbfounded, gawking tourists. He was assailed by the incredible din and exotic smells as he hurried along, oblivious to the loud, insistent pleas of stall owners and beggars.

Lost in the maze of narrow alleys running off the square, the house stood anonymously behind a three-story, tan stucco wall that formed one side of a cramped passageway barely wide enough for two people.

The small, handleless wooden entrance door was nondescript, masking its solid steel core. He pressed the buzzer in the wall beside the door and a CCTV camera mounted high above swiveled to focus on him. After a moment, the guard watching on a screen in the main house pressed the lock-release button. Hearing the buzz, the man pushed the door open. As he stepped inside, the door closed behind him with a soft, pneumatic hiss.

Facing him was a wide, colonnaded courtyard filled with flowering plants, ornamental trees, and shrubs, and centered on a glistening white marble fountain, its spray shimmering in the sunlight. The late afternoon sun seemed filtered here. The splashing water and flower-perfumed air created a secret oasis, a hidden world away from the clamorous, dusty streets outside.

He limped slowly along a flower-lined, flagstoned path to the shaded entrance of the house where two silent, broad-shouldered young men with automatic weapons cradled casually in their arms watched him as he came. The lame man raised a hand in greeting and they nodded slightly as the thick-set figure went by; he was a frequent visitor. Passing under a tiled arabesque arch at the rear of the cool foyer, he entered a large, high-ceilinged room.

Seated in an ivory inlaid chair in the center of the octagonal room, dimly lit by ornamental lamps suspended on long chains from the ceiling, was an aged man. He appeared to be in his eighties, with deep-set eyes, a sharply aquiline nose, and leathery skin, his sunken cheeks covered by a thin white beard. He wore a long, tan woollen Moroccan robe with the hood thrown back.

The room's tiled floor was covered in bright, intricately patterned rugs; plush couches piled with cushions lined the walls. In front of the man was a low wooden table with delicate fretwork, set for tea; another chair stood to one side. His sharp brown eyes narrowed, surveying the approaching figure without expression.

"As-salamu alaykum," the lame man said, looking at the ground in front of the other, his hand on his heart, his head slightly bowed.

"Wa alaykemu s-salaam," the old man replied, gesturing to the facing chair, and then pouring sweet mint tea from a long-spouted, engraved silver carafe into two decorated glasses.

"I trust Allah has preserved you in good health and you are well?" the old man inquired, as he took a sip of tea. But his flat tone told his visitor this was a formality devoid of feeling.

"Yes, thanks be to Allah. And you?" he asked, as he also took some tea to be polite.

"Allah has kept me well. Thanks be to Him."

"And your family?"

"That is a troubling question," he said, looking directly at his visitor who was always surprised by these abrupt transitions. He knew the old man, despite being very traditional, was easily bored with endless ritual greetings.

"How can I help you answer that question?" the lame man asked.

"My mind is disturbed by concern for my youngest sister's only grandson." He paused, and the other man waited for him to go on, taking another sip of tea.

"It has been a year since he went to Sweden to help with my spice importing business. Being young, he became easily bored and restless. This past summer he told me he wanted to learn more about our other business there, and so I paid for him to work for our supplier.

"Now I've been informed that Ahmed is being sought by the Swedish police in connection with a woman's death, and has simply vanished. But Ahmed would never do that without my permission."

He looked directly at the lame man. "I would be grateful for your assistance to discover what has happened and so put my mind at rest."

"I am deeply honored you would entrust me with your family problem."

"I was hopeful, insh'Allah, that you would be willing to help me. Here is the information you will need and funds to assist you," he said, taking a thick envelope from inside his robe and handing it across the table.

"There is a ticket on tomorrow's flight to Sweden." With a hand gnarled by arthritis, he gripped the brass-handled cane resting against his chair and pushed himself up with difficulty. The brief interview was over.

The lame man put his glass down and got to his feet. Taking a few halting steps backward, he placed his hand over his heart as he bowed his head. "Serving you is my great pleasure; lla yhennick," he said.

"Baraka Allahu feek; ttreq ssalama," the bearded man responded, leaning heavily on his cane. He stood there for a long moment, looking after the receding limping figure.

15

GIRLFRIENDS

Wednesday, January 25, 3:30 p.m. Ekman and Rapp were seated in wooden chairs facing a couch occupied by Dahlin's two flat mates. The women appeared bewildered by her sudden disappearance and terrible death weeks later. They couldn't understand how this could have happened to their friend.

"She led a perfectly normal life," said Molla, a tall brunette in her late twenties and the older of the two. "It's really frightening. We don't feel safe anymore, do we, Olise?"

"That's right, we don't, we really don't," said Olise earnestly, leaning forward on the couch. A pale blonde of twenty, she echoed whatever Molla said.

"You know we're looking for a man, Ahmed Chafik. I'm sure you've seen his picture in the papers and on TV. Did she know him, or have you ever seen him around?" Ekman asked.

"If she knew him, she never mentioned it to us," said Molla.

"And if we'd seen that face, we'd have remembered him," added Olise.

"Did anything unusual happen before she disappeared?" asked Rapp.

"No, nothing. We told your officer all about this when we reported her missing," said Molla in an irritated tone.

"Yes, we've read the file," said Ekman. "But it's often useful to go over everything again in case something was forgotten. We know you want to find out what happened to your friend. You do want to help us, don't you?"

"Of course," said Molla.

"Yes, absolutely," chimed in Olise.

"The report said you both had gone out dancing the night she disappeared, but she didn't go with you. Why was that?" Rapp asked.

"She was feeling a little down and didn't want to spoil our fun," Molla said.

"Had something upset her?"

"She'd just broken up with her steady boyfriend," said Olise. "That's enough of a downer for anyone."

"When did this happen?"

"About a week before," Molla said.

"And why was that?" asked Ekman. He knew the answer, but wanted confirmation of what Dahlin's brother had told them.

"She couldn't put up anymore with him being a druggie," put in Olise.

"And worse, he'd started to slap Lynni around. Even though she'd really cared about him. That did it," Molla said.

"He'd become physically abusive?" asked Rapp. It was something she apparently hadn't shared with her brother or he'd have mentioned it.

"Yes, she hated that, really, really hated that," Olise said. "I would too, you'd better believe it."

"What's his name?" Ekman asked to hear it from them.

"Kalle Jakobsson," Molla replied.

"Do you know where he works and lives?"

"He doesn't work. He deals drugs. That was a big part of the problem Lynni had with him. His address and phone number are around here somewhere. Let me look," Molla said. Getting up, she went to a desk against the wall and started rummaging through a drawer.

"Here it is," she said, handing a piece of paper to Ekman.

He glanced at it, giving it to Rapp, who looked at it and put it in his pocket.

"What did you think of him?" Ekman asked Molla.

"He seemed okay at first and we were happy for Lynni, but he gradually changed for the worse."

"Why do men always do that? Go bad, I mean," asked Olise with a petulant frown.

"It's puzzling. We just don't know," said Ekman, straight-faced. "Unless, of course, it becomes a police matter.

"Thank you both for your time. You've been very helpful. Please call me if anything else comes to mind," he said, handing Molla his card.

Outside the apartment building, Ekman turned to Rapp. "What does it look like?"

"The drug pusher boyfriend was abusive. I checked the data base after we spoke with the brother. Jakobsson has no record, but he could have been the other man with Chafik."

"Let's pay him a visit," said Ekman, as they got into their car.

16

AT HOME

Wednesday, January 25, 9 p.m. Ekman was sitting in his study in his oversize green-leather recliner, his hands moving mechanically, adding dark burgundy stitches to the intricately patterned cushion cover in his lap.

Years ago Ingbritt had given him a needlepoint kit to pass the time as he recovered from a badly broken leg in a hip-length cast, the result of a collision with a drunken driver. Stitching had become a calming habit that helped him concentrate. The results, displayed in frames, lined his ochre-colored study together with his collection of antique maps.

Ingbritt had outdone herself with dinner, he thought and had told her so. It had been a very satisfying meal followed by rhubarb pie, his favorite dessert.

Afterward they'd sat close together on the couch with his arm around her shoulders and begun to watch a television program about the lives of chimpanzees. When it came to a segment about their use in medical experiments in the United States, Ingbritt said, "I can't bear to look at this," and picking up the remote from the coffee table, switched the set off.

"It's too upsetting. They need to stop torturing those poor animals, no matter how it may help people. Would they experiment on babies if it might lead to new drugs? Thank God we've banned primate experiments in Sweden. Is there something else we can watch?"

Ekman turned the TV back on, flipping through their favorite channels. "It doesn't look that way."

"Then I'll just go to bed and read for a while. Are you coming up?" she asked.

"I'll be along soon," he said, and went to his study.

Like Ingbritt, Ekman had been disturbed by the scenes of abused animals. He'd seen too much of bestiality by humans toward one another not to be affected. At least animal experimenters were supposed to be finding ways to alleviate human illness. The men who'd raped Lynni Dahlin had no such redeeming rationale: they'd driven her to her death.

Life is hard enough and full of unavoidable loss as it is, he thought. No one, no matter how fortunate they appear, escapes unscathed. All the more reason why no criminal has the right to make life worse for anyone, let alone take that life. If he had a core philosophy that underlay his career as a police officer, this was it.

As he stitched, he reviewed the interview he and Rapp had with Dahlin's ex-boyfriend that afternoon.

17

JAKOBSSON

Wednesday, January 25, 4:45 p.m. Kalle Jakobsson lived in a rundown apartment building with flaking paint on Poppelgatan in one of Weltenborg's poorest neighborhoods. Ekman and Rapp saw that the lock on the lobby door was broken and went in. The sun had set at a quarter to four and it had rapidly become dark.

The dimly lit stairs to Jakobsson's third-floor apartment were littered with refuse and there was a faint stench of urine mixed with the stale odor of fried food.

When they reached Apartment 3B in the back of the building, they took up positions on opposite sides of the door. They didn't really expect anything to happen, but a violent response by a drug dealer to a police visit wasn't unheard of.

Rapp reached over and knocked a few times. They could hear a TV show with the volume turned up high. There was still no response and he tried again, banging loudly this time.

From inside they heard a muffled "Yeah, yeah, I'm coming. Hang on." There was a pause as the speaker moved toward the door.

"Who is it?"

"Police, Jakobsson," Rapp replied. "Open up."

"What do you want?"

"We'll talk inside. Now open the door."

They heard a lock click and the door swung open.

A handsome man in his late twenties with shoulder-length blond hair stood in the doorway. He was wearing a torn tee shirt with the sleeves pulled off at the shoulders and dirty white boxer shorts. His feet were bare.

"Yeah, so what is it?" he asked belligerently.

"Let's take it inside," said Rapp, flashing his credentials. "I'm Chief Inspector Rapp and this is Chief Superintendent Ekman." He gestured to Ekman's towering figure. Jakobsson's face showed his surprise that they weren't street cops. He retreated a few paces into the hallway as Ekman pushed past him. Rapp turned and closed the door. The stale cooking odor was stronger inside.

Jakobsson looked at them for a moment. Then he led the way down the short, narrow hall to a small living room. He turned off the booming, large flat-screen TV in the corner and then shoved a pile of clothes off a faded blue couch.

"Sit down if you want to," he said.

"We'll stand. You sit," said Rapp.

Jakobsson looked up at the two imposingly large men, then sat leaning forward, his hands on his knees.

"So what's this all about?"

"You've heard about Lynni Dahlin's death," said Ekman. It wasn't a question.

"It was all over the news, hard to miss," he said, pointing to the TV.

"You don't seem very upset about your ex-girlfriend dying."

"I was at first . . . real upset . . . but I got over it."

"A fast recovery," said Rapp, his voice heavy with sarcasm.

"She was a great girl. I was sorry she broke up with me."

"How come?" asked Ekman.

"We just didn't see things the same way anymore."

"You mean she'd gotten tired of you slapping her around."

A look of alarm passed over Jakobsson's face. "Hey, it was nothing. I never really hurt her."

"So you say. That isn't what we've heard," said Rapp.

"I had nothing to do with her dying. Nothing, you've got to believe that."

"Why should we believe a two-bit drug pusher? That's what you are, isn't it, Jakobsson?" Rapp asked.

"You can't prove anything. And I've got an alibi. You can't come in here and accuse me," he said defiantly, standing up.

"Sit down, Jakobsson," said Ekman in a harsh voice you didn't argue with. Jakobsson slowly sank back on the couch.

"Tell us about this so-called alibi," said Rapp.

"That Friday night, all night, I was out drinking and partying at a bar. Twenty people saw me."

"We'll need the name of the bar and your witnesses," said Ekman.

"Sure, that's no problem," said Jakobsson, relieved.

"There's a final way you can help clear yourself of involvement, not only in Dahlin's death, but in her rape."

"What's that?"

"Come to police headquarters tomorrow and give us your fingerprints and a DNA sample along with your formal statement and that list of friends."

Jakobsson thought about it for a moment. "That will clear me?"

"Yes," said Ekman, but meant only as the other rapist, not for involvement in Dahlin's death.

"Okay, I'll do it."

"Good. Make sure you're there first thing in the morning so we don't have to come looking for you," said Rapp.

Rapp and Ekman started to leave as Jakobsson got up and followed them down the hall to the door. Ekman turned and stared at him.

"And Jakobsson," said Ekman. "The drug squad will be watching you from now on. You'll want to find another job."

In the street, Ekman said, "What do you think?"

"He seemed willing enough to give us what we need to exclude him from the crime scene, but I still wonder whether he wasn't somehow involved."

"Yes, he wasn't really upset about her death, even though she'd been his girlfriend for some time."

"We'll need to put him under surveillance and see what he does," said Rapp.

Ekman nodded in agreement.

After he'd closed the door behind them, Jakobsson ran his fingers through his hair and shook his head as though to clear it. Going to the bedroom, he picked up his phone where he'd tossed it on the rumpled bed. He'd been given a single-use number for emergencies and he called it now.

"The police were just here. The top brass, for God's sake. I'm scared shitless they'll find out. Why did she have to die? You promised it'd be okay. She'd just be gone for good and nobody would be wise. Yeah, I got paid, but only to put you onto that little bitch because she was going to turn my ass in about the drugs. I didn't get paid enough for this pile of crap you've thrown me into. They said the drug squad will be watching me. So you've put me out of business too, and guess what, I need compensation. Now." He listened for a moment.

"I'll meet you there and you better bring plenty of cash. I can't be bought off cheap anymore."

Tomas put the phone on the table next to his armchair and leaned back, thinking. A little more police pressure and Jakobsson would crack. And his demands for money would always increase. He picked up the phone and called the Keeper.

After he described his conversation with Jakobsson, the other man was silent for a moment.

"Very well," the Keeper said. "We'll deal with him."

18

An Unexpected Death

Thursday, January 26, 5:40 a.m. Ekman had just come out of the shower with a large towel wrapped around his waist when the phone on the bedside table gave a muted ring. He picked it up quickly to avoid disturbing Ingbritt who was curled up on the other side of their queen-size bed.

"Ekman," he said in a low voice.

"Walther, it's Alrik. A patrol near the waterfront has found a body. His ID was on him: it's Jakobsson. He's been strangled. They've cordoned off the crime scene and a forensics team is on the way. I've told them to wait for us and not move the body."

Ekman was silent for a moment absorbing this totally unexpected news. After getting directions from Rapp, he said, "I'll meet you there in forty minutes."

He was about to finish getting ready when Ingbritt propped herself up on an elbow and said, "Walther, what's the matter?"

Early morning phone calls weren't uncommon in his work, but she was concerned.

"It's a new development in the case we've been working on," he said in a reassuring tone, sparing her the grisly details. "I've got to leave right away. Go back to sleep."

But she was already out of bed and pulling on her robe.

"I'll get the coffee started, and you should at least have an egg sandwich."

"You don't have to go to the trouble, but thanks, sweetheart," he said, heading for the dressing room.

It was still black and almost freezing when Ekman pulled up beside the police vans with their winking blue strobes. Brilliant klieg lights on tripods illuminated the crime scene. As he got out of the car, buttoning his heavy overcoat, he could smell the fishy scent of the nearby River Lagan. Through the mist rising from the river, he could make out the outlines of boats docked at the small marina down the cobblestoned street to his left.

Ekman ducked under the blue-and-white tape that cordoned off the area. The uniformed officer logging in personnel saluted and made an entry on his tablet computer as Ekman walked slowly toward the center of the scene, looking carefully about him.

Rapp nodded a greeting. "Jakobsson must have sneaked out another entrance and evaded the surveillance car I placed. He shouldn't have," he said, pointing at the body sprawled just inside a narrow alley between two large warehouses.

"The medical examiner got here a few minutes ago. The photographer and technicians have already worked the scene, but no one's touched him since he was ID'd."

Ekman bent down to look more closely. Jakobsson's once handsome face was distorted in a twisted grimace, a blackened tongue protruding from his wide-open mouth. A thin red line bit deeply into his neck. His fingers were curled into fists.

"Bohlander will have to open his hands carefully," he said to Rapp, who also was peering at the body. "Jakobsson may have gotten hold of something from his killer."

"It looks like the guy used a wire," said Rapp. There was no doubt in his mind that the murderer was a man. He'd never heard of a woman using this method and few would have had the strength.

"Yes," said Ekman. "A garrote is unusual. If he's done it before, it would be a distinctive MO. We'll have to check it out."

Roffe Bohlander was the medical examiner, trim and sandy-haired, in his late thirties. Ekman had found that he wasn't arrogant, as some other examiners he'd worked with were, and his autopsy reports were always revealing. Even more important to Ekman, Bohlander shared his profound respect for the victims. When Ekman attended an autopsy, it was obvious to him in the gentle way the pathologist handled the dead.

Bohlander pulled on latex gloves and, kneeling in his white protective suit next to the body, began to examine Jakobsson. Watching him, Ekman was impressed as the doctor carefully tied plastic bags over Jakobsson's hands.

"I know it's too soon to tell us much, but what do you think, Roffe?" he asked.

"Rigor has set in, but because of the cold it's not possible to determine the exact time of death without getting his internal temperature. I need to put him on a table to give you an answer."

"But roughly, you'd say . . . ?" Rapp persisted.

"Sometime late yesterday evening seems likely. But don't hold me to it."

"Do you think this is where he was killed?" asked Ekman.

"Yes. There's no indication his body was moved. If you've seen enough, I'll take him." Turning, he gestured to two white-suited morgue attendants standing next to a gurney. With some difficulty they maneuvered the stiff corpse into a large, zippered black body bag and, placing it on the gurney, wheeled it to their van, followed by Bohlander.

Rapp nodded to three crime scene technicians who had been waiting to examine the area under the body. As they started their work, Ekman turned to Rapp.

"We'd better get a forensics crew over to Jakobsson's apartment right away. Let me know if anything more turns up. I'll be at headquarters."

19

A Connection

Thursday, January 26, 7:15 a.m. The egg sandwich Ingbritt had made for him had staved off hunger for a little while, but Ekman was now ravenous as he walked into the busy, brightly lit police cafeteria. Perhaps it was standing around in the cold early morning air that had done it. Looking at Jakobsson's body hadn't made him lose his appetite. If the victim had been someone other than who he was, Ekman might have felt differently.

When he'd first seen how a brutal death had ravaged that young, handsome face, he'd been shocked by the horrific transformation. He would do everything he could to find Jakobsson's killer. But Ekman couldn't help feeling that mankind hadn't been much diminished by this death.

He waved to a group of junior inspectors at a table to his left as he came in, but didn't join them. Going up to the counter, he ordered a smoked salmon sandwich with sliced cucumber and a double espresso. He took his food to a table against the glass wall overlooking the interior courtyard.

While he ate, he looked out at the now-bare trees, their branches quivering in a brisk wind, and the old-fashioned wooden benches that offered welcome respite in warmer weather from claustrophobic cubicles. It was the single feature of this new, too starkly modern building that he actually liked.

Checking the clock over the doorway, he saw it was twenty to eight, got up, and took his tray to the kitchen conveyor belt. Before he left, he went over to the counter and paid for two carafes of coffee and a large basket of sweet rolls to be sent up to his conference room. The cafeteria manager didn't like having his assistant provide room service, and wouldn't do it for anyone else, but this was the chief; besides, he was a very generous tipper.

Ekman took the elevator to his office. Holm wasn't at his desk in a cubicle outside Ekman's door. He went in, hung up the hat and coat, sat down, and flipped through his overflowing inbox, but saw nothing important.

At exactly eight, he went in to find all the team members, except Rapp, standing around munching on sweet rolls as they sipped coffee.

"Thanks for this," said Vinter, gesturing to the side table.

"My pleasure," said Ekman, going over to help himself. He was still hungry.

When everyone was seated, Ekman said, "Let's get started."

The corridor door opened and Rapp entered. "Sorry I'm late. I was held up. The chief will tell you why." Tossing his coat over a chair, he grabbed a cup of coffee and a pastry and sat down.

"Alrik, why don't you tell them what's happened," said Ekman.

Rapp went over his and Ekman's interview with Jakobsson late yesterday and the startling murder.

"Forensics hasn't found anything at the crime scene yet that's likely to be helpful, but they're still examining some refuse near the body. Others are going over his apartment right now. So far we've found nothing. Let's hope the autopsy turns up something. Bohlander will be taking fingerprints and DNA to see if Jakobsson was the other man who raped Dahlin. We should know more tomorrow."

The others sat in stunned silence until Holm, looking first at Rapp and then turning to Ekman, said, "Jakobsson must have been involved in some way in Dahlin's death and someone decided to shut him up . . . permanently."

"Yes, when we spoke with him our instincts told us so. I should have pushed him harder," said Ekman. "If I had, maybe he'd still be alive."

"There was no way you and Alrik could have known what would happen, Chief," said Vinter.

"I suppose you're right, Gerdi. It's just that we were apparently much closer than either of us realized to finding the answer to Dahlin's death. It's frustrating."

"Chief," put in Alenius, the usually silent team member, who'd been listening attentively, "I've a question. How did Jakobsson get in touch with whoever met him in that alley?"

Ekman looked at the taciturn detective with surprise, and thought, that's why he's on the team.

"You've put your finger on it, Alenius. Someone could have gotten up to his apartment and they went out together. But the most likely answer is that he called, arranged to meet his killer, and somehow slipped out without being seen. We need to get our hands on that phone," Ekman said.

Turning to Rapp, he asked, "Was it on him?"

"No, it wasn't. And that's strange, because young people never seem separated from them."

"The killer must have taken it," put in Rosengren.

"Yes," said Ekman, "and if he did he must have searched the body for it. Maybe we can find some DNA." Looking at Rapp, he went on, "Alrik, have forensics go over Jakobsson's coat and pockets looking for new DNA. And call the other team at his place and see if they've picked up that phone." Ekman was hoping for a breakthrough if they could discover who Jakobsson called after they'd left him.

Rapp made the call, listened for a moment and then shook his head. "They haven't found one, but they'll keep looking. It's unlikely they'll find it if they haven't already. It would have been lying around in plain sight, not hidden away somewhere."

"We can be pretty sure he phoned from his apartment, right?"

"Yes, but that won't get us anywhere," said Rapp. "As a drug pusher, he probably used a 'burner,' a prepaid, untraceable cell phone. Without the phone, we can't find out who he called."

"But we can find out which mobile towers serve his area," Holm said.

"Whatever type of phone he used, the call had to go through a tower. He probably phoned no more than two hours after you questioned him, most likely right after you left. He must have panicked because he was involved with Dahlin's death.

"We can get a warrant for the numbers that passed through the local towers during those two hours, then we can look for a nonsubscriber number. It's likely to be Jakobsson's and we can get the number he called. If that phone has GPS, we can 'ping' it electronically and get its location. We won't be able to if it doesn't have GPS, but it's worth a try."

"But there could be a thousand regular subscriber calls," protested Rosengren.

"Yes. And sifting through them is what's called police work," Ekman said, while smiling wolfishly at the little inspector. Rosengren knew who would be doing the sifting.

"That's a brilliant idea, Enar," said Vinter, smiling at him. She was very proud of her lover.

"Good thinking, Enar. You're officially appointed our team's techno-geek. And I mean that as a sincere compliment," said a grinning Ekman. "Write up an affidavit for the warrant and I'll take it over to Kallenberg." He was going to have to bring the prosecutor up to date, especially with this latest death. Ekman hoped he wouldn't want to simply take over the investigation himself, but would be willing, at least for now, to rely on Ekman's reports.

"Gerdi, were you able to find out something about Chafik's finances?"

"I spoke with people at the electric utility, the Internet service, and the two department stores that had sent him the old bills we found. Since there's an arrest warrant for Chafik, they didn't argue with me. Fortunately for us, he was something of a pack rat or we'd have had a hard time tracking his accounts because a year ago he started doing everything online. He paid by credit card over the Net."

"Which bank issued the card?"

"It was Scandinaviska Sparbank. I spoke with the manager of the branch he used, but they wouldn't give me access to his account information without a warrant."

"Prepare an affidavit and you'll have it today."

"Rosengren," said Ekman, "what's been happening with the tip line?"

"Mostly crank calls, but I think we've gotten a few good leads, Chief. Chafik was recognized by three callers who said they'd known him. Alenius and I will be interviewing them later today. Better still, a woman in the building where Dahlin was held called to say she'd seen some people going into that apartment. We'll be talking to her first."

"I knew you and Alenius could separate the wheat from the chaff. Good work." Rosengren beamed and Alenius managed something that almost resembled a smile.

"Alrik, what do we know about Dahlin's estate. Did she have a will?"

"There's no will. I guess someone that young thought she wouldn't need one for a long time." He was silent for a moment.

"There's really no estate to speak of and no insurance policy. Her brother will get her personal effects and that's it."

"Okay, let's say the brother is out of it unless something else implicates him. The focus remains on Chafik and Jakobsson. We need to find out everything about them. I'll be speaking with Kallenberg this afternoon and will let him know the affidavits are on the way," Ekman said, looking at Holm and Vinter.

"Although we missed a chance with Jakobsson, knowing he was involved in Dahlin's death gives us another avenue to explore. Let's make the most of it."

20

REPORTING

Thursday, January 26, 11 a.m. Ekman sat gingerly on one of Malmer's instruments of torture, while the deputy commissioner pretended to busy himself with some papers on his desk. Finally after several minutes he lifted his head, his face registering mock surprise at seeing Ekman somehow materialized before him.

"So, Walther, you wanted to see me?"

"Yes, Olav," he replied, not letting Malmer get away with using his first name as he tended to do with subordinates, not out of friendship, but patronizingly.

"You'll have a written report later today; however, I wanted to bring you and the commissioner up to date personally on what's been happening in the Dahlin case."

After Ekman briefed him about the investigation and Jakobsson's murder yesterday evening, Malmer took a moment to ponder the potential media and political risks, his first consideration.

"Do we need a media conference?"

"I think it would be a good idea," Ekman said. "We've already gotten them involved in the hunt for Chafik and they, and the public, will want to know where the investigation stands. News of Jakobsson's murder will also be on TV this afternoon and hit the papers tonight. The publicity is to our advantage because it could generate more leads."

Despite run-ins with the media, and the personal vendetta newspaperman Bruno Haeggman had launched last year, Ekman still believed they could be useful, as long as they didn't get in the way of an investigation.

"I'll speak with the commissioner about the conference and get back to you," Malmer said, and then, turning to his paperwork, pretended Ekman had vanished as mysteriously as he'd appeared.

Later that afternoon, Ekman called on Kallenberg.

"Can I get you some coffee, Walther?"

"Thanks, that would be great," Ekman replied, settling himself into the cushions of the comfortable leather couch.

Kallenberg asked his receptionist to bring them some coffee and biscuits. Taking an armchair facing the couch, he asked, "So how is that case going?"

He listened attentively, his hands steepled, as Ekman described where they were in the Dahlin investigation. When Ekman came to Jakobsson's sudden death, Kallenberg straightened in his chair in apparent surprise.

"This happened last night?"

"Yes, that's what Bohlander believes."

"Incredible. Someone must be very frightened."

With a knock at the door, the receptionist, a short, white-haired woman of fifty, came in with a tray and, smiling, placed it on the coffee table between them, before leaving.

"Thank you, Greta," Kallenberg said.

He poured the coffee and gestured at the plate of chocolate and orange biscuits.

Ekman took a sip and put two biscuits on his saucer.

As Ekman described the warrants needed for Jakobsson's phone call and Chafik's bank account, Kallenberg was silent.

"You realize you'll be invading the privacy of everyone who used those mobile towers?"

"Yes, but the time window is just two hours and it will only be to eliminate calls of regular phone subscribers. Our theory is that Jakobsson's phone was an untraceable throwaway with a unique number. Once it's identified, then we can find out the number he called and take it from there."

"You're assuming, of course, that he didn't call another untraceable phone."

"That's our hope. The search may lead to a dead end, but we can't ignore it."

Kallenberg hesitated. "You're asking me to persuade the district judge to authorize an invasion of privacy of possibly hundreds of citizens on the slender hope of finding a traceable phone number. Does that sum it up?"

"Yes. But it's the best shot we've got at finding a brutal killer."

"Well then, I guess I have no choice except to try and obtain that warrant. I hope the judge will agree with us. The one for the bank account should be easier. Get me the affidavits and we'll see what can be done."

"There's one other thing," Ekman said. "We've had no luck so far finding Chafik and there's a strong possibility he's already fled Sweden. Because there's an outstanding warrant for his arrest, I think we should also issue an international arrest warrant and simultaneously request an Interpol 'Red Notice' asking any country he's in to hold him for extradition."

"Good idea. You'll have the formal Interpol request along with the warrants. I'll leave it to you to get in touch with the right people in Stockholm. Be sure you go through them to contact Interpol. It's the bureaucratic system we've created that we now have to put up with. We wouldn't want anyone getting their nose out of joint," he said with a rueful smile, getting up. "Good luck. I'll look forward to your progress reports."

They shook hands as Ekman left.

Kallenberg sat at his desk thinking about Ekman's request to trace the mobile tower numbers. It was clever, but unlikely to produce any results. Using a throwaway phone without GPS was too common a criminal practice. He decided that anyone Jakobsson had called who was stupid or careless enough to use a traceable phone would be eliminated before being questioned.

21

PRAGUE

Thursday, January 26, 10 p.m. The Medved Dance Club on Myslikova Ulice, a main street in Karimova Namesti, the New Town south of Prague's historic district, was packed. Tomas stood with his back against the bar sipping sparkling water as he watched the crowd gyrating to the DJ's deafening punk rock while colored strobe lights swept back and forth across the huge room.

Tomas didn't regret what had been done to Jakobsson: he'd become an unacceptable danger. The Keeper had called Tomas back later, describing his conversation with Gotz. They both were concerned he might become a loose cannon: he liked killing too much. But they needed Gotz's special talents. Besides enforcement, he was good at breaking in new women, and the occasional boy. It was a form of payment Gotz seemed to enjoy even more than cash.

Since the weekend, Tomas had been searching outside a much-too-risky Sweden for a replacement for Dahlin, but hadn't had any luck with the two likely looking Czech women he'd already approached. They'd both been with friends, and while they'd been interested in him, had been too difficult to extricate.

"Excuse me," she said in heavily accented English. He'd been so lost in thought as he watched the dance floor that he hadn't noticed the woman who'd approached on his left until she'd spoken. He turned toward her. She could have been Dahlin's sister.

"I want to get the bartender's attention and there's no room at the bar."

"Sorry," he said in perfect British English, flashing an even, white-toothed smile. "I'm taking up more than my fair share of space. Please allow me to make amends by getting you that drink. What would you like?"

She hesitated, "Okay, thanks, a Cosmo, please."

He caught the bartender's eye and ordered.

He clinked glasses with her, "Cheers."

"Are you English?" she asked.

"As the occasion demands," he said. "And you're Czech?"

"Actually, I'm Romanian. I'm a graduate student at Charles University." She held out her hand, "Ilinca."

"Tomas," he responded, holding her hand for a long moment. "How come Prague? Do you have family here?"

"No, no one. I got a scholarship: in mathematics."

Better and better. "Where's the boyfriend?" he asked, looking around as though he might appear unexpectedly from the crowd.

"I just started this semester and haven't made any real friends yet."

"This is my lucky night then," he replied, with what he hoped was a dazzling, infectious grin, and meant every word.

22

OPENING DOORS

Friday, January 27, 8 a.m. Ekman looked around the table at his team, noting several glum expressions. Well, he thought, let's hear the bad news.

"Let's start with the Jakobsson murder," he said, turning to Rosengren. "Any luck with those calls?"

"Yes and no, Chief. Alenius and I quickly found an untraceable number in the right time frame. It was soon after you and Alrik left Jakobsson. We thought it was a safe bet that it was his. We tried pinging it to get its location, but it didn't have GPS. Then we tried the number Jakobsson had called. There was no answer, so we tried pinging it too, but got nothing. So that stopped us."

"Well, we were afraid of that, but the possibility had to be pursued. Thanks for the good job checking it out." Ekman was disappointed, but it had been a long shot anyway.

"Alrik, what do we have from forensics and pathology?"

"Jakobsson's DNA didn't match that of the second guy who had sex with Dahlin. They checked his clothing for new DNA, but whoever took his phone was probably wearing gloves. Also, when Bohlander opened his hands, there was nothing. The time of death was what we'd expected, about an hour after we'd spoken with him. The garrote was probably a thin steel wire. We don't have anything on an MO like that in Sweden."

"Okay, so now we know he wasn't one of the two men in the apartment with Dahlin. That's helpful. But he had to be involved in some other way. Maybe he knew Chafik or the other man. What else do we know about Jakobsson?"

"Our street informants confirmed he was just a small-time drug pusher. We're trying to find some of his clients," said Holm. "But I don't think any of them killed him. I believe it was what we suspected before: he must have known something important about Dahlin's death, threatened the wrong people, and had to be shut up."

"Do the rest of you think Enar is right?" asked Ekman. The others nodded their agreement.

"This brings us back to Dahlin. If we pursue things from that end, it could tell us what led to Jakobsson's death."

"We may have something for you there, Chief," said Rosengren, looking more upbeat.

"The woman who saw some people going into the apartment described Dahlin and Chafik pretty accurately. She'd seen him go in and out a couple of times, but she saw Dahlin only once. She seemed drunk or sick, the woman said, because she was leaning on Chafik and he was propping her up before they went in."

"So Dahlin was probably drugged to get her into the apartment. It tells us how they moved her, but that's all," said Rapp.

"I know," replied Rosengren in an irritated tone. "I'm not finished. She also caught a glimpse on another day of an older guy going into that apartment. She's agreed to work with our sketch artist. So we could have a picture of him tomorrow."

"That would be a major step forward, if we can rely on her memory," said Ekman. "Find out more about the lighting conditions in the hallway and how long she saw him. If she actually got a good look at him, we could give the picture to the media."

Turning to Vinter, he said, "Gerdi, what did you learn from Chafik's bank account?"

"When he came to Sweden a year ago, Chafik had a job with a wholesale spice importer, Worldwide Spices AB, in Stockholm. His account showed regular twice-a-month payments from the company that came to 365,000 kronor a year. Six months ago they stopped. Since then there have been monthly electronic transfers that were twice what he'd been making. The really interesting thing is that they came from Al-Amin Bank, in Marrakech."

"Gerdi, I'd like you and Enar to find out what you can about that spice company. Then both of you drive up this afternoon to Stockholm and pay them a visit. Make sure to check in first with the local police. We need to know what Chafik did there, why he left, and where he went afterward. He came to Sweden from Morocco, so the recent payments may have been from family. I'll see if we can find out more about who the money came from.

"We're making progress," Ekman said. "See all of you tomorrow."

23

GRANHOLM

Friday, January 27, 10 a.m. Ekman phoned his friend, Superintendent Garth Rystrom at the National Criminal Investigation Department in Stockholm, hoping he'd catch him in.

"Rystrom," came the familiar voice.

"Garth, it's Walther. How are you and yours?"

"I'm well. How are you doing?"

"As good as can be expected. Garth, we're working on a case you've no doubt heard about: the Dahlin girl. We need your help."

"Whatever I can do."

Ekman described where they were in the investigation. "Our prosecutor has authorized an international arrest warrant for Chafik and a request for an Interpol 'Red Notice.' I've lost touch with who would be best to handle this in the National Bureau. I was hoping you could suggest someone."

"I have just the person in mind. I'll e-mail you the contact information. Let me talk with her first so she'll expect your call. Her name is Valdis Granholm, a superintendent in

International Police Cooperation. She's with the special FAST unit for apprehending internationally wanted persons. We've worked on several cases over the last five years and I think you'll find her easy to get along with."

"Thanks, Garth. I'll look forward to speaking with her."

"You caught me just in time. I'll be out of town on a brief assignment. And if you should meet with Valdis while I'm away, don't be surprised, she's not only very sharp, she's stunning . . . and divorced. But maybe it would be better not to mention that to your charming wife. Anyway, take care of yourself, Walther, and say hello to Ingbritt for me."

Later that morning, Ekman phoned Granholm.

"Garth filled me in on your investigation and what you need. I'll be glad to be your contact with the international agencies."

"That's great. We've also discovered that Chafik had recently been getting large monthly payments from the Al-Amin Bank in Marrakech. Possibly they came from his family there. He'd received a letter from a Fayyad Joumari, who may be an uncle. We'd like to know more about him, and also who was sending Chafik money and why."

"That may be more difficult. Let me talk to one of my colleagues with contacts in the Moroccan Interpol bureau. I'll see what can be done."

"Thanks for your help, it's really appreciated."

Ekman hung up, and pulling himself out of his much-abused desk chair, walked to the windows. For a few minutes, he watched the pedestrians scurrying across Stortorget plaza under a steady, freezing rain, before turning away.

He sat back down and taking the needlepoint cushion cover he'd been working on from a desk drawer, began slowly adding a forest-green thread to the complex pattern. He and the team had agreed that Dahlin's and Jakobsson's deaths were elements of a single, connected case. Ekman hoped that, like the design he was working on, a hard tug on the Dahlin thread would unravel the pattern, revealing the truth.

24

THE VISITOR

Wednesday, January 25, 6:50 p.m. The lame man's flight to Stockholm had been uneventful; he'd slept most of the way. As he came out of the terminal trailing his small suitcase, looking for the taxi stand, he pulled his new overcoat tighter around him. After years in Marrakech he wasn't used to a Swedish winter: it was zero degrees Celsius under a dark grey sky that threatened snow at any moment.

A thirty-five-minute cab ride delivered him to the famous Grand Hotel, overlooking Gamla Stan, Stockholm's ancient heart, where he found that the old man had unexpectedly paid for a suite.

This family matter must really mean something to him, the lame man thought: doubling my normal fee, then a business-class seat, and now this suite. In the two years he'd worked for the old man he'd never known him to be free with money. He must want me to appreciate the importance of this assignment. He shrugged his shoulders and put it out of his mind as irrelevant.

The lame man prided himself on always being coldly rational. While he understood, and used, the feelings that impelled others, *including the old man, it was from an emotional distance he'd never crossed since he was a child. It didn't matter to him whether an assignment from the old man involved one of his many legitimate or criminal businesses: it was all the same to him.*

Peering out the large, second-floor windows, he could see only the harbor lights; the nearby royal palace grounds were shrouded in darkness. The few things he'd brought were quickly unpacked.

He took out his laptop and found what he was looking for without difficulty. There were several Swedish newspaper stories about the search for Chafik and his possible involvement in Lynni Dahlin's death. He had the computer translate them into English and read through each carefully.

After an hour of this, he debated whether to make the phone call now or wait until he'd had dinner. A late-hour call might prove more unsettling to the man he'd phone; he'd often found this useful. It might be better to wait, besides he hadn't eaten on the plane and was hungry. He went down to Matbaren, one of the hotel's Mathias Dahlgren, Michelin-star restaurants.

The lame man had taken his time over an elaborate dinner; it was now ten fifteen. He settled on the elegant, green-and-white striped couch in the living room. A phone was within easy reach on the mahogany end table. Finding the number he was looking for among the papers the old man had given him, he lifted the receiver and got an outside line.

25

SPICE MERCHANTS

Friday, January 27, 3:30 p.m. Gerdi Vinter and Enar Holm were sitting in the office of the manager of Worldwide Spices waiting for him to appear. His secretary, a plain, heavyset blonde woman in her forties, had told them he was in a meeting and would join them shortly.

They looked around the starkly furnished room with its cheap wooden desk, single steel filing cabinet, an old TV set, and two thinly padded guest chairs. The manager's desk was bare; there were no family photos. The walls were undecorated except for a large, unframed map of the world, held up by push pins, to the left of the manager's desk. The office told them nothing about the manager or the firm, except that extreme frugality appeared to be the company motto.

They'd made good time driving up the E4, arriving in Stockholm two hours before their appointment. Going directly to the city police headquarters at Kungsholmgatan 43, they'd identified themselves to the desk sergeant who called upstairs. A grey-haired inspector came down to meet them and they explained that they were in Stockholm following a lead in the Dahlin investigation. He was curious about how that was going, but they didn't provide any details. They knew Ekman would prefer they keep it that way.

Holm found a convenient parking space down the street from the spice company's warehouse at 420 Frihamnsgatan, near the docks. When they'd first driven into the neighborhood, they'd looked for a convenient place for a quick lunch, and spotted an Indian restaurant two blocks away. They decided to try it, and leaving their car, walked over.

When they came in, they were surprised to see that this small, hole-in-the-wall place was filled with customers eager to take advantage of the reduced lunch prices, and it seemed, tasty food. They were lucky to find a table.

"We made a good choice," said Vinter, as she used a piece of naan bread to scoop up another bite of her palak paneer.

"Yeah, they've got a great buffet," Holm said, glancing over at the long table against the far wall. Customers were moving back and forth, ladling samples onto their overflowing plates from the row of twelve covered chafing dishes set out on a white linen tablecloth.

Holm picked up another forkful of tandoori chicken and paused before putting it in his mouth.

"So do you think the company's legit?" he asked. They'd been talking only about their future plans together on the drive up and hadn't discussed what Vinter had found out about the spice importer.

"It looks that way. They've been in business for six years and have had contracts with major supermarket chains like Coop Forum and ICA MAXI."

"Then it's been a good business."

"Good enough. The Tax Agency told me that last year they had gross sales of around 330 million kronor."

"Who owns it?"

"A holding company controls the stock, which isn't unusual, except that this one's based in Rabat, the Moroccan capital."

"Don't keep me in suspense. Who's the real owner?"

"I have no idea. Maybe Ekman can find out, but otherwise it's a dead end."

"Perhaps using your feminine wiles, you can pry the information out of the manager," Holm said, grinning.

"My womanly charm is focused only on you, sir, as you very well know," she replied. They'd been hopelessly in love for more than a year.

"In that case, let's see if I can be the persuasive one," Holm said, looking at his watch as he pushed his chair back. "I'm going to grab another plateful, and then we'd better head over."

They looked up as the manager, a good-looking man in his thirties, wearing a conservative suit with a yellow tie, came into the office.

"I'm really sorry to have kept you waiting, inspectors, an unexpected meeting," he said apologetically, coming forward with his hand out, as they both stood up. "I'm Thore Ostlund."

He gave them a broad, friendly smile, as they all shook hands before he moved behind his desk and sat down.

"Now, how can I help you?"

"We're looking into the disappearance of one of your employees, Ahmed Chafik," said Vinter.

"Actually he's a former employee," Ostlund said, giving her a wide grin that showed his white teeth. "Chafik left, let's see, it was last summer, about six or seven months ago. I can get you the exact time."

"That would be helpful. We'll need the dates of his employment. Did he say why he was leaving and where he was going?"

"As I recall, he told me that he wanted a job with more advancement possibilities. But he didn't say where he was going to find it," he said.

"What did he do here?" asked Holm.

"Well, we're a small wholesale firm with a limited office staff, but with more people in the warehouse. He was an administrative assistant handling shipment invoices and accounts receivable."

"Was his work satisfactory?"

"He was okay with routine paperwork, but wasn't creative; he never came up with any ideas to improve things. My impression was that he was fairly dull."

"I'm sure you've heard that we're looking for him in connection with the death of a young woman," said Vinter.

"Yes, I saw the story in the papers and I was shocked. Chafik was a quiet guy. He didn't socialize with people here after work and so I don't know anything about his private life, but he certainly didn't seem like the type who'd be involved in a woman's death."

"What type would that be, Herr Ostlund?" asked Holm.

"Well, a rowdy, a tough guy, I suppose. I don't really know," he replied with a disarming smile.

"Sometimes the people you'd least suspect surprise you the most," said Vinter.

"I guess that's right. I'm sure you meet all kinds in your work."

"We'll have to interview your employees about their contacts with Chafik, so we'll need their names, addresses, and phone numbers," said Holm.

"Is it really necessary to discuss this with all our employees?" Ostlund responded, apparently taken by surprise.

"This is a criminal investigation, Herr Ostlund. And yes, it's necessary," replied Holm.

"Just a moment," said Ostlund, getting up. "I'll ask Marta, my secretary, to start on that list."

He went out of the room for a few minutes, and then came back and sat down.

"Is this a profitable company, Herr Ostlund?" Vinter asked. She already knew the answer, but wanted to hear what he would say if her question threw him off balance.

"We do all right," he said, his face showing some surprise. "Business has grown over the past six years and we've been lucky to land some major contracts even competing against really big companies like McCormick. Our supplier, a spice factory in India, has given us a competitive edge in pricing."

"Do you own the company, Herr Ostlund?" Holm asked, although he knew the answer to this question too.

"No, although I wish I did. I just manage it."

"Who is the owner?"

"It's an outfit in Morocco. A holding company. Marta will get you the address and phone number." He wants to impress us with how cooperative he is, Holm thought.

"Do you have frequent contact with them?"

"It's not frequent. Mostly I send them monthly reports and they call if they have any questions."

"They must trust you a lot," said Vinter.

"They should," he replied with a dazzling toothy smile. "I do a great job for them. But we also have an annual audit by an accounting firm. Besides, I'm a really honest guy," he said with a laugh.

Where have I heard that before? thought Holm.

"Do you mind if we look around the warehouse?" Holm asked.

"No, not at all," Ostlund replied, with a surprised look. "I have some things I need to attend to, but Marta will get you the information you asked for and show you our facility. Give me a call if you have any further questions," he said, standing, and smiling broadly gave each of them his card.

He buzzed for his secretary and when she came in asked her to show their visitors around after she'd given them the information they wanted. She nodded, regarding them with a heavy, expressionless face.

"And good luck with your search," he called out, as they headed down the hall behind Marta.

Sitting inside a company delivery truck in the far corner of the large, chain-link fenced parking lot, Gotz watched with narrowed eyes as the two inspectors moved along the warehouse loading dock. They were questioning two workmen who were putting cartons of boxes filled with spice packets into trucks. After observing them for a few more minutes, he lit a cigarette, started the engine, and drove out of the lot.

They questioned the seven employees who were working that day, but discovered nothing of interest about Chafik. Telephone interviews would have to do for the other employees, but if significant information seemed likely, they'd have to return.

In the car on the way back to Weltenborg, Holm asked Vinter what she thought about Ostlund.

"He smiles too much," she said.

26

A PORTRAIT

Saturday, January 28, 6:20 a.m. Ekman was getting dressed in his usual three-piece, black suit. He couldn't conceive of wearing anything else to the office, Saturdays were no exception, although he tolerated his detectives' casual weekend clothes. He scowled at his reflection in the dressing room's full-length mirror, noticing how the vest he was trying to button was straining to contain his stomach. I've got to do something about this, he thought, or I'll soon have to buy new clothes.

But downstairs he heard Ingbritt preparing breakfast and realized he was much too hungry to just grab a bite of dry toast and a cup of black coffee. Well, I'll use restraint at lunch and dinner, was the excuse he gave himself. He knew this was a rationale for a personal failing, but told himself no one is without some flaw: this was his.

As he came into the brightly lit, yellow-painted kitchen he saw that Ingbritt was wrapped in her quilted, flower-patterned robe. It was dark outside and the sun wouldn't be up for almost two hours, but the room was cheerful.

"So what fabulous repast have you prepared for us this morning, my sweet?"

"It's not 'fabulous'," she laughed, "but it should be satisfactory. I'll serve."

The kitchen table was set with a blue linen cloth and white china. Ekman pulled back his chair and sat down rubbing his hands as Ingbritt placed in front of him a plate of mackerel fillet in tomato sauce on brown bread, topped with cucumber slices. On the sideboard were more bread, assorted cheeses, slices of ham, and a large cinnamon roll.

"I say this is 'fabulous' and I won't be contradicted," he said, as he picked up his knife and fork.

Over strong, black coffee and plates of the cinnamon roll, the two sat quietly, looking through the morning papers, until Ekman, glancing at the kitchen clock, saw it was almost seven fifteen, and got up.

"Time I got started," he said, heading down the hall for his coat and hat.

As SHE often did, Ingbritt went to the front windows to watch him leave. She worried constantly whether he'd return safely because his work exposed him to the constant threat of danger. The risk had diminished as he'd risen in rank, but she knew it was always there.

Everything that mattered most in her life revolved around this reserved, sensitive man she'd married when she was very young. She knew he loved her, and understood she was sometimes fragile. He tried to reassure her by constant attentions: flowers, unexpected gifts, and remembered birthdays and anniversaries.

Writing filled her time while he was at work. The award-winning children's books she wrote distracted her from persistent worry about the danger her Walther faced. Her books transported her to a simpler, brighter world where, in the end, love always prevailed. It was her refuge from the menacing reality she had to live with every day.

It was minus-three degrees Celsius and Ekman could see large, falling snowflakes glistening in the light from the house as he backed down the driveway. He drove cautiously along snow-slicked Brunnvägen, his defroster and wipers on high. Twenty minutes later, he parked his black, Volvo S80 in the police headquarters' underground garage and then headed up the stairs to the cafeteria on the second floor to order coffee and sweet rolls for the team.

At eight exactly, Ekman went into the conference room to find his team members milling around the side table, eating Wienerbröd pastries and sipping coffee.

He poured himself just a cup of black coffee before sitting down at the head of the table, as the others took their usual places.

"Thanks for coming in on a Saturday. Overtime pay is good, but I know you'd just as soon have the day off. Let's see if we can't make this the last Saturday we spend on this case.

"Gerdi and Enar, what can you tell us about that spice company?"

"It looks like a successful, legitimate business," said Holm, describing what they'd learned about the company, Chafik's employment, and the absentee Moroccan owner.

While he was speaking, Ekman had noticed that Vinter was frowning.

"Gerdi, what do you think?" he asked.

"Chief, I agree with Enar that the business is exactly what it appears to be. The employees we questioned didn't know anything useful about Chafik and seemed okay. But I've got a vague feeling that something is wrong, although I can't put my finger on it. I guess it's because I didn't like the manager, who was trying too hard to ingratiate himself. And the woman who's his secretary seemed rather strange, and was clearly reluctant to tell us about Chafik. These are just my very subjective impressions and probably don't mean anything."

"Your intuition is usually exactly right. We'll keep it in mind. But give me the information about that foreign owner and I'll see what more we can learn."

Ekman turned to Rosengren. "How did that witness work out?"

Rosengren reached into a folder in front of him and distributed a facial sketch of the older man the woman tenant had seen in the hallway.

"She came in and spent two hours with our artist. It looks detailed enough for people to recognize him," he said.

"What about the lighting in the hall?"

"She only saw him that once, but said there was enough light to get a good look at him."

"Okay, now we have something concrete to give the media. I'm going to ask the commissioner to call a conference. It may take some time to organize, so it will probably be Tuesday morning. Alrik, you and I will be handling it. The rest of you will also want to be there," Ekman said, looking around the table. "But be unobtrusive, and if someone asks you anything, refer them to me.

"Enar and Gerdi, now that you've met some of the people at the spice company, I'd like you to check the background of all the employees. Let's see if there's anything that can substantiate what Gerdi's radar detected."

"Rosengren and Alenius, you've done such good work sifting the wheat from the chaff, I want you to handle the

phone calls we'll get when that sketch hits the media." The
two seemed about to protest, then evidently thought better
about it and simply slumped in their seats with downcast
expressions.

"And Alrik, you and I will be working together on the
Moroccan connection. I think it would be a good idea for us
to get to know our international contact in Stockholm better.
As soon as I can arrange a meeting, let's plan on driving up
there. Have a good Sunday everyone," Ekman concluded, getting up. "I'll see you at the media conference."

27

RAPP

Sunday, January 29, 12:30 p.m. Alrik Rapp's Sunday had started off well enough even though it was another grey day with freezing rain beating steadily against the windows of his small house with its carefully tended yard.

He'd made fancy sandwiches for brunch for his teenage daughter, Mia, and himself, and then settled down to finish reading the Sunday papers with his black Lab, Balder, lying beside his easy chair.

Life as a single, male parent hadn't been easy. His wife had died ten years ago of liver cancer when Mia was eight. Although he was only thirty-six then, he'd never remarried. Between long hours at work and raising his daughter there had been little time or money for a social life. He'd been fortunate early on to find a nanny for his pretty little girl, an older woman who loved Mia. Retired last year, she came to visit as often as she could, but Rapp was now on his own as a father.

He was browsing through the sports section when Mia came in, carefully made up, and wearing a bright yellow raincoat, matching hat, and high, black boots.

"Where are you headed in this miserable weather, honey?" he asked. "Do you really have to go out?" He wanted to spend the day with his daughter, take her to a movie, and then maybe dinner at a local Italian restaurant she liked.

"I'm meeting some friends. We'll be together all day and I'll probably be back late tonight."

Rapp was hurt, but tried to smile anyway. He didn't want her to feel he was always hovering over her, although that's exactly what he would have preferred to do.

"Are these friends I've met?"

"It's Adela," she said, naming her best friend, "and a couple of guys she knows."

"But you don't?"

"No, but you don't need to be worried. If Adela likes them, they're okay."

"Mia, I'd feel better if you at least knew these men."

"Well, the only way to get to know new boys is to meet them, right?" Now she sounded annoyed.

"I'm just concerned for your safety, honey. There are a lot of dangerous types out there." He couldn't help thinking about the Dahlin girl and what had happened to her; it preyed on his mind.

"Don't be such a worrier, Pappa, I'll be fine," she said as she went over to kiss him good-bye.

"Leave your mobile on, Mia, and please call if you need anything, okay?"

"If it will make you feel better, sure. And don't wait up, please," she replied, in an exasperated voice, and turning, headed out the front door.

Rapp sat there, staring at the closed door. If something should happen to her, he didn't know what he would do. His job was important to him, but she was the real center of his life. Mia was gradually finding her way to becoming an

independent adult. She no longer wanted his constant attention, yet he knew he would always be there, quietly watching
over her, terribly afraid that one of the tragedies he dealt with
every day could overtake her despite his best efforts.

She found him anxiously waiting up when she finally
came home at eleven thirty that night.

28

NORLANDER

Monday, January 30, 10 a.m. After yesterday's rain, the sky had been washed a cold, crystalline blue. Bright sunlight streamed through the large windows of Commissioner Elias Norlander's fifth-floor corner office overlooking Weltenborg's central square. It wasn't the usual Spartan police office: it had been decorated at the commissioner's expense with dark antique furniture, oil paintings in gilded frames, and intricately patterned Persian rugs.

Ekman was sitting on a soft, brown leather couch, with Norlander and Olav Malmer in armchairs facing him. Norlander's slender, Saville Row-suited form contrasted sharply with his deputy's short figure in a rumpled tan jacket. Where Malmer was abrupt, abrasive, and tone-deaf to others, Norlander was smooth, conciliatory, and politically astute. They were childhood friends and Malmer was very loyal; Norlander made allowances for him.

"So, Walther," Norlander said, "you think you need a media conference now?"

"Yes, commissioner," Ekman replied, describing how they'd come up with the sketch of an unknown man. "They can help us publicize the picture. A briefing might also quiet them down. As you know, they've been clamoring for more information about the Dahlin case."

"Are you going to tell them about the suspected link to the Jakobsson murder?"

"It's only conjecture, so I don't propose we discuss it. Alrik Rapp will be with me at the briefing. He's never done one of these before and the exposure will be good for him."

"I agree that not discussing the possible Jakobsson connection is the right approach until we know more. And I'm sure you and Alrik can handle the conference. It doesn't sound like Olav and I need to be there."

Ekman realized he was distancing himself from the case until it seemed likely to be resolved; then Norlander would suddenly become very accessible to the media.

"You suggested tomorrow afternoon. How about one? That will give them plenty of time to get it on the evening TV news and in the morning papers."

"That sounds fine, Commissioner."

"I'll have our public relations officer set it up," added Malmer, reminding them he was there.

Norlander rose. "Thank you for your hard work, Walther."

"And let's hope this briefing helps you finally solve these cases," said Malmer, a parting shot as Ekman headed for the door.

29

KALLENBERG'S PROBLEM

Monday, January 30, 2 p.m. Arvid Kallenberg was pacing back and forth in his office, glancing occasionally at the police sketch in his hand. Ekman was sitting, watching the usually imperturbable prosecutor.

When he'd told Kallenberg about the press conference he hadn't seemed agitated until Ekman had shown him the portrait of the unknown man. Then he'd gotten up and started to pace.

"Is something wrong, Arvid?" Ekman asked.

Kallenberg resumed his seat behind his desk and placed the sketch in front of him.

"Walther, I know you think the media might help identify this man and it would aid your investigation, but there's a problem."

"What is it?"

"Tell me again why you're interested in him."

Ekman described in detail the sighting of the man entering the apartment Lynni Dahlin had escaped from. "He may be the other man who raped her."

"But he was seen on another day, not the one she died."

"Yes, but his involvement could be significant anyway."

"You're proposing to distribute a picture that could be any one of hundreds of men who vaguely resemble this sketch," he said, pointing to it. "And you'll inevitably get dozens of calls from people who think they know who it is."

"That's likely. We'll just have to sort through them."

"While you and your team are doing that, which could take any number of days, suspicion of involvement in a horrible crime will fall on every single man your callers identify."

"That's possible, but we'll ask the people who call not to jump to conclusions."

"After you've sorted through those calls, you'll have to question all the men who could be this individual, isn't that so? It would take even more time to check alibis, and so on."

"You know all that is normal police work, Arvid. I don't believe it can be avoided."

Kallenberg ran his hands through his hair. "You're right, Walther, but as you can tell, I'm extremely uncomfortable about this entire business."

"What is bothering you in particular?" Ekman asked in a neutral tone. He wasn't quite certain why Kallenberg was reluctant to give the sketch to the media, but thought it was curious.

"It's just possible I know the man in your sketch. I'm certain he couldn't be involved, but I have a duty to tell you. If it comes out that he's being questioned it will cause not just him, but his family, great distress, and I don't want to put them through it.

"In my mind, I'm multiplying this situation hundreds of times over. I don't know if we're morally justified doing this on the slim chance that something helpful may come from all we'll be putting many innocent people through."

"I understand your feelings, Arvid, but I don't think we have a choice. We can't just ignore an obvious means of identifying a potential rape suspect. We'll try to be as careful as possible. Who do you think you recognized?"

Kallenberg was silent for a moment. "It looks somewhat like Bengt Engblom. He's been my internist for years. But I can't conceive that it's him."

Ekman took out a small, black notebook, and made an entry. "We'll check it out."

"For God's sake, do it quietly. If it got out, it could ruin him." Kallenberg dropped his serious manner and laughed abruptly. "Then where would I find another really good internist?"

Ekman wondered if that was the only reason that lay behind Kallenberg's reluctance.

30

CONFERENCE

Tuesday, January 31, 1 p.m. Rapp was standing at the podium while a noisy crowd of reporters milled about in the auditorium's aisles as TV crews positioned their cameras. Looking over their heads, he saw the other team members standing at the back.

"Ladies and gentlemen, please take your seats so we can get started," he said, his voice booming too loudly before he stepped back from the microphone and cleared his throat. He was a little nervous at running his first media conference.

Gradually people took their seats and the hubbub subsided.

"Thank you for coming. I'm Chief Inspector Alrik Rapp and with me is Chief Superintendent Walther Ekman, who is heading the Lynni Dahlin investigation," he said, turning to Ekman who was several paces behind him. Ekman, glancing around the room, raised his hand, acknowledging the crowd.

"We need your help asking the public to identify a possible person of interest in the Dahlin case. We have a police sketch of a man we'd like to speak with," Rapp said, holding up an oversize version of the sketch with the phone to call in big red numbers along the bottom. The TV cameras focused in on it.

"Fru Sahlin will give you the picture before you leave," he said, looking at the media relations officer standing to one side of the platform near a table with a pile of photos.

"We'll try to answer any questions you have," said Rapp.

Several hands went up and he pointed to a short woman in the front row.

"How was this man involved in Dahlin's death?" she asked.

"We don't know that he was, but we'd like to speak with him because he was seen in the immediate vicinity."

Rapp indicated a well-dressed man several rows back.

"You haven't told us why Dahlin was on that roof in the first place. Was she trying to commit suicide, or did this man push her out that attic window?"

Ekman came to the microphone. "At this point in our investigation it's not clear if she was trying to kill herself. And as Herr Rapp has said, we don't know if this man was at all involved.

"Please ask your readers and viewers not to jump to any conclusions, even if they think they recognize him. Many men who have absolutely nothing to do with this case may resemble the sketch. We'd appreciate it if you'd emphasize that people need to just call with their information, and leave it to us to sort it out." Ekman felt he'd now tried as best he could to satisfy Kallenberg's misgivings.

"You haven't released the autopsy findings. When will you do that?" The question was asked in a belligerent tone by a disheveled Bruno Haeggman, the chief investigative reporter for *Sydsvenska Nyheter,* one of Sweden's largest papers. He'd hounded Ekman mercilessly during the Grendel case last year, almost destroying his reputation.

Ekman looked hard at Haeggman and replied in a controlled voice, "Herr Haeggman, as I'm sure you know, this information can't be released yet. It would be premature and damage our investigation. The report will be made available as soon as we can responsibly do that."

"More bureaucratic stonewalling," said Haeggman loudly. "The public has a right to know what's going on." The TV cameras had swiveled to cover him.

"We recognize the public's right, Herr Haeggman, and will provide all the information we can as soon as we can," Ekman responded in a mild tone. He turned and looked at Rapp pointedly, meaning call on someone else.

"Okay, if you're so sensitive to the public's rights, tell us how the Kalle Jakobsson murder is tied in," said Haeggman with smug satisfaction.

How did he pick up on that so fast, thought Ekman?

"We don't know if Herr Jakobsson's death is connected."

"Well, maybe my readers will figure it out faster than you apparently can. Read all about it tomorrow in the *Sydsvenska Nyheter*. It may help your so-called investigation," Haeggman said, his voice heavy with sarcasm, as he turned and stalked out, the TV cameras zooming in on his departing figure.

31

DINNER WITH HAEGGMAN

Tuesday, January 31, 7:30 p.m. Ekman was digging into
a dish of raggmunk . . . potato pancakes with fried pork and
lingonberries . . . as he recapped the press conference for
Ingbritt.

"So Haeggman turned it into a public relations disaster for
us, just as he intended," he said, grimacing around a mouthful
of pancake and reaching for his glass of Dugges ale.

"I hate that man; he has no conscience," said Ingbritt.
"Why does he keep attacking you?" Ekman saw that she'd
become agitated.

"There's no point in getting upset. Haeggman's an egoma-
niac, always on the prowl for stories that tear people down, so
long as it gets him an attention-grabbing headline and more
readers. It's what he lives for."

"I don't know how you have the patience to put up with it."

"That's the first time you've ever accused me of having too
much patience."

"And it may be the last," she replied, smiling as she calmed
down. "So, was he right after all about the Jakobsson murder?"

"Unfortunately. He must have found out from Dahlin's brother or her flat mates that Jakobsson had been her boyfriend until just before she disappeared. Then he tied the two deaths together so it would give him a sensational story. Of course, he made me look like an idiot when I said we hadn't made the connection."

"But you had."

"Yes, but not for public consumption. After all, there's just our best guess that Jakobsson must have known something about Dahlin's death and had to be shut up."

"An informed guess based on years of experience."

"Mine, Alrik's, and the team's. It's good enough for us, however it's not 'ready for prime time,' as they say."

"When do you think you'll have the evidence you need?"

"Ingbritt," he said with a laugh, "when we catch the men behind Dahlin's death, force them to admit what they did to her, and then get them to confess who killed Jakobsson."

"But even when you find the monsters who drove that poor woman to her death, they may never admit to killing Jakobsson."

"Exactly," Ekman said, pointing a finger at her. "You've hit the nail on the head. We'll probably need to offer a reduced sentence to one of them in exchange for that information. It's the most likely way we'll get evidence that could persuade a court. I didn't want to make the connection public because the killer could become alarmed at the increased attention and feel more at risk. Then any accomplice, knowing who killed Jakobsson, may have good reason to think he could be next."

"That miserable Haeggman isn't just harming you, he's hurting the investigation, and endangering someone who might identify the murderer."

"That's what I'm afraid of. But enough of this distasteful subject," Ekman said, as he wiped up the last traces of food from his plate. "Let's focus on something more appetizing. What do we have for dessert?"

The next morning, Haeggman's story was on the front page above the fold. The sketch of the man they were looking for had been on television news last night, but had been relegated to an inside page of the paper so that Haeggman's story would get the most attention.

As he read it over breakfast, Ekman had another surprise. The reporter had somehow found out . . . maybe he'd bribed a morgue attendant . . . that Jakobsson had been garroted. It was information about the killer's MO that Ekman had hoped they could keep to themselves.

Goddamn him, he thought. He's fucking up this investigation for a byline and there's no way to stop him.

32

BREAKFAST WITH IVAR

Thursday, January 26, 9:05 a.m. *The lame man looked up from his menu and stared across the table at the other man, who seemed unaware he was being watched as he decided what to order.*

When the lame man had called last night, speaking in lightly accented English, the voice at the other end of the line had at first shown surprise, then quickly recovered. The lame man had proposed a breakfast meeting at his hotel, but the other man had insisted on this nondescript café hidden on a side street in the old quarter.

He's afraid someone might recognize him, the lame man thought; he doesn't want to be seen with me. That's interesting; he must know people who frequent my posh hotel. All he'd been given by the old man in Marrakech was a contact phone number for the supplier. Now he knew much more.

He guessed the man was in his fifties. Tall and fair haired, he was dressed in a dark business suit.

"I'll be wearing a red tie and sitting at a table in the back," *the man had said.*

The lame man had taken a taxi from the hotel. When he entered the small café, filled with the aroma of freshly ground coffee, there were only a few customers. It made it easy to pick him out. As he walked toward the table, the man stood and extended his hand; the lame man briefly shook it as they sat down.

"We haven't exchanged names, but you can call me Ivar, if you like," the Keeper said, smiling. "What shall I call you?"

The lame man looked at him for a moment before replying. "Karim, will do."

"Okay, Karim," the Keeper said. "You probably noticed that I was rather surprised by your call last night."

"Why was that?"

"Because I'd already told your boss's assistant that Ahmed had simply stopped coming to work. We still have no idea where he is."

"As you can tell, that didn't satisfy my boss. He has a personal interest in Ahmed; it's a family matter."

A middle-aged waiter came over. "Have you decided, gentlemen?" he said in English, for the benefit of the obviously foreign customer.

Ivar ordered an open-faced ham and cheese sandwich, and coffee. The lame man, orange juice and muesli with yogurt.

"I'm sorry your trip to Sweden seems a waste of time. But if you haven't been here before, perhaps I can suggest some attractions that might interest you."

"I'm not here as a tourist," the lame man said in a flat tone.

"I understand. But there's no harm in mixing business with a little pleasure, is there?"

"Perhaps not." They sat there in silence until their food arrived.

"How do you like the Grand?" Ivar asked, as they ate.

"It's all right."

"Have you worked for your boss for a long time?"

"For a while."

"Is he difficult to deal with?"

"Not particularly."

Ivar's attempts at conversation were going nowhere and ground to a halt. It was several minutes before he spoke again.

"I was thinking you might like to see where Ahmed worked. It's about an hour south of Stockholm. I could drive you there."

"That would be helpful," the lame man said, as he took a last spoonful of muesli.

"When would you like to go?"

"Today or tomorrow. The sooner the better."

"I have some business to attend to today, but I could meet you near here at ten a.m. tomorrow. I'll be in a black Land Rover parked just down the street," Ivar said, and gestured to the waiter for the check. When it came, he paid in cash; the lame man didn't thank him.

They shook hands again outside the café and turned in opposite directions. The lame man decided to stroll around the old quarter. He would play the tourist for at least that day.

33

LUNCH WITH GRANHOLM

Wednesday, February 1, 9:30 a.m. Rain was coming down in torrents from a cold, iron-grey sky, obscuring the windshield despite the furiously working wipers, as Ekman and Rapp headed up the E4 for lunch with Valdis Granholm.

"I should have checked the weather before arranging this," Ekman said, concentrating on driving in the cloudburst.

"I won't argue with that," said Rapp, his feet tensed on the floorboard.

The team meeting that morning had been disappointing; there was no significant new information. Alenius and Rosengren were following up phone calls about the sketch, but nothing looked promising at this point.

Vinter's check of the spice company's employees had uncovered only one with a criminal record, a truck driver named Vigert Gotz, who'd served four years for aggravated assault and was released two years ago.

They'd have to keep hoping the sketch would produce the lead they were looking for.

After the team meeting, the two of them had sat in Ekman's office trying to figure out their next steps before heading to Stockholm.

"Unless the sketch generates something besides crank calls and false leads, we're at a dead end," said Rapp, his downcast face showing how unhappy he was with this conclusion.

"Maybe," said Ekman thoughtfully. "But there's still the Moroccan connection. I'm hoping that besides coordinating the international hunt for Chafik . . . which may locate him if we're lucky . . . Granholm can find something there that can help."

"It's a long shot."

"Yes, but what else do we really have, unless we find Chafik?"

The rain had stopped by the time they arrived a few minutes before twelve thirty. They found a convenient parking space and headed into the imposing, modern national police headquarters on Nora Agnegatan.

Valdis Granholm was a tall, extremely attractive forty-two-year-old with a mass of distinctive red hair. After exchanging introductions in her small, fourth-floor office, the three walked around the corner along rain-wet streets to Scheelegatan. They were heading to La Dame Noire, an old-fashioned French restaurant, a favorite of Granholm's.

"Bonjour, Madame," said the beaming, portly maître d'. "A pleasure to see you again. Your table is ready, please follow me." He led them to one set for three in a back corner with a view of the cozy, retro-decorated restaurant, and handed them elaborate, printed menus.

Ekman looked up from the one he'd been studying. "This all seems really tempting. What would you recommend, Valdis?"

"If you'd like potato pancakes with bleak roe as a starter, it's quite good here."

"And for a main course?"

"I often get the lamb fillet with savoy cabbage."

"Are those what you're going to order?"

"They are," she replied with a smile.

"Then that's what I'll have too."

Rapp had been silent during this exchange. "Why don't we get three orders? The kitchen will love us for making their job simpler," he said, grinning at her.

When they'd first met Granholm, Ekman had noticed that his chief inspector seemed instantly taken with this striking, red-haired woman. Rapp had stared at her so much that she'd finally turned to him with a quizzical expression and he'd hastily averted his eyes, looking everywhere else around her office.

As they ate, Ekman observed Rapp struggling manfully to keep from looking too long at Granholm. She was focused on Ekman as they discussed the Dahlin case, only glancing at Rapp occasionally to include him in the conversation.

Ekman explained where the case stood and how they believed it tied into Jakobsson's murder. Granholm listened attentively without interrupting.

Concluding his recap, Ekman threw up his hands in frustration and said that he and Rapp were stymied, at least for the moment. They hoped she could suggest some new avenues to explore.

"I wish I could tell you the search for Chafik outside Sweden was making progress," she said. "But so far we have nothing, even though I've been badgering my Europol contacts unmercifully. And the Interpol 'red notice' also hasn't produced any results."

Ekman cut a piece of his lamb steak and chewed it slowly. "What about the family link I'd mentioned before, the possible uncle, and the money Chafik was receiving from Morocco?" he asked.

"I spoke with the head of Interpol's Moroccan bureau about the uncle in Marrakech, Fayyad Joumari, and he's worth looking into."

"And?" interjected Rapp. Granholm turned and looked at him without expression. He's not doing himself any favors with her, thought Ekman.

"*And* he's known to be involved in criminal activities."

"Do they know what kinds of things?" asked Ekman.

"Apparently he's a very shadowy figure, always just in the background, but he could be a major mover in drugs and prostitution. The money sent to Chafik came from an account set up by a small leather goods company. Our Interpol contact made some quiet inquiries at the Al-Amin Bank in Marrakech. It seems the company is owned by a relative of Joumari."

"This could be the tie-in to the Dahlin case we've been looking for," Rapp exclaimed enthusiastically. "It's what we've suspected all along, Walther. It was more than just a one-off rape."

"You may be right, Alrik, but we mustn't jump ahead of ourselves. We'll need to establish a clear link between the rape in Sweden and a possible prostitution operation in Morocco. Then we have to identify those who committed the rape, find hard evidence to arrest them, and convince Kallenberg he has enough for a court to convict. We have a long, difficult road ahead."

Rapp was silent for a moment. "You're absolutely right, Walther," he said in a dejected tone. "I guess I've become too excited about what could be a way forward."

"You see," he said apologetically to Granholm, "I realize that I need to get some distance. I'm raising a teenage daughter on my own and I've probably become more wrapped up in this case than I should be."

She looked surprised that this tough, muscular cop, who'd been frankly looking her over, was also a single parent and so emotional.

"The Dahlin case could be part of an international trafficking operation," said Granholm quietly. "In my work, we're seeing more and more of this in Europe and everywhere else. It's the dark, underside of global commerce."

"Valdis," said Ekman, "please ask your contact to find out as much as possible about Joumari. Also we've uncovered another connection with Morocco. The wholesale spice company where Chafik worked is owned by a holding company in Rabat and we need to know more about it. Here's an address and phone number for them," he added, handing her a slip of paper.

"I'll get started on this as soon as I get back." Turning to Rapp, she said, "Alrik, you have nothing to apologize for. I have a young daughter at home too." And she smiled at him for the first time.

With a dessert of melted chocolate over vanilla ice cream, followed by a double espresso, a satisfied Ekman insisted on picking up the check. They both shook hands with Granholm and said good-bye outside the restaurant.

"Well," said Ekman, as they headed back to Weltenborg, "that was a productive meeting, besides, the lunch was very tasty. And after a rocky start, you seem to have made some headway with the lovely Fru Granholm, who Garth Rystrom tells me, by the way, is divorced." He grinned at Rapp.

"I wasn't trying to impress her."

"Yes, I know. That's what impressed her."

That same morning, another driver had also been heading north from Weltenborg. Fredrik Haake was pleased they'd found a replacement, but he was exasperated that the man he only knew as the Keeper insisted he come to the farm. He'd tried offering even more money to have the new girl brought to Weltenborg, but the Keeper had been adamant over the phone.

This new one was supposed to be very much like the dead woman. Anticipating a two-hour session to make up for the long drive, he felt his groin stir as he thought about what he would do with her.

He was too preoccupied as he drove to notice the nondescript car that followed him, keeping well back.

34

AT THE FARM

Friday, January 27, 10 a.m. *The lame man found the Land Rover where Ivar had told him it would be. Getting in, he just nodded in response to the other man's, "Good morning."*

"We've got a nice day for a drive, for a change," said the Keeper, as he pulled away from the curb under a bright, cloudless sky.

"How was your day yesterday?" he asked.

"I looked around the old quarter."

"If you're interested in antiquity, you should try to visit the Vasa Museum. It's got a completely preserved seventeenth-century warship. Really remarkable."

"I may do that," the lame man said, looking out the window.

They lapsed into silence, exchanging occasional comments about the scenery on the drive to the farm, as Stockholm, and then the countryside, rolled by.

When they pulled into the side yard of the old farmhouse, the lame man got out and looked around at the house and barn, as the man he called Ivar joined him.

"What's in the barn?"

"It's where we store the product," the Keeper responded.

The lame man just looked at him. *Why doesn't he simply say "women"?* he thought. *He's avoiding what he really does.* The lame man had always acknowledged to himself what he did. He thought it important to accept reality as it was, otherwise you could be blindsided by your own delusions.

They walked over to the farmhouse and up the porch steps. Gotz had been expecting them and opened the door,

"Has the new shipment arrived?" the Keeper asked.

"Came in late last night." Gotz replied. "Marta is with her now. I was just waiting for you to get here before I went over."

"This is our visitor, Karim," said the Keeper, introducing him.

He looked closely at the big man facing him. *He's the enforcer,* the lame man thought.

"Gotz," the other man said, extending his hand, which the lame man shook.

"I'll see how she's coming along," Gotz said, as he turned and walked out.

"He's quiet and very helpful, multitalented," said the Keeper, smiling.

The lame man looked around. "Is this where Ahmed worked?"

"Here, and at our other holding facility."

"There's more than one?"

"We had another in the city. That's where she got out, as you probably know from reading about it. Now there's just the barn here. No one gets out of that. How about some coffee?" the Keeper asked, as they headed down the hall. "I could use another cup."

They went into the kitchen where the Keeper began grinding some beans.

"I always insist on freshly ground," he said. "It makes all the difference."

As they sat at the kitchen table sipping steaming mugs of coffee, Ivar said, "Now that you're here, Karim, perhaps you'd like to mix a little pleasure with business. I don't know what your tastes are, of course, but I think we can accommodate them. Right now, there are four fully trained, very pretty young women here. Our new one isn't ready just yet and is being broken in right now." He paused and smiled, "She only arrived from Prague last night, although I understand she's actually Romanian. In a few weeks, I expect she'll be available in Marrakech."

"I'll wait until then," the lame man replied, his face expressionless.

"As you wish," said Ivar, in a casual tone.

"What is your facility here like?"

"There are five rooms with adjoining bathrooms on the upper level of the barn and as business continues to expand, we plan to construct four more on the ground floor. The two bedrooms in this house are for staff. Please feel free to look around anywhere here and at the barn."

"Thanks, but that won't be necessary," the lame man said. "Then business has been good?"

"We've been fortunate."

"Most of your 'product' comes from Eastern Europe?"

"Yes, and I intend to draw from that area exclusively from now on. I have to admit, it was a serious flaw in our business model to use Sweden, or other Scandinavian countries. Extractions are too noticeable."

"All your clients come here?"

"Yes, it ensures security, even though it somewhat limits our customer base. The only exception was one client who insisted we bring the Dahlin girl to Weltenborg so it would be more convenient for him. He paid quite a bit extra for that privilege; it was another mistake that won't be repeated."

"And Ahmed was looking after her?"

"Yes. Apparently it only took a few minutes for her to get out."

"Ahmed was not careful enough, was he?"

"*No one is perfect.*"

"*It must have been very upsetting for you.*"

"*It did create some difficulties, but nothing we couldn't handle.*"

"*Did Ahmed come back here afterward?*"

"*No. I thought that unwise. It would draw police attention to this place if he were found here. I met him in town and gave him quite a bit of money. We agreed the police would soon identify him because he'd rented the apartment where she was kept. I told him to find a small hotel for the night and call me the next day so we could figure out what to do. I planned on getting him out of Sweden as fast as possible and on his way back to Morocco.*"

"*But he never called?*"

"*He simply vanished. How he did it, I have no idea. We haven't heard a word from him since that night.*"

"*You must be concerned that the police will eventually pick him up, here or elsewhere in Europe.*"

"*It is a little worrisome. But he's certainly shown his ability to evade them.*"

"*As I'm sure you can appreciate, my boss is anxious to locate his grandnephew and assist him. Since he found him this job he feels it's his special responsibility to bring Ahmed safely home to the family.*"

"*Of course, of course. And I want to do everything I can to help, but I don't know what that would be under the circumstances.*"

"*I understand,*" said the lame man, getting up. "*Thanks for showing me your excellent facility.*"

"*My pleasure entirely,*" said Ivar, rising. "*If you've seen all you want, we can head back to Stockholm.*"

As he pulled up in front of the Grand Hotel an hour later, Ivar said, "Karim, it's been good meeting you. Have a pleasant stay in Stockholm and a safe journey back to Marrakech. I'm looking forward to many more profitable years doing business with your boss."

"I'll certainly let him know that," said the lame man, as they shook hands, and getting out of the SUV, he headed into the hotel.

He sat on the couch in his suite, thinking about his visit to the farm. Seeming relaxed and glib, Ivar was much too casual about Ahmed being caught. Therefore, he'd lied. Why? Because Ahmed, searched for by police throughout Sweden and Europe, had become a danger to them: on the run, he'd always be a threat to their operation. And they hadn't just kept him locked away at the farm. He'd wanted to go there to find that out.

When Ivar had offered to let him inspect their entire facility, he'd decided that Ahmed wasn't there. Moving him anywhere else would have been too risky. He must have been killed and his body disposed of, probably by their enforcer, that man Gotz.

The lame man picked up the phone and called Marrakech.

35

ANOTHER DEATH

Thursday, February 2, 8:20 a.m. The team meeting that morning had been brief. Rosengren and Alenius were still following up leads from the police sketch, and Ekman had assigned Vinter and Holm to help them. The four middle-aged men they'd so far been tipped off about had solid alibis for the night Dahlin had died, as did Kallenberg's internist.

Ekman was sitting in his office, mulling over this frustrating case, when Rapp burst in without knocking.

"Walther, there's been another killing," he exclaimed, the words falling over themselves in his excitement.

Ekman was startled.

"Who is it?"

"Believe it or not, it's Fredrik Haake, chairman of the Sodra Sverige Bank. I just learned a few minutes ago that he was found beside his car in the bank garage. Our sergeant at the scene says it looks like he's been strangled . . . with a wire."

"Jesus Christ," said Ekman, who normally never swore out loud. This murder had to be connected to the Jakobsson case, and therefore to Dahlin. It could be the break they'd been looking for, but he realized that starting now the pressure on them would become enormous.

"Do we know anything else?"

"As soon as I heard, I pulled up a picture of him on the Net," Rapp said, putting the photo on Ekman's desk.

Looking back at him was the man in the police sketch.

"He's the man in the hallway," Ekman said, in his astonishment stating the obvious. At that moment there was no doubt in his mind that Haake was the second man who'd raped Dahlin.

In more than thirty years as a police officer, he'd had several cases involving prominent individuals who'd turned out to be criminals. He still found himself amazed by people who had everything and who, out of blind arrogance, threw it all away.

"What's happening now?" he asked, as he stood up.

"The area's been cordoned off, and a forensic team and pathologist are on the way."

Walking over to grab his hat and coat, Ekman said, "Let's go."

Haake lay with his face to one side and most of his dark-suited body under his black, Bentley Mulsanne sedan. The garage wasn't brightly lit, and Ekman decided that unless you looked closely he wouldn't immediately have been noticed lying there hidden in the car's shadow.

Because Haake's parking space was on the top floor of the three-story underground garage, the garage entrance was cordoned off by blue-and-white police tape. The entire floor would have to be processed as a crime scene.

Turning to the pathologist, Dr. Bohlander, who'd arrived just after them, Ekman said, "Roffe, can we get him out from under there?"

Bohlander gestured to two morgue attendants, gloved and in white coveralls, who'd been standing back waiting for instructions. They placed a white plastic sheet next to the car, and bending down, one took Haake's shoulders and the other, his head, as they carefully lifted his rigid torso a few inches and shifted it from under the car, placing it two feet away on the sheet. They repeated the operation with his knees and legs.

Bohlander, dressed like the attendants, knelt beside the body and, turning Haake's head gently, exposed more clearly the bright red line deeply incised along the base of his throat.

"Does it look like the same technique used on Jakobsson?" asked Rapp, as he peered down at the corpse.

"I'd say so, from just looking. Like Jakobsson, it appears that a wire garrote was used. Of course, I'll have to take measurements to see if it went as deep and the same amount of pressure was applied."

"What was the approximate time of death?" Ekman asked.

"I'd say it was probably last night, say between eight and ten p.m. But that's preliminary, of course, and don't hold me to it."

"When you have him on the table, please get a DNA sample, Roffe. We need to compare it with one from the Dahlin case."

Bohlander looked surprised. "Really . . . Fredrik Haake?" he said, knowing they were looking for a match to a second rapist.

Ekman just nodded.

"From the position of the body, it looks like Haake was getting into his car when he was attacked from behind," observed Ekman.

"Yes, his reserved parking space has his name on it," said Rapp, pointing to the wall behind the car. "His killer knew where to find him."

"What's in his pockets, Roffe?" Rapp asked.

The doctor carefully checked them, removing a wallet, key ring, and handkerchief. He handed each item to the gloved crime scene technician standing behind Rapp, who placed them in clear plastic evidence bags.

"There's no phone?" asked Rapp.

"I didn't find any. Maybe it's in the car or fell under it. If you've got what you need, I'll take him," said Bohlander, standing and turning to the attendants who had brought up a stretcher. Lifting the corpse into a zippered black body bag, they placed it on the gurney, strapping it in place before wheeling it out, followed by the pathologist.

Two body-suited forensic techs examined the car, looking under it, and in the immediate surrounding area, but didn't find a phone. A police tow truck had driven in to haul the car away when they'd finished. A half-dozen other techs had begun to systematically examine every inch of the entire garage floor.

"If he was killed last night, how come no one reported him missing?" asked Rapp.

"Yes, that's interesting. Of course, he could have been leaving on a business trip. Have them check the car's trunk for luggage, and Alrik, make sure to get the videos from the garage's security cameras.

"Speak with his secretary and any assistant, and ask them not to contact Haake's family. And get the entire team over here. Start some of them interviewing the person who discovered his body, and the garage attendants. The others will need to speak with the bank's senior staff and find out if Haake had particular problems lately, like difficult business deals . . . or enemies.

"I'm heading to his house to inform his wife."

Ekman had brought the grim news to too many families. He dreaded this part of his job, but when he led a murder investigation, never delegated it.

The man who'd followed Fredrik Haake on his last day alive, stopped when he saw the farm buildings a half kilometer away. He pulled his car well off the muddy track and behind dense shrubbery where it couldn't be seen from the lane or the buildings.

Reaching for his camera with a long telephoto lens mounted on a tripod, he got out and made his way to a wooded rise overgrown with bushes. The rain had ended, but the ground and wild grass were dripping wet. Hidden in the undergrowth, he focused the lens on the buildings. For three hours he remained there, virtually immobile, with the camera fixed on the buildings.

When he saw two men and a woman emerge from the barn, the camera whirred as he took frame after frame. One of the men was Haake, whom he'd known for years. Now that he had photos of these others, he planned on returning here to follow them and discover who they were.

Haake's picture had been plastered across the papers and on TV screens above the question, "Do you recognize this man?" Yes, he thought, he'd immediately recognized Haake, and knew him for what he was beneath the haughty exterior.

When Haake headed back to Weltenborg, the man followed. He left his car on a side street and walked the few blocks to the bank garage Haake had entered.

His car was backed into a dimly lit, reserved place with his name in white lettering on the wall. The man crouched behind the car and waited. He had infinite patience.

Haake appeared an hour later. As he opened the car door, the man sprang forward and with gloved hands slipped the killing wire noose over his head, gradually tightening it, while Haake desperately grabbed at the wire as it cut deeper into his neck. The man muttered a few words in Haake's ear as he applied inexorable pressure until the windpipe gave and Haake went limp.

He pulled the bloody garrote loose with some difficulty and dropped it into a plastic bag. Searching Haake's body, he found his phone and shoved it in his own pocket. It might have some revealing numbers on it.

Looking down at Haake's sprawled body, he felt no guilt, only deep satisfaction that his plan was becoming reality: he'd moved one step closer to his goal. With a little luck the police would think the garroting linked Haake's death to Jakobsson's.

The man walked rapidly from the garage, taking care to shield his face with the hood of his parka.

36

FRU HAAKE

Thursday, February 2, 10:40 a.m. The Haake house, hidden behind dense woods, was invisible from the main road, and was reached down a long, brown pea-gravel drive. It looks more like a French chateau than a Swedish country house, thought Ekman, as he pulled into the circular, Belgian bloc-paved parking area fronting the house.

He hadn't called ahead. When he rang, a beefy, middle-aged man in a white shirt, black vest, and trousers, opened the iron-bound oak door.

"I'm Chief Superintendent Ekman from the Weltenborg police," he said, showing his identification and handing the man his business card. "Please tell Fru Haake I need to speak with her immediately. It's urgent." Looking the man over, Ekman decided that he probably also handled security for the Haakes.

The man led him into a two-story atrium hall and said, "I'll let her know you're here." He hurried up a large, winding staircase on the left, leaving Ekman standing in the hallway.

A few minutes later, he reappeared, following Haake's wife down the stairway.

Fru Haake was wearing what Ekman thought was a Chanel pants suit, dark blue with white trim. A heavy gold bracelet hung around the hand she extended to Ekman.

She's quite attractive and elegant, Ekman thought. She looks like the wife of a bank chairman.

"I'm Kajsa Haake, Chief Superintendent. Marten said it was urgent. Has something happened?" Her face was tense at this unexpected visit from a senior police officer.

"Can we sit down somewhere, Fru Haake?"

"Of course. Marten," she said, turning to the house-man who stood to one side, "please take Herr Ekman's coat and hat, and bring us some coffee and biscuits in the music room." Ekman thought she was trying hard to maintain the appearance of normalcy in an abnormal situation.

He handed his things to the man who hung them in a concealed guest closet behind them.

"We'll go this way, Herr Ekman," Fru Haake said, leading him down the wide hallway, and turning through high, double doors on the right.

The cream-colored room was enormous under a fourteen-foot ceiling, its walls hung with brightly colored abstract paintings. He could see that three, tall french doors along the far wall opened onto a flagstone terrace overlooking a sweeping expanse of lawn.

What looked to Ekman like an elongated Giacometti sculpture stood in one corner. Taking pride of place, was a marquetry inlaid grand piano with Bösendorfer inscribed in gold lettering, above the keyboard.

"That's a fine looking piano," Ekman said to break the ice. "Do you play?"

"Yes, whenever I can find the time. Years ago, I even thought of becoming a concert pianist." She glanced over at it with a look of regret. "It's a marvelous instrument. The piano tuner was here a few days ago and said it was the finest piano he'd ever worked on."

She sat down at one end of an oversize yellow, Chippendale sofa and gestured to Ekman to join her. He took a seat at the other end.

"What is this visit about, Herr Ekman?" she asked in an apprehensive tone.

"Fru Haake, I'm afraid I have very bad news. You must be brave," he replied. "Your husband was found dead this morning in the garage at his bank."

A hand went to her mouth. "Oh, my God. Did he have a heart attack?"

"No. I'm sorry to say he was murdered."

"Murdered? That can't be. Are you sure?" Her voice was strained and her carefully made-up face looked increasingly tense.

"Unfortunately, there can be no doubt. He was strangled."

"This is incredible." She took out an embroidered handkerchief that had been tucked in a sleeve and dabbed at her eyes. Ekman thought it was mostly for effect. The new widow didn't seem particularly grief-stricken.

"Who can have done such a horrible thing?"

"That's what we need your help to find out."

"But I don't know anything that could possibly be helpful," she protested.

"That's typically what family and friends of murder victims think, but they may know more than they realize."

The houseman came in carrying a tray with a silver coffee pot, two delicate porcelain cups on saucers, and a plate of assorted biscuits. He put the tray down on the teak coffee table in front of the couch.

"Thank you, Marten," Fru Haake said as he turned and left, closing the doors behind him.

"Would you like coffee, Herr Ekman?" she asked, as she tried to regain the role of self-assured hostess.

"If you're having some, I'll join you."

She poured with a shaking hand, passing him a cup, and moved the biscuit plate toward him. "Please, help yourself," she said.

"Thank you," Ekman replied, taking a biscuit. He hoped that the familiar ritual of sharing coffee would create a sense of normality in a world that had abruptly changed for her. He needed her to speak frankly during a difficult conversation.

"It's important in any investigation, but particularly this kind of crime, to move as rapidly as possible, so I hope you feel able to answer some questions now."

"Yes, of course. I want to assist you any way I can, although I can't imagine what that could be."

"Background information is extremely important in these cases. Even small details can be significant. Some of the questions I have to ask will seem unnecessarily personal, but your answers can be a great help, so please be absolutely open with me."

"Go ahead," she said, raising her head and looking Ekman directly in the eyes. "Ask."

"Was your husband planning to leave on a business trip yesterday?" Ekman said, starting with a low-key question.

"No, I don't think so."

"But if he was, he would have mentioned it?"

"Not necessarily. He didn't usually discuss business matters with me."

"Were you concerned when he didn't come home last night?"

"No, not really. If he was going to be away, he usually phoned, but not always."

"So there were other times when he didn't return home and didn't let you know?"

"Yes."

"Were those frequent?"

"No, just occasional."

"Do you know the terms of your husband's will?" Ekman asked, changing the subject abruptly.

She looked surprised, but answered readily. "Yes, of course. We are each other's sole heirs."

"What was your overall relationship with your husband?"

She paused. "We were friends. It wasn't like that at first, but over the years we drifted apart. We mostly led quite separate lives."

"Then you both had intimate relationships outside your marriage?"

She hesitated again. "I have. I assume he did too."

"So you're not aware of what your husband did in this regard?"

"No, and I didn't inquire. He didn't either. I've already told you, it was just understood between us," she said, her voice rising.

"Please consider this next question very carefully. You've become an extremely wealthy woman now that your husband is gone. Can you think of an intimate friend who would want to eliminate him so he might marry you?"

"That's ridiculous. I would never let any of those relationships threaten my marriage, and my partners knew from the beginning that I would always stay married to Fredrik Haake.

I have never had a secret plan to marry someone else, if that's what you're thinking," she said with a note of defiance.

She knows exactly where I'm going with these questions, Ekman thought. Despite her denials, he couldn't ignore the possibility that she'd decided to rid herself of an unsatisfactory husband. And without the divorce that might cost her half his money under Sweden's community property laws. She could have found a willing partner to help her, considering how much was at stake.

"We'll need the names of these men and the dates involved," Ekman said, and saw that she was about to refuse.

"Our inquiries will be very discreet. It's essential that we speak with them because otherwise we won't be able to eliminate them as possible suspects. You can't be absolutely certain that one of them didn't see things differently than you, and was ready to act on his feelings."

"I can't believe it. But if it's that important, I'll e-mail you the information later today," she said with obvious reluctance.

If his suspicions about a possible accomplice were right, Ekman wondered whether they'd really get all the names. They'd have to dig a bit to make sure she hadn't intentionally left someone off the list.

"We'll also need to interview your staff."

"Is that really necessary?"

"I'm afraid it is. My officers will be here later today to take their statements. Please make sure they're available. How many are there?"

"Besides Marten, who runs the house and sometimes drives me, there are two maids, the cook, and the gardener."

"Do any of them live here?"

"Marten and the cook each have two-room suites above the garage."

That must be quite a garage, thought Ekman.

"Fru Haake, thank you for being so open with me at this difficult time," Ekman said, standing. "And now I'd like to see Herr Haake's study. There may be something among his papers that could help us."

She looked surprised, but just nodded, as she got up.

They left the room and he followed her farther down the hall to a door on the left, which she opened for him, and then stood aside.

Ekman went in and peered around the comfortable, masculine room, lined on two sides from floor to ceiling with books. A large, mahogany desk, bare except for a brass lamp and a few mementos, faced windows looking out on a garden. A red leather armchair with a reading lamp behind it stood in one corner of the room.

In the corner opposite it was a tall, glass cabinet with miniature bronzes on three shelves. Curious, Ekman went over and saw that they were a collection of Daumier caricature busts. How strange, he thought, a cultured rapist. But why not? Didn't Hitler fancy himself an artist?

Going back into the hallway, he closed the study door. Then, reaching into his jacket, he took out a package of police seals and pasted two of them along the doorjamb above the knob, and two below, preventing the door from being opened without breaking them. He knew he had no authority to do this, yet it needed to be done, and he didn't believe the widow would challenge him.

Turning to Fru Haake, who'd been watching with a look of amazement, he said, "We need to treat Herr Haake's study as an extension of the crime scene. My officers will search the room later today, and until they do, it needs to be undisturbed. I'm sure you can understand why.

"If there's nothing further you can tell me now, I'll be leaving."

She frowned, but said nothing, leading him back to the entrance hall. The houseman, who'd been waiting there, retrieved Ekman's things and helped him on with his coat.

"Thanks again for your assistance, Fru Haake," he said, offering his hand.

"Good-bye, Herr Ekman," she replied, ignoring the proffered hand and turning away, walked up the staircase.

Back in his office that afternoon, Ekman and Rapp were going over his conversation with Haake's wife.

"Do you really think she could have had him killed?" asked Rapp.

"It's a possibility we have to explore. We'll need to see his will to find out if she really is his only heir."

"But doesn't the garrote tie his murder to Jakobsson's? She had no reason to be involved with that."

"If she planned Haake's death, maybe that's what she and whoever did the actual killing want us to believe. She could have seen the police sketch, recognized her husband, and decided that now was the perfect time to have him killed, using a garrote to link his death to Jakobsson's and Dahlin's. It would divert us from suspecting her, as we otherwise naturally would. After all, she has a great deal to gain from Haake's death, and by her own admission, there was no love lost between them."

"So we're looking at a copycat murder?" Rapp asked.

"Perhaps," said Ekman. "But maybe whoever killed Jakobsson wanted to prevent us from sooner or later having a little chat with Herr Haake."

37

INSPECTION

Monday, January 30, 10 a.m. The lame man sat in Thore Ostlund's office, as the manager responded to his questions about Ahmed Chafik. The answers were the same he had given the police on Friday, he said, as he described Chafik's employment. The lame man already knew the answers, but wanted to hear what Ostlund would say.

It was the same tune Ivar had sung: Ostlund knew nothing about what had happened to Chafik after he left the company. The lame man had decided Ivar was lying. He suspected Ostlund also was lying.

Then he changed the subject by asking about the spice company's current condition and future plans. As the manager described the company's operations, he listened carefully. What Ostlund was saying had unexpectedly become important to him.

After his conversation on Friday with the old man, he'd had the weekend to himself to wander around Stockholm. The next day, he'd decided to follow Ivar's suggestion and took a taxi to the Vasa Museum on Djurgården Island. He wasn't prepared for the startling impact of the huge seventeenth-century ship, the most perfectly preserved warship of that time, sitting in the museum's immense central hall as though it had just sailed in.

He spent Sunday morning at his hotel, but after lunch he became restless. Borrowing a hotel umbrella, he walked through a light rain the few blocks across the Kungsträdgården Park to the large Nordiska Kompaniet store on Hamngatan. He browsed for an hour among some of its 100 departments, finally deciding on a pair of comfortable black walking shoes. The rest of the day he relaxed in his suite trying to finish the Simenon novel he'd brought from Marrakech.

When he'd explained to the old man his reasons for thinking Ahmed had been killed, there was such a long silence that he thought the call had been dropped.

"What is your advice?" the old man had finally said.

He was surprised. This was the first time he'd been asked his opinion about anything. Perhaps age has made the old man uncertain of himself, he thought.

"I'd recommend doing nothing right now. Although Ahmed's death must eventually be avenged, it's important not to disrupt your business relationship with these people. I'd give it time and see what develops."

"You've confirmed my own thinking. I will wait, and, insh'Allah, the right moment will come. While you're in Stockholm, I would like you to visit my spice company and give me your impression of how it's being run, and the people there. I rely on your sound judgment."

"I'm deeply flattered that you put such trust in me. I will do my best, insh'Allah, to justify it."

After they'd hung up, he sat for several minutes mulling over the conversation. I wonder if he's begun to think of me as a possible successor and wants to learn if we see things the same way. It had never occurred to him before because he wasn't a relative.

Perhaps there was no one else in the family the old man thought could take over, and now had to look outside.

After all, why not, the lame man thought, I've worked for him for the last two years, and he's always been well satisfied. He smiled to himself at what could be an unexpected turn of good fortune.

Ostlund had appeared strangely unsurprised by the appearance of the man who called himself Karim, and claimed to represent the owner. He'd just blandly accepted it.

The manager must have known about me, the lame man decided, and been expecting my visit. The only way he could have learned about me was from Ivar. Besides Ahmed working for both of them, what was their connection? And was the old man aware of it? He decided to put these questions aside, until he could learn more.

"So," Ostlund concluded, "that's where things stand. Contracts are in place and business is looking up. It promises to be a profitable year. The owner should be pleased."

"That all sounds satisfactory, but I'm not an accountant," the lame man said, shrugging. "More of a business consultant."

"Of course," Ostlund said. "Please satisfy yourself, and the owner, that all is in order."

"Now," the lame man said, standing, "I'd like to see your facility and meet your employees."

"I'll be glad to take you around," said Ostlund.

His secretary was sitting at her desk outside his office.

"This is Marta, the woman who keeps things running smoothly here," he said, referring to the lame man, simply as "our visitor."

They walked into the front office and the manager introduced him to the two men there, explaining what each did. In the adjoining warehouse, they went through the same procedure with the five female workers. The women were packing plastic *bags of spices into cartons labelled with the company's logo. Going out onto the adjoining loading dock, three men were putting the boxes into delivery vans.*

At the last truck bay, the workman had his back to them, busy with what he was doing. When he heard them, he turned around as Ostlund said, "And this is Gotz, our delivery foreman."

The lame man kept his surprise from showing, as he said, "I believe Herr Gotz and I have already met." Gotz's face was blank, but his eyes narrowed. He said nothing.

Ostlund's face betrayed his astonishment. He recovered quickly and said, "What a coincidence. Karim, you've certainly been getting around since you got here."

"Yes," said the lame man. "Sweden has much to interest a visitor."

To Gotz, he said, "Good seeing you again," as he and Ostlund headed back to the manager's office to say good-bye.

When the lame man had gone, Ostlund called Gotz to his office.

"When did you meet him?" he asked.

"At the farm, last Friday," Gotz replied. "He was looking around, trying to find out what happened to Ahmed."

"He asked me about Ahmed too. He acts like he doesn't know about the connection between the company and the farm, but seeing you here makes it obvious."

"So what?" said Gotz. "Who cares why this guy's playing dumb, they can't want to screw everything up, it would only hurt them too."

"You're right. But maybe they're thinking about changing our arrangement. That's what we need to figure out," said Ostlund, as he reached for the phone.

38

INVESTIGATION

Friday, February 3, 8 a.m. The team members had come in early and were standing around drinking coffee and talking excitedly when Ekman entered.

He took his seat at the head of the table, as the others quickly sat down.

"I know you've all seen the newspaper and TV coverage of the Haake murder. Because of his prominence, and his strong resemblance to the sketch of one of Dahlin's rapists, it's become a media sensation. The pressure to come up with answers is growing by the hour so we'll be meeting every day, including weekends, until we close the case.

"I have to brief the commissioner," he said, taking out his pocket watch, "in thirty minutes. We've got a lot of ground to cover, so let's get started." He turned to Rapp.

"Alrik, did the garage cameras give us anything?"

"We got some clips of a guy walking into the garage and leaving that floor around the right time Wednesday evening. He was wearing a hooded parka that hid his face, but he was a big man, moving quickly."

"Okay, that may help when we have a suspect. Did we ever find Haake's phone?"

"It wasn't in the garage, his office, or home. Maybe the killer took it."

"That's interesting. There may have been something on it that his murderer didn't want us to see. Have we heard anything from Bohlander yet?"

"He's putting the time of death where he'd originally suspected, between eight and ten, Wednesday evening. DNA results aren't back, but they'll confirm Haake was Dahlin's other rapist, or I'll buy coffee and pastries for everyone for a year," Rapp said, as the others laughed.

"Bohlander did say that the incision on Haake's neck was a little wider than on Jakobsson's. He thought the wire used was different. Jakobsson was killed with ordinary hardware store wire, but the one used on Haake was somewhat thicker."

"That's interesting," Ekman said. "Has the killer changed weapons, or are we looking at two different killers? Perhaps Haake's murder was a copycat? It's something we need to consider. Who handled the interviews at the bank?"

"I did, Chief," Holm replied. "First, we spoke with the woman, Annika Bremer, a bank teller, who found Haake's body. She spotted it when she came to work Thursday morning at 7:20 and parked on that floor. She assumed it was Haake because he was lying next to his car and called bank security immediately. I think we can rule her out as being involved."

"What about Haake's senior colleagues? Anything interesting there?"

"Gerdi and I spoke with the chief operating officer, and then with the bank's treasurer, who also heads planning." Holm turned to her.

"The bank is in good financial shape, according to them," said Vinter. "In fact they'd begun talks about a merger with another bank they didn't want to name. They didn't know of any business or personal problems Haake had."

Holm continued, "Several lower-level employees who'd worked with Haake said he was personally hard to take. He was a tough boss, usually arrogant and abrupt, although he could put on the charm when he had to."

"Let's find out more about that proposed bank merger. Enar, make them understand that in a murder inquiry every-thing's on the table, and that we can get a warrant for the documents we want. It will make life easier for them to coop-erate. Tell them we'll try to keep the merger confidential, unless it was a reason for his death."

Ekman turned back to Rapp. "How did things go at Haake's house?"

"Rosengren, Alenius, and I interviewed the staff. Nobody liked Haake, and a couple of them, a maid and the cook, said they'd planned to quit. Apparently he was a hard-nosed bas-tard at home, as well as at the office."

"Alenius and I searched his study," said Rosengren. "There were just the usual bills and papers, nothing of interest."

"I thought there should be something more, so I spoke with his wife about where else there might be documents," said Rapp, "and after hesitating a bit she opened a safe for me in their bedroom closet. There was jewelry, a fair amount of cash, and passports. The usual. And a life insurance policy, and a will, dated a year ago." Rapp opened a folder in front of him and passed out copies.

"As you can see, his wife gets everything. Just as she told you, Walther."

"These confirm that she had a strong motive," said Ekman, explaining the copycat murder theory he'd discussed with

Rapp. "But it doesn't mean she and one of her lovers killed Haake.

"The other theory is that Haake, like Jakobsson, knew too much. After the sketch went public, he would sooner or later be identified as one of Dahlin's rapists, so someone decided he had to be shut up before we could get to him."

"I think the second theory is right," said Vinter. "Haake wasn't an opportunistic rapist who just happened to come across a woman who'd vanished a couple of months before. He was a customer. It feels to me more and more like there's a trafficking ring operating."

"After speaking with Fru Haake," said Rapp, "I don't think she planned her husband's murder, mostly because she didn't have to risk killing him to be very rich. I've had the same feeling as Gerdi all along: there's a trafficking ring."

"I'd say the same," put in Holm.

Rosengren and Alenius nodded agreement.

"I think all of you are right, but to be safe, Alrik, let's check out her lovers before we put the copycat theory on the back burner. And we also need to take a closer look at Haake's house staff."

Ekman got up. "Now I'd better brief the commissioner."

39

THE TRADE

Wednesday, February 1, 11 a.m. The sky over the old man's patio was grey and the fountain didn't sparkle with sunlight as it had on his last visit, but the temperature was still a comfortable twenty degrees Celsius. He breathed in deeply: the scent of flowers lingered on the air. Most of all, he was glad to have shed his heavy overcoat; he'd had enough of the Swedish winter.

When he'd called Marrakech on Monday afternoon to report on the spice company, he'd been surprised. He'd started to ask a question, but the old man had cut him off abruptly, saying "Come see me," and then hung up.

Yesterday's flight from Arlanda had been as smooth and uneventful as the one that had brought him in. On the plane, he'd considered the answers he'd come up with to his questions. It was becoming clearer to him why the old man wouldn't discuss things over the phone. When he landed, he took a taxi to his apartment in the modern part of the city and arranged an appointment for the next morning.

As he limped up the flagstone path to the house he saw that the same two guards were in place: it looked like they hadn't moved. He nodded to them as he went under the overhanging portico and wordlessly, they nodded back. The old man was seated in his usual place in the large octagonal room with a tea service on the table beside him. It looked like he hadn't moved either.

They briefly exchanged ritual greetings and mutual inquiries about health as Joumari poured them each a glass of mint tea and then, suddenly as usual, brought up what had brought the lame man back.

"*What did you think of my spice company?*"

"*It appears to be well-run and successful.*"

"*And . . . ?*"

"*It also provides a good means of moving something other than spices from India.*"

"*I was hoping you would discover this,*" *said the old man, and a rare, twisted smile lit up his lined face.*

So it was a test, just as I thought, the lame man decided.

"*Also there's an exchange arrangement with the supplier of women,*" *he said.*

"*Just so. And how does all this work?*"

"*You provide drugs to them wholesale; they handle distribution themselves so you needn't be concerned about operating a network from here. They also provide women at a wholesale price, and the ships that deliver your spices to Sweden return with them here.*"

"*And what do you think of this arrangement?*"

"*It works well, as long as the people involved also work well.*"

"*Do you have concerns about them?*"

"*Yes. They risked upsetting everything by allowing that woman to escape and killing Ahmed. These were serious mistakes that make me question the judgment of the man, Ivar, who runs their side.*"

"*What would you do?*"

"*The spice company drug operation has to be protected because it produces the highest profits.*"

"*Yes, it does.*"

"*I was told the police had been making inquiries at the company in their search for Ahmed.* Insh'Allah, *they won't return. But any police attention to the company is a danger that should have been foreseen.*"

"*I agree.*"

"*The police are focused on Ahmed and the woman. If the investigation continues, the entire arrangement could unravel. The women part of the business should be shut down. It's become too risky.*"

"*But it's very profitable,*" the old man said in an irritated tone.

"*Sometimes one has to make a sacrifice. It's only temporary. The business can be continued with another supplier not connected with the spice company and the drugs. Combining the two operations has been profitable and convenient for everyone, but it's become too dangerous. Separating them protects both businesses, especially since police activity in Sweden is intensifying.*"

Joumari *was silent for a moment.* "*You are right,*" *he said finally, with obvious reluctance.* "*It's a shame to do it, but* insh'Allah, *our larger interests must be protected.*"

"*The difficulty will be in persuading Ivar to shut down that side of their operation completely. He may be tempted to supply women to other groups, but doing that could still attract police attention to your drug trade.*"

"*How do you propose to persuade him?*"

"*I would point out the increased risk we are all taking, and offer him a reduced price for the drugs to offset some of his loss on the women.*"

The old man was taken aback. "*Must I lose even more money?*"

"*Unfortunately. I think it's an unavoidable part of the sacrifice.*"

"And if he is still unwilling?"

"Then he must be replaced. It would be payback for Ahmed, whose death he probably ordered."

"Do you have someone in mind?"

"There are limited possibilities, the most promising seems the spice company manager, a man named Ostlund."

Joumari looked thoughtful. "You have given me unwelcome, but sound advice. When will you return to Sweden?"

"Tomorrow, if it can be arranged," the lame man said, not looking forward to the biting cold again.

"A plane ticket, your hotel reservation, and additional funds will be delivered to you later today," said the old man, pushing himself erect with his cane, as the lame man also stood.

He was surprised when Joumari came over, put a hand on his shoulder, and kissed him on both cheeks.

"May God bless you; have a peaceful trip," the old man said.

As he left, the lame man was quietly elated. He'd passed the test. Perhaps he'll adopt me as his son, he thought. That would ease my transition as his successor, although the family won't be happy about it. I'll have to watch my back.

40

PRESSURE

Friday, February 3, 8:30 a.m. Norlander and Malmer were standing in the commissioner's office talking, when Ekman knocked and entered.

"*God morgen,* Walther," Norlander said. "It's good to see you. Why don't we sit over here." He led the way to two arm-chairs, gesturing to the couch for Ekman.

"Olav and I were shocked, as you must have been, by Fredrik Haake's murder."

"You're right, Commissioner. So was everyone on my team. But it did solve our search for Dahlin's other rapist."

"He looks like the sketch, but are you certain he's the one?" asked Malmer.

"We're waiting for DNA confirmation, but his strong resemblance, and the fact that he was garroted like Jakobsson, clinches it in my mind."

"This murder of a prominent businessman, who looks like the rapist you've been searching for, together with the two related deaths, has made for a media circus. They're going to

keep up relentless pressure until we close the case," said Norlander. "Where are we now?"

Ekman briefed them on the investigation and the alternative theories they'd developed, concluding with, "It's still too
early to say definitely, but my team and I believe a human
trafficking ring is behind all these deaths."

"And when do you think you'll shut them down?" asked
Malmer.

"When we identify them, and then assemble enough evidence," Ekman replied in a neutral tone to this idiotic question. "We have a long way to go."

"That's understood," said Norlander, looking pointedly at
Malmer. "But Walther, this is no longer just a local case. It's
attracting national attention. I have every confidence in you
and your team, but speed has become critically important."

"Considering that Haake was murdered only the night
before last, I think we're moving remarkably fast, Commissioner," said Ekman.

"I agree, absolutely. But the media and the public don't
understand how painstaking police work has to be in order
to find, arrest, and eventually convict criminals. Because this
case has become such a sensation, I think you should plan on
calling in the national CID."

Norlander saw that Ekman was about to protest.

"This is no reflection on you or your team. It's just that
more resources are needed to wrap this up as fast as possible.
Why don't you see if your friend Garth Rystrom is available?"

Ekman was silent for a moment. He resented having his
ability being questioned, but after dealing with bureaucrats
for decades, he recognized when to bow gracefully to the
inevitable.

"If that's what you want, Commissioner, I'll call him this
morning."

"Excellent, Walther, excellent," said Norlander, getting up, as the other two also stood. "Knowing you, Walther, I'm sure you'll soon have good news for us."

Ekman went down to his office and called Rystrom. After he'd explained the situation, he said, "So do you think you can give us a hand?"

"The case sounds intriguing, Walther. Have your commissioner call my boss, and assuming it's okay, I'll plan on coming down first thing tomorrow."

"Thanks, Garth. I'll look forward to seeing you."

Then he called Kallenberg's office. He needed to brief him right away. Kallenberg's assistant told him that the prosecutor was at a meeting in Stockholm and wouldn't be back until late that night. Ekman asked for an appointment the next morning at ten.

"Yes," he told her. "I realize tomorrow's Saturday, but he'll want to see me anyway. It's urgent."

That evening, discussing the case with Ingbritt over dinner, Ekman sounded despondent.

"We're really at a dead end. I don't know where we go from here unless we somehow come up with a new lead. Maybe Norlander was right: we need help. Perhaps Garth can think of something."

"It's always like this, Walther, when you're starting," she replied, and reaching across the table patted his hand. "Don't get discouraged. You'll find a way. You always do. And make sure you invite Garth for dinner tomorrow. It will be good to see him again."

After they'd cleared the dishes, Ingbritt went upstairs to read in bed.

Ekman sat in his study in his big leather recliner while he went over the case. In his long career as a police officer, he'd gradually become famous as a criminal investigator, fame he didn't want. Now he wondered whether he still deserved this recognition. He felt old and tired.

Maybe I've lost whatever ability I had, he thought. It happens to everyone sooner or later, your mind doesn't work the way it used to, you just run out of juice.

Okay, enough. He straightened himself in his chair. Stop beating yourself up, Ekman, it's a bad habit. As Ingbritt said, find a way. He sat there and thought hard, but couldn't come up with anything.

41

SUSPICION

Thursday, February 2, 1 p.m. *The lame man was relaxing on the flight back to Sweden by working out chess problems on his tablet computer. After an hour of this he became bored and decided to check the* Sydsvenska Nyheter *website. As the pages came up, he had them translated into English, and saw breaking news about the murder of Fredrik Haake.*

Thore Ostlund was in his office, meeting with Ivar, when Marta came in without knocking. She was visibly flustered and spoke breathlessly.

"There's a news story on TV about Fredrik Haake. He's been murdered."

Ostlund exchanged surprised looks with Ivar.

"Calm down, Marta," Ostlund said.

"And close the door on your way out," added Ivar. She left, slamming the door behind her.

Ostlund turned on the TV and switched to SVT Channel 24 news.

They watched in silence as the first details of the murder were reported.

"What the hell is going on?" Ostlund asked, staring at Ivar, as he turned off the TV.

"I'm not sure, but it's not all bad, despite losing the money we were going to get out of him. When his picture went public I don't mind telling you I was starting to sweat. The police were getting much too close and Haake would have folded quickly."

"So you think Gotz just took it on himself? I told you he likes killing too much. He's become a goddamn loose cannon."

"Maybe. But he's indispensable right now. I don't have a replacement who can do what he does for us."

"But we can't let him think we're ignoring this, or he'll get completely out of control."

"Okay. Call him in, right now. And tell Marta not to say anything."

When Gotz came into the office the other two were standing.

"Sit down, Gotz," said Ivar in a harsh tone.

Gotz looked puzzled, but sat down.

"Why did you do it?" asked Ostlund.

"Do what?"

"Kill Haake, strangle him. There's no use denying it," said Ivar.

Gotz looked astonished. "When did this happen?" he said, glancing up from one man to the other standing over him.

"He was found this morning in his bank garage; but you know that," replied Ostlund.

"Like hell I do," Gotz replied, his voice rising. "This is the first I've heard about it." He was visibly indignant and got to his feet.

"This is bullshit." He turned to Ivar. "You know I wouldn't do something like that without talking it over and getting your okay. Besides, he was a good customer. Why would I do it?"

"If you say so, then we need to rethink what's happening," Ivar replied.

"If Gotz didn't do it, who did?" asked Ostlund, turning to Ivar.

"And why?" said Ivar. "That's the basic question."

After they'd both apologized to Gotz, he stalked out, still pissed.

"Do you believe him?" Ostlund asked.

"I don't know," Ivar replied. "He may have thought Haake had become too much of a risk to all of us and decided to act on his own. Now he doesn't want to admit he did it without consulting us."

"So what should we do?"

"Just accept what he told us. What else can we do? We need him."

"What about Karim? Do you think the Moroccans are planning something?"

"They haven't said anything to me. I checked at his hotel yesterday and he's gone; I assume, back to Marrakech."

"I've got a bad feeling that things are changing, and not in a good way."

"Look, Haake's death prevents the police from getting closer to us. Nothing else has happened. So, for God's sake, stop worrying."

But Thore Ostlund had become increasingly worried and since Dahlin's death had been thinking about how he could get out before everything fell apart.

42

A CONNECTION

Saturday, February 4, 7 a.m. Ekman came downstairs dressed in his usual black, three-piece suit, just as Ingbritt was placing bowls of muesli with filmjölk, soured milk, on the table.

He looked surprised at this frugal breakfast. "Is this all we're having?" he asked in a plaintive tone.

Ingbritt looked up. "It should be, Walther. We're both putting on too much weight. But it's not," she said, and going to a cupboard, took out rågkusar flat rolls, Herrgårdsost cheese, tomato slices, and a tube of Kalles cod caviar spread, and placed them on the table.

"Is that better?" she asked, smiling.

"Much," he replied, as he sat down and started in on the cereal.

"When will you be back?" Ingbritt asked later over coffee and the kanelbulle cinnamon rolls she'd also brought out against her better judgment.

"It's probably going to be a long day. But I'll be home for dinner around seven at the latest and I'll bring Garth with me."

"I'll fix something nice for us, so don't have a big lunch."

"Crackers and water only," he said with a laugh. "Will that do?"

"Perfectly," she replied.

As Ekman backed down the drive it was zero degrees Celsius and snow had begun falling rapidly from a leaden sky. There was thin, weekend morning traffic on the drive down Brunnvägen to headquarters.

When he got to his office, he found Garth Rystrom already there looking out the window at snow beginning to blanket an almost empty Stortorget Square.

He turned when he heard Ekman come in and hang up his hat and coat.

"Garth, it's good to see you," Ekman said. "Did you just get in?"

"No, I decided to come down last night, and it's probably a good thing I did."

"Where are you staying?" Ekman asked.

"At the Thon," he said, naming a hotel a few blocks from headquarters.

"Are you sure you don't want to stay at our place? We'd be delighted to have you."

"Thanks, Walther, but I thought I'd just remain at the hotel."

Rystrom was a good-looking, blond-haired man with light blue eyes and pale skin whose unlined face made him appear much younger than his midfifties. Ekman couldn't help wondering if his long-married friend might be seeing another woman while he was in Weltenborg, and then dismissed the thought as unworthy.

"Well, if you change your mind, you know you're always welcome. But you have to have dinner with us this evening or Ingbritt is going to be very disappointed."

Rystrom hesitated before he said, "I'll be delighted to see her again." But Ekman thought he'd quickly changed other plans for that evening.

The team was already seated when Ekman and Rystrom came into the conference room.

Ekman looked around the table. "You all know Garth Rystrom. He's kindly agreed to help us, as he did last year." Rystrom had been crucial in finally resolving a horrific case.

"It's good to see you all again," Rystrom said. "I hope I can be of some help."

Ekman sat down at the head of the table and Rystrom took a seat at the other end, next to Rapp.

"Okay," Ekman said. "Let's get started. Alrik?"

"We've gotten the autopsy report and Haake was strangled between seven and eight Wednesday evening. From the width of the wound, the wire used was slightly thicker than the one that killed Jakobsson, and was applied with even more force. A little more and it would have cut through his spine. Also, DNA confirmed what we thought: Haake was definitely the other man who'd raped Dahlin. He was the really brutal one who'd raped her anally." Rapp looked grim as he said this.

"Now we're on firmer ground than before," Ekman said. He turned to Holm. "Enar, what have you got?"

"Chief, I didn't get anywhere with the bank about their merger plans. They said it was too preliminary and sensitive to discuss. If we want the information, we'll have to get a warrant."

"All right, I'll be meeting with Kallenberg this morning and ask for it. Prepare an affidavit, please."

"Who checked the list of Fru Haake's lovers?" Ekman asked.

"We did, Chief," responded Rosengren, looking over at the taciturn Alenius. "There were five of them over the last four years. None of them look good for the killing; they all have solid alibis for when Haake was killed."

"Could you double-check those alibis?" put in Rystrom. "I always get suspicious when people are too quick to come up with them and they're too strong. Most folks can't remember what they were doing yesterday,"

Ekman nodded and said to Rosengren, "Garth's right. Take another look to be certain." Rosengren frowned, but said, "Whatever you want, Chief," pointedly ignoring Rystrom.

"Also," Ekman added, "while you're at it, double-check the dates she gave when she was involved with each of the men. If there are any unusually long time gaps between them, it could mean she left someone off the list."

"Will do, Chief," said Rosengren.

"What about the house staff?" Ekman asked, looking around.

"I did the research," said Vinter. "They have completely clean records, except for Marten Hult, the houseman. Two years ago, he finished serving four years for drug dealing and grievous bodily harm. There's been nothing since then."

"How long has he been working there?" asked Rystrom.

"He started shortly after he got out of prison."

"Gerdi, ask Fru Haake if they knew about his conviction when they hired him," said Ekman. "And try to get her to tell you more about him."

Vinter nodded.

"Maybe it was this ex-con who put Haake in touch with the trafficking ring," said an excited Rapp.

"It's an interesting possibility. After Gerdi talks with Fru Haake, why don't you bring him in for a quiet chat, Alrik?"

43

KALLENBERG INTERVENES

Saturday, February 4, 10 a.m. Arvid Kallenberg was thinking about Haake's murder as he gazed at trees in the small park beside the courthouse. Thickly falling snow was beginning to wrap white shrouds around their bare limbs when Ekman knocked and came in.

"Good morning, Arvid," Ekman said.

"Good morning to you, Walther," Kallenberg replied. "Although it's not so good after all." He gestured to the windows. He was casually dressed in a heavy, cable-knit white sweater and black slacks.

"I assume you want to talk about Fredrik Haake's murder," Kallenberg said.

"Yes, with all the attention it's getting and the media inquiries you're bound to have, I wanted to make sure you had the latest information on the investigation." Mostly, however, Ekman wanted Kallenberg to be comfortable with what he was doing so he wouldn't consider taking over the investigation himself.

"I appreciate that, Walther. I've gotten several questions from them already, but referred them to your public information office. They won't be satisfied with that, of course, and so pretty soon I expect they'll be swarming over both of us," Kallenberg said with a laugh.

Ekman reviewed where the investigation stood, what they'd discussed at that morning's meeting, and the new information about Marten Hult. Explaining that the bank was stonewalling, he handed Kallenberg an affidavit for a warrant for the bank's documents relating to the proposed merger.

"And you should know that Norlander had me bring in Garth Rystrom from the CID. He joined us this morning."

Kallenberg was silent for a moment as he considered this.

"Walther, with all the media pressure, and CID now in the picture, I think I've got to be more directly involved." He saw the momentary look of dismay that flitted across Ekman's face. "It would look strange if I weren't.

"I really do have absolute confidence in you, but considering everything, I need to be at your team meetings from now on. Don't worry, I want you to continue to lead the investigation. I'll just try to be a helpful observer."

But Ekman knew that at any moment the prosecutor could simply take over. His attempt to ward off what was probably inevitable hadn't worked.

44

Fru Haake Confides

Saturday, February 4, 2 p.m. Marten Hult opened the door when Gerdi Vinter rang.

Right after the team meeting, she'd called to arrange a visit with Fru Haake.

"What is this about now?" Kajsa Haake had asked, sounding exasperated.

"I'd rather discuss it with you personally," Vinter replied.

"All right, if you must. I'll see you at two."

Vinter looked at Hult carefully, taking in his muscular figure and stolid face.

"I'm Inspector Vinter, Fru Haake is expecting me."

Hult just nodded, and opening the door wide, let her into the foyer. He took her coat from her and hung it in a closet.

"Come this way, please," he said, preceding her down the corridor to the room in which Ekman had had his interview.

He knocked, opened the door, and said, "Inspector Vinter," then turned and went back down the hall.

Vinter was surprised by the size of the room and looked around before focusing on the slender woman, dressed in a grey pants suit. She'd put down the magazine she'd been reading and gotten up from the couch.

She came forward and offered her hand, "I'm Kajsa Haake," she said in a flat tone.

Haake suggested they sit on the couch.

"Would you care for some coffee, Inspector?"

"No thank you, I'm fine," Vinter replied. She didn't want to drag out this meeting, just get the information she needed and leave.

"What can I help you with?"

"As part of our investigation, we've been reviewing the backgrounds of your house staff."

Haake looked startled.

"It's part of normal routine in a murder investigation," Vinter said. "One of your staff has a criminal record. Were you aware of it?"

"You mean Marten. And yes, he told my husband about it when he was first interviewed. Fredrik believed that everyone deserves another chance. So do I."

"Have you had any reason for second thoughts about him?"

"None at all. He's worked here for two years and has been very satisfactory."

"It's vital in an investigation of this kind that you be completely frank, Fru Haake, and we appreciate the information you gave Herr Ekman. It's been extremely helpful. But now I must ask you to be equally open with me. What is your personal relationship with Marten Hult?"

Kajsa Haake was silent for a long moment. She looks distressed, thought Vinter: she doesn't want to tell me.

45

DINNER WITH RYSTROM

Saturday, February 4, 6:50 p.m. The plow had piled snow in tall drifts on each side of the road, but strong gusts of wind had blown some of it back. The surface was slick in places with patches of black ice that glittered dangerously in his headlights. Ekman drove slowly, glancing occasionally in the rearview mirror to make sure Garth Rystrom's following car was all right. He'd suggested that they travel together and that Rystrom at least spend that night with them, but he'd declined.

As Ekman saw the lighted windows of his house and pulled into the drive, he felt the same warm sense he always had coming home. It was his refuge from the often-horrific world he faced every day. He opened the garage with a remote and drove forward into the brightly lit space, leaving room in the driveway for Rystrom's car.

They both entered the house from the connecting side door. Ingbritt had heard the garage door open and was standing in the hall waiting for them, a broad, welcoming smile on her face. She gave Rystrom a tight hug.

"Garth, it's so good to see you," she said. "It's been too long."

She took his coat and hat and hung them in the hall closet.

"Both of you go into the dining room and relax," she said, "I know you must be hungry. Dinner will be ready in five minutes."

Ekman was surprised; they usually ate in the kitchen. Going down the hall toward the front of the house, he went into the old-fashioned, wainscoted dining room with Rystrom and saw that Ingbritt had set three places with her grandmother's china and silver. A crystal vase of blue and yellow irises stood in the center of the white damask-covered table.

She's gone all out, Ekman thought. Well, why not. We don't see Garth very often.

He sat down at the head of the table and gestured to the chair on his right for Rystrom.

"For this evening, the house rule is no shop talk," Ekman said. "Politics, religion, and sports only, nothing as controversial as murder cases,"

"That's okay with me."

"So who's your pick in the bandy championship next month?" Ekman asked, referring to the popular ice hockey-like game.

"Well, I should root for the home team, Stockholm's Hammarby IF, but I really like Västerås SK."

"Good choice. They're mine too. So much for sports." Ekman knew neither one of them had the time or inclination to follow the teams closely.

Ingbritt came in wheeling a serving cart with bottles of liquor and wine.

"What would you like, Garth?" Ekman said, going over to the cart.

"Maybe just a small glass of wine. I've got to drive later, but it should have worn off by then."

"What's the main course?" Ekman asked Ingbritt.

"I thought you and Garth might enjoy roast duck," she said, "and so I opened that bottle of good Barolo we've been saving, to go with it."

"That all sounds wonderful."

"Garth, let me pour you some of this." He raised the half-filled glass and inhaled. "It's even better than I'd hoped," he added, handing Rystrom the glass.

As she set the first course on the table, Ingbritt asked, "How are Myrie and the children, Garth?"

Rystrom had two grown daughters and several grandchildren. He paused before answering and said, "The girls and the little ones are fine."

"And Myrie?"

"We separated three months ago."

There was a long silence until Ingbritt said, "I'm so sorry to hear that, Garth. Do you want to talk about it?"

"Not really. There's nothing much to tell. We'd just grown apart. I guess twenty-six years of me was more than she could take."

Police officers were notorious for having broken marriages. The irregular hours and constant, grinding pressure of dealing with crime was too much for many relationships.

Ekman looked closely at his friend.

"Is there anything we can do, Garth, to help make things easier?"

"No, Walther. But thanks for asking."

The dinner was delicious, both men said and thanked Ingbritt profusely. But after Rystrom's revelation, conversation had lagged. Right after the dessert of rhubarb pie, Rystrom looked at his watch and said he'd better be heading back to town. He seemed anxious to leave.

They said their good-byes, and Ekman and Ingbritt watched from the doorway as Rystrom's car pulled out of the drive.

I was right after all, Ekman thought. There's another woman. And she's waiting for him at his hotel.

46

HULT INTERVIEW

Sunday, February 5, 8:45 a.m. Icy rain coming down in sheets from a cinder grey sky had shrunk the snowdrifts alongside the road, but frozen on the surface making driving treacherous, as Ekman headed to his office. He'd gotten up unusually late, and only had time for a hasty bowl of hot oatmeal and a cup of coffee, instead of their usual, large Sunday breakfast.

Ingbritt had said, "Please be careful, Walther, it looks bad out there."

He'd grunted agreement as he pulled on his hooded parka and hurried to the garage.

Rapp had called at seven thirty that morning to tell him he was bringing in Marten Hult. They planned to start the interview at ten. Ekman had called Rystrom to let him know.

The three men sat on one side of the table facing Hult. He looked without expression from one to the other, but Ekman thought he was probably intimidated and wanted him to stay that way.

"It's ten a.m., February 5. This is a formal interview with Marten Hult. I'm Chief Superintendent Ekman, with me are Superintendent Rystrom, and Chief Inspector Rapp," he intoned for the video cameras peering down from the walls of the stark white interview room.

"Do you know why you're here, Herr Hult?" he asked.

"I was asked to come and give a statement, something about Fredrik Haake's death. It's a hell of an inconvenience on my day off. I already spoke with your inspector at the house and told him everything I know. Which is exactly nothing."

"We appreciate your cooperation," said Rystrom. "However, there may be some information you've preferred not to share with us. For example, how you used your prison connections to put Haake in touch with the people who kidnapped the Dahlin woman he raped."

Hult was obviously startled and didn't answer for a moment. "I've got nothing to do with that."

Rapp said, "We don't believe you, Hult. Every time you deny something we know, you dig yourself in deeper. Make it easier on yourself and tell us who you sent Haake to."

"You've got it all wrong. I never did anything like that." But he didn't sound convincing. Ekman thought he was lying. Was he afraid to give them the name of his contact?

"I don't have anything to tell you. Can we get this over with? There are things I need to do today."

"Would one of those things be fucking the late Herr Haake's wife?" asked Rapp, suddenly switching the subject. Gerdi had briefed them the previous afternoon about Kajsa Haake's revelations.

Hult's jaw dropped. He hadn't expected such a brutal frontal assault.

"I don't know what you're talking about."

"Of course you do," said Ekman. "And it makes you a likely suspect for Haake's murder."

"Now wait a minute, wait a minute," a flustered Hult said, his composure gone. "All right, I admit it, we've fooled around, but I had nothing to do with his death. And I've got an alibi."

"Yes, Fru Haake has said you were in the house Wednesday evening. It's convenient that it was the cook's night off and so there's no one else to confirm it."

"It's the truth."

"Why should we believe you, Hult, or her? You've a record of violence. Maybe getting rid of Haake would have opened new possibilities with the lady that she welcomed. She's a rich widow now, and you already have an inside track, so to speak," said Rapp.

"She'd never go for it. I'm not her type—except in bed."

"Do you know about her other lovers?" asked Rystrom.

"Yeah, I know and don't care."

"If she picked one instead of you and he suddenly died, who do you think we'd come looking for?" Rapp asked.

"I told you I'm okay with it. If she marries one of them, that's all right with me."

"Then you'd be out of both your jobs: as houseman and lover," said Rapp.

"So I'll find another job. And there are plenty of other women."

"When did you and Fru Haake first decide to kill her husband? Was it right after the Jakobsson murder? Is that why you used a wire, so we'd think it was connected?" asked Ekman.

Hult turned pale. "I already told you I had nothing to do with it. We never talked about it and you can't prove otherwise," he replied in an agitated voice.

"Suppose we believe you. Maybe Fru Haake planned the killing with one of her other lovers," said Ekman.

"She wouldn't do that. She's not that sort of person."

"Maybe you don't know her as well as you think," said Rystrom.

Hult paused. "You've got her all wrong. Haake left her alone. She got along with him fine. There was no reason to kill him."

But now he's considering it, thought Ekman. Maybe this will start a rift between them that we can exploit.

"It's something to think about, isn't it? This interview is over . . . for now," said Ekman, standing.

"We'll want to speak with you again, Hult. Don't leave Weltenborg without notifying us. The constable at the door will show you out."

The three were seated in Ekman's office going over the interrogation.

"How did he seem to you?" asked Ekman.

"Very nervous," said Rapp.

"But anyone would be, under the circumstances," said Rystrom.

"Do we agree he probably put Haake onto the trafficking ring?" asked Ekman.

Rystrom and Rapp both nodded.

"So how do we get the information out of him?" Ekman said.

"All we can do is keep the pressure on about Haake's murder. He might think that giving us the name of his contact would get us to ease up on him as a murder suspect," said Rystrom.

"I agree," Rapp said.

"He's still a strong possibility as the killer. Could he have planned it with Haake's wife?" Ekman asked.

"Yes, and she gave him his alibi," answered Rystrom.

"A rich widow who couldn't stand her late, unlamented husband is a hell of a motive," said Rapp.

"But unless one of them cracks, we've got no evidence," said Ekman.

"So we keep after both of them," said Rapp.

"But if they're innocent, there's no way for them to prove it," Rystrom added.

"We have to assume they're guilty until our other theory bears fruit. Justice demands it," Ekman said with a twisted smile.

47

NEW ARRANGEMENT

Friday, February 3, 11 a.m. *There was a knock at the door of Karim's suite at the Grand. He got up from the living room couch, limped down the hallway, and opened the door to Ivar.*

"Please come in," *he said and led the way back into the living room. He gestured to the couch and sat in a facing armchair. Ivar took off his coat and hat and placed them beside him.*

There was a coffee service with two cups on the low table in front of the couch.

"Would you like some coffee?"

"Yes, thanks, that sounds fine. It's another miserable day out there."

Karim poured cups for both of them.

He could tell from Ivar's voice that he'd been surprised when he'd called last night. Ivar evidently hadn't expected him back so soon. He'd again resisted the idea of meeting at the hotel, suggesting instead the café they'd met in before. But Karim had been insistent that they needed privacy for this meeting. He wanted it to take place on his terms.

"That was a fast round trip. I assume you went back to Morocco?"

"It was a little stressful, but I had to meet with my principal. There were some questions that could only be discussed in person."

"But now you have your answers?"

"Yes, and we need to talk about them."

"Are you and your boss unhappy with our arrangement? It's been very profitable for all of us."

"You're right, it's been quite successful, but things have changed. The girl's public death, the search for Ahmed, and now the murder of your prominent client, Fredrik Haake, have focused too much police attention on the women side of the operation."

"That's a temporary situation. We'll keep a low profile for now. Things will die down after a while and return to normal."

"My boss and I don't agree. We think the risk level has become too high. If the police should uncover one side of the business, the other side would quickly follow. And that's where most of the profits are, for both of us. It's in our mutual interest to protect the drug operation."

"What do you propose?" Ivar said in a friendly tone.

"You need to get out of women trafficking immediately."

"What if we just stop the reciprocal arrangement?"

"That won't be good enough. The police could unravel your drug distribution network if they uncover the trafficking business, whether that side of it is with us or someone else."

"What if I could guarantee that the police investigation will soon end, marked 'unsolves'?"

"How could that be?"

"Let's just say I have highly placed connections."

Karim considered this for a moment.

"We can't risk it. There's too much media attention for these deaths to be swept under the rug, even by 'highly placed connections.'"

"If we agree to your idea, we'll lose fees from our clients here. And we'll both lose money on the women's resale in Marrakech."

"We recognize that. We'll just have to absorb the loss. To make this easier for you, we're willing to reduce the price of the drugs."

"By how much?"

"Five percent."

"That's not nearly enough. Twenty percent."

"Eight."

"Fifteen."

"Ten, and that's our final offer."

"It won't begin to offset our loss," Ivar said.

"We're each going to take a hit, but it's the safest course."

"And if the police investigation does end, what then?"

"Then we can revisit this, but as of now, this new arrangement holds."

"I'll agree . . . for now."

"You'll have to start shutting down your trafficking operation."

"It will take at least a week. The ship isn't due to arrive until then."

"They'll be the last shipment."

"And we'll have to notify our clients. They'll be extremely unhappy."

Karim shrugged. He couldn't care less about discomforted perverts.

Ivar picked up his hat and coat as they both got up.

Karim walked him to the door.

"I can't honestly say it's been a pleasure doing business with you," Ivar said.

"Look at it this way. We'll all be able to breathe easier with this new arrangement."

"Perhaps," replied Ivar. "We'll see." He turned and walked down the hall toward the elevators.

Karim watched him leave for a moment before closing the door and limping back to the living room.

He picked up the phone and called Marrakech.

"He accepted the deal," he said, and hung up. But he was troubled; Ivar had agreed too easily. If he reneged, he would have to be dealt with.

48

NEW MEMBER

Monday, February 6, 8 a.m. The team members were in their usual places around the table, but the chair on Ekman's left was now occupied by Arvid Kallenberg. The others glanced at him, but said nothing. The prosecutor had never chosen to join them before.

Ekman introduced him. "The media attention this case is getting has persuaded Prosecutor Kallenberg to participate in our meetings." Then he turned to him. "Would you like to say a few words?"

Kallenberg looked around the table. "First, I want to congratulate all of you on how quickly you've developed this investigation. Chief Ekman has been briefing me on your progress and I'm impressed with the work you've done. Second, I want to assure you that he will continue to lead the investigation. He has my complete confidence and support. My role will be limited to observing, and perhaps making a few suggestions." He turned to Ekman.

"Thanks," said Ekman. "Okay, let me bring everyone up to date." He summarized the interview with Marten Hult and the conclusions the three interviewers had reached.

"What do the rest of you think?"

"I agree, Chief," said Holm. "Hult is the most likely contact for Haake with the traffickers."

"The most likely, but not necessarily the actual one," said Vinter.

"But Gerdi," said Holm, "what else do we have to go on? Haake wouldn't have just run into them at a bankers' meeting."

"You're outvoted, Gerdi," said Rosengren. "Alenius and I also think Hult's the contact man."

"But Gerdi does have a point," said Rystrom. "While Hult looks like our best bet, we can't be certain."

"We should be very careful before implicating this man in a criminal conspiracy," put in Kallenberg. "If it should leak, we could ruin an innocent person and expose the police to damages."

"You're right," said Ekman. "But we need to convince ourselves that he's not involved. I think we should tap his phone and put him under twenty-four-hour surveillance for the next week. If nothing turns up, then we can assume Gerdi is right and we have to look elsewhere. Will you agree to that?" he asked Kallenberg.

The prosecutor was silent for a moment. "All right, but just a week."

"I'll be glad to bring in my technical people and surveillance teams," said Rystrom.

"Thanks, Garth. We'll need the help," Ekman said. He meant it, but from now on he knew he'd have to struggle to retain control as both the prosecutor and his friend from Stockholm CID became increasingly involved.

49

GRUNDSTRÖM

Monday, February 6, 2 p.m. Enar Holm and Gerdi Vinter sat in his imposing corner office across a large mahogany desk from Håkan Grundström, the bank's new CEO. He was a well-built man of fifty, who was observing them with considerable distaste written on his handsome, craggy face.

"This warrant is outrageous," he said. "It's ridiculous and much too broad. I'm seriously considering having our counsel fight this in court. You have no reason to see dozens of documents relating to our proposed merger. They can have no conceivable bearing on Fredrik's death."

He slapped the warrant against the palm of his left hand. Grundström could delay them, but a court battle could hurt the bank's carefully nurtured reputation as a scrupulously law-abiding pillar of the community, and might damage the merger they'd gone to such pains to promote.

"You'll have to let us make that judgment," Holm said in a flat tone. "In a murder investigation there's no way to tell if some background document might provide critical information."

"I can assure you that that will not be the case in this instance. But I guess my word isn't going to be good enough for the police."

Holm was adamant. "You can start by telling us the name of the bank you're proposing to merge with."

"All right, but you must agree to keep this confidential. If it got out it would affect the stock prices of both our banks and possibly endanger the merger."

"If it has nothing to do with the murder, as you've said, then it will remain confidential. But we can't make any guarantee if it turns out to be a factor. I'm sure you can understand that, Herr Grundström."

"Okay, as long as we're clear on the ground rules. It's Nordbank," he said, naming one of the largest banks in Sweden.

Vinter raised her eyebrows in surprise. "Because of their size, I assume they're proposing to buy your bank."

"That's right."

"And you'll head the merged bank?" asked Holm.

"No. I expect it will be their current CEO."

"So you'll be out of a job?"

"Not at all. I'm to be the chief operating officer at a substantial increase in compensation."

"But you won't be the CEO."

"Not for now. However their current head is planning on retiring in less than two years and I'd be the logical choice as successor."

"How did Herr Haake feel about the merger?" asked Vinter.

"He was very much against it. He'd been trying to persuade our board to turn down the offer."

"Why was that?"

"Because he'd no longer be chairman and CEO. Unlike me, he'd have found it impossible to be in a subordinate position, even for a few years. Besides, they didn't want him in any capacity."

"So he was going to be forced into retirement if the merger went through."

"Yes, it was his age: he was sixty-two. Their board wanted younger leadership."

"Could he have succeeded in stopping the merger?"

Grundström paused for a moment. "It's hard to say. Probably not, but he'd convinced a few key members of our board to vote against it. Nordbank had made a generous offer in stock and cash and most of the board would realize something of a windfall if the merger went through."

"And would you also benefit financially, Herr Grundström?" asked Vinter.

"Yes, I guess I would." He stared with tightened features at each of them, and then said in a harsh voice, "You're not suggesting that I had any reason to kill Fredrik, are you, because that would be an outrageous idea."

"Not at all, Herr Grundström. As we told you, we're just gathering information," Vinter replied.

Holm and Vinter were using two computers to look through the DVDs Grundström had given them in response to the warrant, searching for e-mails between Haake and his bank's board members.

"It's clear that Haake was really upset about the merger," said Holm. "Look at this one."

Vinter came over and read the screen over his shoulder. Haake had written to all the board members a week before his death, denouncing the merger and arguing for the bank's continued independence. He'd concluded by offering to double the directors' compensation.

"He sounds frantic," said Vinter.

"Yes, he was desperate to stop the merger. But he may have had a better chance of succeeding than Grundström said. I found this one too. It was two days before Haake was killed."

He changed screens to an e-mail from one of the directors to each of the others. It indicated that a majority of the board had decided to side with Haake and oppose the merger.

"With Haake gone, however, everything changed."

"Yes. He was the one, real obstacle," Holm said.

"So Grundström and those directors who supported the merger had every reason to want him out of the way."

"But who was willing to kill him over this? We need to take a look at the finances of Grundström and the board members who wanted the merger."

"There are going to be a lot of unhappy bankers when we go digging around."

"True, but upsetting the smug and powerful is half the fun of the job, right?" said Holm.

50

IVAR'S PLAN

Saturday, February 4, 5 p.m. *Ivar and Thore Ostlund were sitting in facing armchairs with drinks in their hands in the living room of Ostlund's spacious apartment in Södermalm, a trendy section of Stockholm.*

Ivar had been laying out Karim's proposal for Ostlund.

"So you see, they want us to get out of the women business entirely."

Ostlund was silent for a moment. "They may be right. It's become increasingly risky."

"Yes, it's risky, but it's always been. We knew that when we started. With the drugs, it's made us both rich. We shouldn't panic now and just get out. It's taken years to build up a clientele. If we drop them and then things quiet down, we'll never get them back. And it's not everyone who has a taste for what we've been providing."

"I don't know. You may be right. But it feels like things are closing in, and I have to tell you, Ivar, I'm getting more and more uncomfortable. Why don't we just pull back until the search for Ahmed dies down?" Ostlund asked.

"If we're going to stay in the business, I think we need to keep on doing exactly as we have. That search will go nowhere."

"You sound very certain about that."

"I am. Trust me on this," Ivar said.

"Assuming you're right, how are we going to deal with Karim?"

"We'll send Marrakech all the women we have now, tell them we've dropped the business, and take the 10 percent cut in the drug price."

"But we're not really getting out?" asked Ostlund.

"No, we'll just find another wholesaler outside Europe to take new women off our hands when our clients are through with them. It shouldn't be difficult to locate someone. There's plenty of demand in the Middle East and Southeast Asia for well-trained European women."

"What do you think Karim will do if he finds out?"

"They could stop doing business with us entirely. But I don't think they will. Our drug distribution network has functioned too well for them. They'd have to start from scratch again, find another distributor and try them out, and that could be very expensive.

"No, I think they'll bitch about it and take back their 10 percent cut, probably retroactively. But we can live with that. We won't be any worse off than before the new arrangement. My guess is that they're already looking for another supplier of women, an outfit not connected to their drug business," Ivar said.

"If we ship all our current supply to Marrakech this week, how will we manage to hang on to our clients? It takes time for me to find the right women."

"They need us much more than we need them. We'll just tell them we're restocking with exciting new merchandise and it will take a few weeks."

"I'm going to have to scramble then to pick up new goods," Ostlund said.

"It'll be worth it. And Marta and Gotz will have a good time breaking them in. They've both seemed on edge lately. Marta has become even bitchier than usual. And despite his denials, we both agree that Gotz probably killed Haake."

"That's a real problem. I think he's out of control, and he's endangered us by a killing that's turned up the heat."

"We'll increase his take and Marta's, and feed them new women; that should keep them in line," Ivar said.

"I hope you're right. If Gotz kills again on his own, no matter how useful he is, we'll have to get rid of him."

51

AN ENGLISH BREAKFAST

Tuesday, February 7, 5:30 a.m. Ekman had slept badly, tossing and turning during the night and getting up twice to use the bathroom, a sign, he thought, of impending old age. He'd groped his way cautiously in the dark, not wanting to turn on a light and disturb Ingbritt.

The second time he'd gotten up, she'd stirred and raising herself on an elbow, asked, "Are you all right, Walther?"

"Yes, I'm fine, just need to pee. Go back to sleep."

Ingbritt turned on the bedside lamp and looked at the alarm clock. "It's time I got up anyway," she said, throwing off the duvet and reaching for her quilted robe on the chair next to the bed. She pulled on the housecoat, slipped her feet into warm, sheepskin-lined mules, and headed out the bedroom door for the stairs to the kitchen.

Ekman took longer than usual in the shower, letting the steaming hot water run over his neck and back. Those muscles often ached, another sign of advancing age? Or perhaps just stress, and the wet heat felt good.

Looking at himself in the full-length mirror as he dressed, he glanced at his expanding belly, and shook his head. He was going to have to exercise and tighten things up. But when would he find the time? Since Haake's murder, this case had become all-consuming. He felt relentless pressure.

As he came downstairs and into the warm kitchen, the scent of frying bacon became stronger and he could hear it sizzling in the pan.

"I thought this morning I'd do something different and cook us a real English breakfast."

"That sounds terrific and smells even better," he said.

Their usual breakfast sandwiches were fine, but this was a welcome change on a cold winter's day.

Ingbritt served them each glasses of fresh orange juice, and plates piled with four strips of streaky bacon, two fried eggs, mushrooms, grilled tomatoes, and beans, accompanied by a rack of whole wheat toast, marmalade, and a pot of black coffee.

"This looks marvelous. What a great idea," Ekman said, rubbing his hands as he pulled out a chair and sat down.

After they'd finished, and were lingering over second cups of coffee, he'd gone to the front door and retrieved the two morning newspapers on the stoop, covered in plastic that was wet from the now heavily falling snow.

Going back into the kitchen, he threw away the wrappings and handed a paper to Ingbritt. Both newspapers had front page stories about the investigation of Haake's murder. The still fruitless, ongoing search for Ahmed had slid to a sidebar in one, and a brief paragraph on the third page of the other.

"Haeggman is at it again," said Ekman. "Everything is a mess, nothing is happening, and it's all my fault, as usual." He held up the paper, punching the story hard with a finger.

"Walther, you mustn't let him upset you," Ingbritt said, observing his reddening face. "You know it's bad for your blood pressure."

"You're right, you're right. I should know better by now. He'd get a kick out of it if he knew he was getting to me. I shouldn't give him the satisfaction."

Ekman looked at his watch. It was 7:20. He folded the paper carefully and put it on the table.

"Time to get going," he said. "Thanks again for the breakfast. It was a treat."

Ingbritt watched through the living room windows as his car pulled slowly out of the drive and turned toward town on the freshly plowed road.

She had worried about him for about a year. He was still energetic and deeply involved in his work, but something was missing. A certain sense of joy in life seemed to have drained out of him since their son's death. She wondered if it would ever return.

52

SUSPECTS

Tuesday, February 7, 8 a.m. When Ekman came into the conference room, he saw that everyone was there except Kallenberg.

He waited five minutes before beginning, letting the others chat among themselves, and debated whether to delay longer for the prosecutor. He decided it wasn't his problem; Kallenberg knew the meeting time.

Just then the prosecutor came in and took his seat.

"Sorry to hold you up," he said to Ekman. "The roads were worse than I'd thought."

"Okay everyone, let's get started," Ekman said. "Garth, how is the Hult surveillance going?"

"Everything's in place, but nothing of interest has happened so far. He's phoned a few friends, just routine conversations. Alrik's checked these people out, however, and he can tell you about them. Hult's been to a couple of local bars and we've sent someone in to watch. He had a drink or two then left. No contact with anyone."

"Alrik?"

"Neither one of his phone buddies has a record. They talked about sports mostly and a new girlfriend one of them has been dating. Nothing relating to Haake or trafficking."

"Rosengren and Alenius. Anything?"

"We double-checked the alibis of Haake's wife's lovers. They still hold up," said Rosengren.

"But we also took another look at the dates she gave us, and you were right, Chief, there's been a recent gap that looks as though she's left someone out," Alenius said.

"She's been very active for an old broad," Rosengren added, "and hasn't had any trouble finding new guys, so why the break? It doesn't add up."

"Gerdi, you had a productive talk with Fru Haake," said Ekman. "Why don't you have another chat with her and see if she's been holding out on us."

"Will do, Chief," Vinter said.

"Enar and Gerdi, what did you find out at Haake's bank?"

"We may have something interesting," said Holm. "There was a good reason they didn't want to give us information about their merger."

"Haake was against it," Vinter continued. "Nordbank wanted to buy them out, offering heavy cash and stock incentives, but wouldn't have him as CEO, and in fact, didn't want him at all. They thought he was too old and should just retire."

"So Haake launched a campaign to stop the merger and had persuaded a majority of his directors to go along with him two days before he was killed," said Holm. "The new CEO, Håkan Grundström, and the directors who wanted the merger, would lose a lot of money if it didn't go through."

"We'd like to take a look at Grundström's finances, and those of the directors who wanted the merger, to find out how badly they needed it," said Vinter. "We'll have to get warrants to examine their financial records," she added, glancing at Kallenberg, who'd been listening intently.

Ekman looked thoughtful. "Gerdi, you and Enar may have discovered an important new piece of the puzzle," he said. "I think we should follow through on your idea. Prepare affidavits for the warrants."

"I hate to disagree, Walther," Kallenberg interjected. "This would be nothing more than a fishing expedition and it could become a serious problem. These are very prominent people. We have no substantial reason to suspect that any of them had a hand in Haake's death."

"Arvid, I understand your reluctance, but *all* of us," he looked at Kallenberg directly, "are under a lot of public pressure to solve Haake's murder quickly. Every avenue has to be explored, even if it might mean upsetting a few important people."

Kallenberg was silent for a moment. "How many directors are we talking about?" he asked Vinter.

"Six, including Grundström."

"All right, you'll have your warrants. But do your search as unobtrusively as possible. And don't interview any of them until you clear it with Herr Ekman and me. Is that acceptable, Walther?"

"I think that's the right approach, Arvid."

Ekman turned to Holm and Vinter. "Be discreet. This could be very touchy and we don't need more problems."

"Got it, Chief," Holm replied.

53

LUNCHEON SPECIAL

Tuesday, February 7, 1:15 p.m. Ekman and Rapp were seated by a rear window in Ekman's favorite restaurant across Stortorget Square from headquarters. They'd both ordered the smoked salmon plate lunch specials, and were sipping beers as they waited for their food.

Under a dismal sky, few cars and fewer pedestrians had braved the biting wind and deepening snow. The temperature was steadily dropping and icicles had formed on the stilled bronze fountain in the center of the plaza.

"Do you think we'll get anywhere with those bankers?" Rapp asked.

"It's a long shot in my opinion. They would have to be very desperate to commit murder to get their hands on extra cash. Bankers are likely to have other, less drastic means of bailing themselves out of financial difficulties."

"So should we call off Enar and Gerdi before they accidentally stir up a hornet's nest?"

"I don't think we can. It's an avenue that has to be explored even if it leads nowhere."

Ekman was sitting facing the front door and saw two heavily bundled figures enter. He didn't know them for a moment, and then saw it was Garth Rystrom and, when she threw back the hood of her parka, he immediately recognized Valdis Granholm's red hair.

He stood up, waved to them, and said to Rapp, "We've got company."

Rapp turned in his seat and a look of surprise crossed his face.

Rystrom and Granholm came over to the table.

"I thought we might catch you here," Rystrom said to them. "Can we join you?"

"Please do," said Ekman. Rapp had gotten up and pulled over two extra chairs.

"I didn't know you were in town, Valdis," Ekman said.

"Garth and I came down together."

"Garth, you should have told me. Ingbritt would have been delighted to have had both of you over for dinner."

Ekman knew that his instincts had been right: Granholm was the woman who'd been waiting for Rystrom at his hotel.

"I'd love to meet her. Perhaps we can arrange something in the next few days."

"How long will you be in Weltenborg, Valdis?" asked Rapp.

"Until the weekend. Garth and I will be returning to Stockholm Saturday, and then he'll come back down again Sunday night."

The waiter came over. "Can I bring you something?" he asked the new arrivals.

Rystrom looked questioningly at Granholm. "Yes, I'm starving," she said, as the waiter gave them two menus.

While they waited for their food, Granholm brought them up to date on her inquiries.

"There's still nothing about Chafik. He seems to have just vanished. But we've had better luck finding out more about Joumari.

"He's elderly, believed to be in his eighties, and, as we know, for fifty years he's been thought to be a major figure in drugs and prostitution, not only in Morocco, but throughout the Middle East. He's very secretive and always acts through several cutouts.

"Recently there've been quiet attempts to build a drug case against him, but no one in the prosecutor's office has gotten anywhere. Potential witnesses, and his biggest competitors in the business, have a funny way of simply disappearing or changing their minds. Again, nothing has ever been traced directly back to him, but his reputation on the street is that he's extremely dangerous to cross."

"That's very helpful information. Have your contacts been able to find out anything about who actually owns the spice company where Chafik worked?" Ekman asked.

"The Rabat holding company is a paper front. The attorney who acts for the real owner won't tell my Moroccan contact anything."

"It's suspicious that whoever owns the company is so secretive," said Rapp.

"Yes, but there could be tax or family reasons for that," said Rystrom.

"Possibly, Garth, but I think Alrik's right. It's got to be Joumari's company," Ekman said. "Look what we know: Chafik's a relative of Joumari; he rapes the Dahlin woman; her kidnapping and death is connected to a trafficking ring; Joumari runs a major prostitution operation; Chafik vanishes and can't be found anywhere in Europe. What are the odds that Joumari's not involved?"

"We should take another look at that spice company," said Rapp.

"I agree. Garth, I'm going to ask Kallenberg to authorize phone taps and surveillance on the company. We'll need your help in Stockholm."

"You'll have it."

"And Valdis, we need to work closely with your Moroccan Interpol office. I'd like to find out more about what's happening at that end."

"I'll speak with him today," Granholm said.

Their lunches arrived and everyone was quiet while they concentrated on the food.

After Rystrom and Granholm had left, Ekman turned to Rapp.

"Well, what do you think?" He meant about the new directions the case was taking.

"They're lovers," said a visibly downcast Rapp.

54

FRU HAAKE—AGAIN

Tuesday, February 7, 2:30 p.m. Gerdi Vinter and Kajsa Haake were seated in the same room where Vinter had first interviewed her. Haake was twisting a handkerchief around her left hand as she spoke.

"I don't know why you people are persecuting me. Don't you realize I've just lost my husband? You have no feelings." Her eyes grew moist as she said this.

"We're deeply sympathetic, Fru Haake. But our job requires us to do more than sympathize. We have an obligation to you, and to society, to find your husband's killer. So please bear with us during our investigation. We have to pursue every possibility, and that means asking sometimes painful questions."

"I understand, but it's difficult to put up with all this prying into my personal life, which has nothing to do with Fredrik's death."

"You have to let us judge what may be relevant."

"All right. Let's get this over. What do you want to know now?"

Vinter had been speculating about who the lover could be that Fru Haake hadn't wanted to disclose. There was one interesting possibility and she decided to try a direct approach.

"What is your relationship with Håkan Grundström?"

She was silent for a moment. "He was my husband's colleague at the bank. We socialized frequently with him and his wife. Nothing more."

Vinter looked at her closely. "Fru Haake, I don't feel you're being entirely frank with me."

"You can feel whatever you want, but I've said all I'm going to."

"Let me be very clear. You can tell me what I need to know here in your home in the next few minutes, and then I'll leave and not bother you again, or you can come with me to police headquarters for a formal interview that will take many hours and be conducted by men who will be much less sympathetic than I am." Vinter's voice had grown harsh as she said this.

"You're an unkind person. That's why you have your job. You enjoy doing this. You enjoy humiliating others."

"That isn't so, and you know it. Please, Kajsa, make this easy for both of us."

"Håkan and I have a personal relationship. There, I've said it, are you satisfied?"

"I'm glad you decided to tell me the truth. I have just a few more questions. How long has this been going on?"

"For the last six months. We've been very discreet because of his position at the bank."

"Are you in love with him?"

Fru Haake didn't reply immediately. "I think so."

"Have you thought about marriage?"

"Håkan separated from his wife a year ago and is divorcing her. And yes, after Fredrik died we talked about getting married. I haven't wanted to say anything because I know it would throw suspicion on him, even though it's ridiculous. He'd never hurt anyone, let alone kill them. Now, have I told you everything?"

Vinter stood up. "Thank you for being candid, Kajsa. I won't trouble you again." She knew she wasn't being entirely candid herself. If the investigation focused on Grundström, Kajsa Haake would have to be formally interviewed, and could find herself on the witness stand at his trial.

55

KALLENBERG BALKS

Tuesday, February 7, 4 p.m. Ekman was quietly fuming, and trying not to show it. He was seated in Arvid Kallenberg's office and had just laid out the rationale for phone and physical surveillance of the spice company. The prosecutor had flat-out refused to authorize it.

"Arvid, we need to find out more about what's going on at this company. It's likely that Joumari owns it and, if so, he's probably using it for illegal purposes."

"I understand your argument, Walther. But you have no evidence that would justify surveillance of what your inspectors have said appears to be a legitimate business. Because it's owned by a Moroccan holding company and Chafik worked there, doesn't mean Joumari owns it, and even if he does, that there are illegal activities."

Ekman knew Kallenberg could sometimes be a legal nit-picker, but under the circumstances he couldn't understand why Kallenberg was digging in his heels this way.

"I think that since we've decided to pursue all possible leads, excluding this one frankly doesn't make a lot of sense."

Kallenberg frowned. "Even if you're right, I can't see how it could help us with Haake's murder."

"Well, we know that Chafik and Haake raped the Dahlin woman. If the company is involved in Joumari's prostitution operation, a falling out could have led to Haake's death."

"That's a really big 'if,' Walther. I'm very reluctant to start investigating legitimate businesses on the basis of sheer speculation. What sort of country would we have if this became routine procedure? A police state? Get me something more to go on and I'll reconsider.

"Besides, the company is outside our jurisdiction; we'd first need to clear anything we did with the Stockholm authorities. It could become too complicated. For now, let's leave the company alone.

"After all, we're taking a close look at Hult and those bank directors. Let's see where those inquiries go. We don't want to spread ourselves too thin." Kallenberg leaned back in his desk chair.

"Walther, we shouldn't argue. It's important for us to work together amicably. We can revisit this issue later."

"All right, Arvid. You're the boss. But please note my disagreement," said Ekman, getting up. He was angry, but kept his features under control.

"Duly noted," replied Kallenberg. Coming around his desk he put a hand on Ekman's shoulder as he walked him to the door.

56

FISHERMAN'S CATCH

Wednesday, February 8, 10:35 a.m. The *Annalisa* lurched in the green swell. A white-crested wave broke high over her plunging bow as the herring trawler headed farther into the Kattegat strait separating southwestern Sweden and Denmark.

The poor catch so far that morning, and reports from other Swedish boats of fish running closer to Denmark, had persuaded the dark bearded captain, Jörgen Blohm, to try his luck in that direction. He stood on the deck, oblivious to the icy, wind-driven spray, scanning the leaden horizon with binoculars for signs of other vessels.

Blohm went over to the wheelhouse door and, opening it, yelled over the stiff wind to his mate to hold to the south-southwest course. His heavily gloved hand holding tightly to a rail running along the wheelhouse, he carefully made his way to the stern. He wanted to check the midlevel ocean trawling net suspended from the tall boom and spread out deep in the sea behind the boat.

Going back into the wheelhouse he looked at the sonar screen for signs of a herring school. There was nothing.

Shrugging, he went over to the carafe on the sideboard and poured himself a cup of black coffee. After twenty years at sea he was accustomed to disappointment and had learned to be patient. So far, his patience had paid off; he now owned the *Annalisa,* named for his wife.

"Jörgen," said his mate, a sturdy thirty-year-old, "there's something on the screen."

Blohm went over to see. Yes, there was something, but it wasn't the familiar pattern made by a school of herring. Damn, whatever it was, it was fouling his net.

Calling down the companionway hatch to the two seamen who'd been taking a break, he said, "I need you on deck. We have to clear the net."

The men quickly pulled on their slickers and scrambled up the ladder.

Blohm went with them to the stern and activated the power block on the boom that gradually hauled up the huge net.

Lowering it to the deck, they could see a large object caught in the mesh.

"Let's get it out of there, boys," Blohm said.

The seamen pulled the net open and each taking an end of the object pulled it out of the netting and onto the deck.

Blohm took his gutting knife from its sheath and cut the rope holding the canvas tarp together. Reaching over, he pulled the tarp open.

Staring back at him from empty sockets was the ashen, bloated face of Ahmed Chafik.

57

A BODY AND A SUSPECT

Thursday, February 9, 7:15 a.m. Ekman had come in early that day. He wanted to sit down with Rystrom to go over where they were before that morning's meeting, and had left a note on Rystrom's desk.

Hanging up his hat and coat, he decided to try and reduce the pile of papers that had evidently been reproducing by themselves in his in-basket.

On top was a report of a man's body that had been fished out of the Kattegat yesterday morning. The corpse was now at the forensic pathology lab in Linköping, where they'd discovered that he'd been strangled with a wire. They were estimating the time of death as several weeks ago. A full autopsy report would follow. Some grisly photos were attached.

Ekman looked at what remained of the man's face. He was barely recognizable, but Ekman believed it was the man they'd been hunting for without success since Lynni Dahlin's death. DNA tests would confirm whether it was Chafik, but he felt sure it was.

From the deteriorated condition of the body, someone must have decided shortly after Dahlin died to get rid of Chafik. This strengthened his conviction that a trafficking ring was involved. Chafik apparently had become too much of a risk for them to leave walking around. Find this ring, and they'd find his killer, and probably Jakobsson's and Haake's as well.

A few minutes later, Rystrom stuck his head in the door. "You wanted to see me, Walther?"

"Come in, Garth, and take a look at this," Ekman said, holding up the report.

Rystrom sat down and began to read. He flipped through the photos and looked up.

"It's Chafik, isn't it?"

"Yes, I think so too."

"They must have thought he'd become too much of a problem."

"Exactly. But now we know for certain that there's a trafficking ring."

"There doesn't seem to be any point in waiting for DNA confirmation. I'll tell Valdis so she can call off the international search."

"Good idea. What do you think about informing the media?"

Rystrom considered this for a moment. "It can't hurt and might produce some new leads."

"And it will at least resolve why we haven't been able to find him. The press have implied we're imbeciles." Ekman was thinking about Haeggman's stories about the hunt for Chafik that had as much as said that the police, and especially Chief Superintendent Ekman, were hopelessly incompetent.

"So where do you think this leaves us with Dahlin's death, and the Jakobsson, Haake, and now Chafik murders?" Ekman asked.

"Well, we know they're all connected, and the murders were probably committed by the same man, since they all involved a garrote," Rystrom replied.

"And our suspects?"

"So far we haven't any."

"This is a record of accomplishment we'll refrain from sharing with Herr Haeggman," Ekman said.

"But we do have reason to suspect that this Moroccan crime boss, Joumari, may be involved. When are we going to take a closer look at that spice company?" Garth asked.

"Not for a while, and maybe not at all. According to our esteemed prosecutor, we'd be indulging in police state tactics."

"Shit. We both think something's going on there."

"Yes, but Kallenberg wants stronger grounds than mere suspicion, even if it's informed by our combined half century of police work."

"So where do we go from here, Walther?"

"I hate to admit it, but I'm not at all sure."

Rystrom looked at his watch. "It's eight. Maybe the others will have some suggestions."

The other team members, and Kallenberg, were already seated when Ekman and Rystrom came into the conference room.

"Good morning, everyone," said Ekman, as he took his place at the head of the table next to Kallenberg.

"I have some news. Ahmed Chafik has been found."

The others appeared startled.

"When did this happen, Chief?" asked Rapp.

"Yesterday morning. He was pulled out of the Kattegat. Linköping says he was strangled with a garrote around the time Dahlin died."

"Well, that's another dead end," said Rosengren, and then sniggered at his unintentional pun. His partner, Alenius, stifled a rare smile.

"We now have three killings and the Dahlin woman's death to investigate," Kallenberg said. "Walther, public scrutiny is going to increase even more."

"Yes, I'm very aware of that, Arvid. All the more reason to explore every possible avenue," Ekman said, looking hard at him.

Kallenberg didn't respond.

"Gerdi, why don't you bring us up to date?"

Vinter summarized her conversation with Kajsa Haake. "She admitted that Håkan Grundström is a recent lover, and that they've been talking about marriage since her husband's death. Enar and I also uncovered some interesting financial information," she said, turning to him.

"Five of the six directors who wanted the merger are wealthy," Holm continued. "The merger would just make them richer. But Grundström really needs the money. He borrowed heavily to place a huge bet three years ago on a start-up technology company that went under last year. He's had to take out a second mortgage on his house, and with his divorce, he'll barely be able to cover running expenses."

"The merger, and marriage to a wealthy widow, would more than solve all his financial problems," said Vinter.

"Then he had every reason to want Haake out of the way," said Rapp.

"Enough to kill him?" asked Rystrom.

"It's a real possibility," said Ekman. "There could be two killers: the man who murdered Chafik and Jakobsson, and a copycat murderer who killed Haake. Grundström may have decided that doing away with Haake would get him what he desperately needed and imitating the Jakobsson killing would

cover his tracks. We should have a serious conversation with
Herr Grundström."

"I agree, but for God's sake, be civil. He's very well connected," Kallenberg said.

"We're always civil these days, Arvid. I haven't used a
rubber hose in years," Ekman said.

58

THE LAST SHIPMENT

Thursday, February 9, 9:15 a.m. Karim had just finished a leisurely late breakfast in the Grand Hotel's Terrace restaurant and was idly watching through the large windows as traffic and pedestrians moved along the broad street under a chill, pale grey sky. Across the way, boats were docked in the narrow Stockholms Ström bay.

He'd had a pleasant week in Stockholm acting like a typical tourist: wandering around medieval Gamla Stan, visiting museums, the royal palace, sampling restaurants, and doing sporadic shopping.

When he'd phoned Ivar a few days ago, he'd been assured that everything was on track. The ship they'd been waiting for had arrived and they were shutting down their women trafficking operation as agreed. Ivar invited him to observe them do it.

A 1:40 that morning he'd sat in Ivar's Land Rover and watched a van pull up to the gangplank of the *Kharon*, a small, rusted freighter with Liberian registry that had brought in a shipment of drugs from India concealed in lead foil packets hidden in sacks of spices. It had arrived at the Frihamnsgatan docks, near the spice company's office, two days before, passed customs' inspection, and unloaded its cargoes. The ship would be leaving on the next high tide.

They'd sat in silence as Ostlund and Gotz carried five heavily drugged women up the gangplank and onto the ship. They would be kept half drugged on the 2,000-mile voyage to Casablanca, and the three-hour drive to Marrakech.

Ivar and Karim sat there until all the women had been taken on board and the two men had gotten into the van and driven off.

"Your buyers will be looking forward to trying these new women out," Ivar said as he started the Land Rover. "When these shipments stop you'll have some very disappointed customers."

"They'll get over it," said Karim in a voice that indicated he didn't care. Besides, they'd soon find another supplier not connected to their drug business. "What's important is not risking our drug operation here and in the rest of Scandinavia."

Ivar changed the subject. "Will you be staying on in Stockholm?"

"No. I'll be heading back Saturday."

"I assume the drugs will come in on the same schedule as before."

"Yes. Nothing will change."

"And our 10 percent discount will continue."

"That was our agreement and we'll stick to it. Just as we expect you will."

"Of course." But Ivar had other plans.

59

GRUNDSTRÖM INTERVIEW

Friday, February 10, 10 a.m. Advokat Birghir Edgren's face wore an expression of amazement. With eyebrows raised over watery blue eyes and partly open mouth, he looked from Ekman to Rystrom. They were seated in an interview room across the table from him and his client, Håkan Grundström.

"Gentlemen," he said in his polished, aristocratic voice, "you can't be serious. Herr Grundström, a murderer? It's the most bizarre accusation I've ever heard in forty years of practicing law."

"It's not an accusation, Herr Edgren," said Ekman. "We're just conducting a murder investigation. And we'd simply like to know what Herr Grundström was doing on the evening of Wednesday, February 1, when Fredrik Haake was killed."

"You can go ahead and tell them Håkan," Edgren said.

"I was at home."

"The entire evening?" asked Rystrom.

"That's my recollection."

"Can anyone verify that?"

"I don't think so. My wife lives apart from me and the cook had prepared dinner and left before I came home around six o'clock. Can anyone verify where *you* were?" Grundström asked.

"I'm not the one being questioned, Herr Grundström, because I had no reason to kill Herr Haake."

"Are you implying that Herr Grundström did?" asked Edgren. "A fantasy."

"Perhaps not as fantastic as you think, Counsellor," said Ekman.

"What is your relationship with Fru Haake?" he asked Grundström.

"We're good friends."

"Maybe more than friends?"

Grundström hesitated and looked at Edgren before answering. Edgren nodded. "We have a personal relationship."

"You mean you're lovers?" asked Rystrom.

"Yes."

"For how long?"

"The last six months or so."

"So you were fucking your boss's wife for half a year before he conveniently died?" Ekman asked in a harsh voice.

"There's no need for that kind of language," interjected Edgren.

"I'll use whatever language I want. It's accurate enough, isn't it, Herr Grundström?"

Grundström had turned red and was obviously controlling himself with difficulty. He didn't reply at first. "Look, you need to understand: Kajsa and Fredrik were leading separate lives long before she and I got involved."

"Since Haake died, you and Fru Haake have been considering marriage?" Rystrom asked.

"She told you that I guess. Yes, we've talked about it. But that's all."

"Now that Haake's dead she's a very wealthy widow, isn't she? That makes her a prime candidate for marriage and even more desirable from your point of view, doesn't it?" Ekman asked.

"Her finances have nothing to do with my feelings for her."

"Considering your own precarious financial condition, isn't that pure bullshit?"

"Herr Ekman, I must ask you to treat my client with more respect. He's been a pillar of this community his entire life. He has an impeccable reputation, which you seem intent on tarnishing without any cause."

"This is a formal interview in a murder investigation. My concern is with finding a murderer, not protecting your client's reputation. So you'll have to excuse me if my questions seem too brusque for his, and your, delicate sensibilities."

"Walther," said Rystrom, "Herr Edgren has a point. Please forgive my colleague, gentlemen. He's been under a lot of strain lately, as I'm sure you can understand."

"My client's participation in this interview is purely voluntary. If Herr Ekman doesn't change his attitude and moderate his language, we'll simply leave."

"Your help in our inquiry is sincerely appreciated," said Rystrom. "Herr Grundström, the point Walther was trying to badly make," he looked over at Ekman and shook his head in mock dismay, "is that you've been experiencing some financial difficulties lately. Isn't that right?"

Again, Grundström looked at Edgren before answering. "A company I'd invested heavily in went under unexpectedly. For the moment, it's left me in an uncomfortable financial situation."

"Which the merger with Nordbank would go a long way to fixing, right?" Ekman said.

"The merger is a good deal for our bank and its stock-holders."

"Haake was trying to put a stop to it and had convinced a majority of the directors. But with him suddenly dead, opposition to the merger collapses, and you stand to make a much-needed bundle. As an added attraction, the rich widow you've been screwing becomes available for marriage. How strangely well-timed it's all been for you, Herr Grundström," Ekman said.

"Now that does it," said Edgren, getting up. "Come on, Håkan, we're leaving."

Grundström stood, as Ekman and Rystrom also got up.

"You can walk away now, Grundström, but we're not finished with you yet," said Ekman.

"We have our eye on you, and no high-powered attorney can protect you forever. We have good reason to believe you killed Haake, and you can be sure that sooner or later we'll have the evidence to put you away. Your precious reputation won't save you."

"If word of these scandalous accusations should somehow leak out, Herr Ekman, we'll know where to look and you'll pay a heavy price. Remember that," said Edgren as he stalked out of the room with Grundström at his heels.

"That was quite a performance, Walther," Rystrom said.

"Long ago in school I'd toyed with the idea of acting. This was an opportunity I couldn't pass up. You don't think I was too rough on him, do you?"

"Not if he's guilty. But if he's innocent, he must be royally pissed. Kallenberg wouldn't say you followed his request to be 'civil.'"

"That's too bad. Grundström will get over it if he's not our murderer."

"Unfortunately we didn't learn anything new."

"It wasn't likely we would. We knew he'd lawyer-up when we asked him to come in. If he's Haake's killer, he now understands we suspect him and that his position won't shield him."

"Do you think he and Haake's wife planned the murder together?"

"I don't see it," Ekman said. "If he did it, it was his idea. She didn't have enough to gain to make it worth her while. Besides, I don't think she hated Haake, she was just tired of him.

"The best we can hope for is that we've shaken up Grundström sufficiently for him to make a mistake. We need to set up a phone tap and surveillance."

"Will Kallenberg agree?"

"He'd damn well better."

60

Scoop

Saturday, February 11, 6:30 a.m. The headline above Haeggman's byline on the front page of that morning's *Syd-svenska Nyheter* screamed **Murder Spree Continues; Police Baffled**.

Ekman read the story through. Haeggman implied that Chief Superintendent Ekman, heading the investigation, was incompetent and should be replaced before there were more killings. It wasn't the first time Haeggman had said this sort of thing; they had a long-standing mutual antipathy.

He slapped the paper hard on the table. The breakfast dishes rattled and Ingbritt looked up with a start.

"What is it, Walther?" she asked.

"That bastard Haeggman somehow discovered that Ahmed Chafik has been found murdered. We were going to let the media know after DNA tests confirmed it was him, but there's been a leak, and he's jumped the gun to get his damn scoop."

"Are you sure it's Chafik?"

"Sure enough, even though he was barely recognizable."

"Well, at least you can stop the search now."

"We've already called it off. That's probably how Haeggman found out. And he's putting the blame on me for not already solving that killing, and the others."

"Is the case really going badly, Walther?"

"Which one? We've now got three murders and a death."

"They're all connected, aren't they?"

"Maybe. Although there's a good possibility that the Haake murder was an unrelated copycat killing. Yesterday, I grilled a suspect, a banker named Grundström, who stood to gain a great deal from Haake's death."

"And?"

"And if Grundström's guilty, he now knows we're onto him and maybe the pressure will make him slip up."

"But if he's innocent, Walther, how will he prove it?"

"He can't. The only way we can be sure he's innocent is if we catch the real murderer."

"Forgive me for saying so, but it just doesn't seem right."

"It isn't. That's how the system works. If I could figure out a better way to get at the truth, believe me, I would."

"You're doing the best you can."

"Yes, but it may not be good enough." His lips were drawn down in a despondent line as he shook his head in frustration.

61

REVENGE

Saturday, February 11, 5:15 p.m. Karim was sitting in
the octagonal room in Joumari's house, watching as the old
man poured mint tea for his two visitors. Beside Joumari,
facing Karim, was Joumari's grandnephew, Askari Harrak, a
muscular man of thirty with a black stubble beard. He was
wearing a too-tight tan suit with a shirt open to a gold Hand
of Fatima pendant.

Harrak was famous for his violent temper and for plunging headlong into dangerous, risky schemes without caring
about consequences. But nevertheless, he could be persuasive;
family members tended to defer to him. Despite this, Karim
nursed a hope that Harrak's erratic behavior and bad judgment would eventually persuade Joumari to rule him out as
a successor.

Karim had read Haeggman's story on the early morning
flight to Marrakech. The discovery of the body confirmed
what he'd suspected all along: Ahmed had been killed to
silence him.

Harrak had evidently read the same story online and brought the news to Joumari. He hadn't stood up when Karim came into the room, just nodded.

Tea had followed the ritual exchange of greetings, cut short as usual by the old man.

"How did you find things in Stockholm?" Joumari asked.

"Everything went well. As I told you on the phone, they accepted the new arrangement, but it took some persuading. I was there watching when they loaded the last shipment of women."

"How much of a discount on the drugs were you able to negotiate?"

"They wanted 20 percent, but I got that down to 10."

"Five would have been better," Harrak said.

Joumari cast him an irritated glance. "Yes, but Karim did well. I am satisfied."

"But we cannot accept what they did to Ahmed," Harrak said.

"No one accepts that, Nephew. I have been waiting for the right moment."

"Now that we know he's dead, murdered, the moment has come. We must act."

"I will decide when we will do that," Joumari said sharply.

"I don't speak for just myself. When we learned of Ahmed's murdered body being discovered, the family decided to meet this afternoon. It was agreed that we must avenge Ahmed's death or lose honor. The entire world now knows he was murdered. We have to take revenge. I need hardly tell you that, Uncle." Joumari had a well-earned reputation for ferocious acts of vengeance.

Karim thought it was a bad sign that the meeting had been held without Joumari.

The old man was silent for a long moment. "If we do this now, our drug business will be interrupted until we can find a new distributor. And this would be happening at the same time we're searching for another supplier of women. Has the family considered this?"

"Yes, Uncle. We know there will be a heavy price. But if we don't act now when the world is watching, we will lose credibility and territory forever. There are many competitors waiting for us to show any sign of weakness."

Karim had said nothing during this exchange. He was listening intently as he heard the balance of power in the family shifting. If Joumari resisted the group's decision, he could lose control completely.

The shrewd old man understood this very well and raised his eyes to the ceiling. "Then, *insh'Allah*, let it be done."

He looked at Karim. "You will be the instrument of our vengeance. Destroy those who have dishonored our family."

Karim got up and placing his hand over his heart, silently bowed his head to Joumari before turning and limping slowly from the room.

62

BLOCKED

Sunday, February 12, 10:30 a.m. Ekman had been sitting in his office thinking about the team's unproductive morning meeting when he got a call from Norlander that he wanted to see him. He was surprised because the commissioner almost never appeared on weekends.

When he went in he saw that Malmer and Kallenberg were there.

"Please sit down, Walther," Norlander said.

Malmer said, "Good morning," but Kallenberg just nodded. He hadn't been at the team meeting.

"Walther, you can imagine how disturbed we all were by yesterday's newspaper story about Chafik. Olav and I have received numerous calls from papers and TV stations about it, as I know you probably have as well."

Since yesterday, Ekman had brushed off half a dozen requests for comment with a brusque, "I can't talk about an ongoing investigation."

"That's true, Commissioner," he said.

"We've all seen stories like this before. I guess it's the price we have to pay for trying to protect the public." He sighed. "I want to assure you that's not why I asked you to join us."

"I appreciate your support, Commissioner."

"What has disturbed me more than that story is a call I got yesterday from Birghir Edgren, an old friend of mine, about an interview you conducted on Friday with his client, Håkan Grundström. He said you were repeatedly disrespectful to Herr Grundström, a highly regarded banker, and actually abusive, even after Edgren had asked you to restrain yourself. Is that right?"

"I wouldn't characterize our conversation that way, Commissioner. I'm sorry Advokat Edgren troubled you, but he's given you a distorted picture of that interview. Let me explain why we were speaking with Herr Grundström." Briefly Ekman sketched out the reasons he was considered a suspect in Haake's murder, what they'd learned from the interview, and the rationale for the tough line he'd taken with him.

"I see," said Norlander after a moment. "Thank you for putting it in context, but I'm still concerned, Walther."

"Didn't I ask you to be civil when you interviewed Grundström? And didn't you assure me you would?" asked Kallenberg.

"I told you we'd stopped using a rubber hose, Arvid," said Ekman with a laugh, trying to lighten the conversation. It fell flat.

"Walther, it's understandable given the difficulty you've been having with the Haake case, that you were, how shall I say, extremely zealous, in questioning Herr Grundström. But trying to intimidate him was a mistake. He's not only a well-known banker here in Weltenborg. As Birghir explained to me, Grundström's on track to head one of the largest financial institutions in Scandinavia. Naturally he has powerful friends in Stockholm. Some of them are members of the National Police Board." He looked directly at Ekman.

"I understand, Commissioner." What Ekman really understood was that Norlander was concerned about protecting his own prospects for advancement.

"I guess that now is not the best time to ask for a phone tap and surveillance of Grundström," he said, turning to Kallenberg.

"That's very perceptive, Walther," Kallenberg replied in a dry tone.

"Get ideas like that completely out of your head," said Malmer.

"Walther, we all appreciate that you have your hands full with these investigations," said Norlander, glancing over at Malmer, "and, of course, none of us want to impede your work. But until something clearly implicates Herr Grundström in the Haake murder, I think it best to leave him alone."

"As you wish, Commissioner," Ekman said in a neutral voice. But he was seething. An avenue that might have led to Haake's killer had just been closed off.

63

NEW APPROACH

Sunday, February 12, 8:20 p.m. Ekman was sitting in his study thinking about the conversation he'd had with Ingbritt after dinner.

She'd been telling him about speaking earlier that day with their daughter, Carla, when she saw that Ekman wasn't listening.

"What is it, Walther? You seem totally preoccupied."

"Sorry. I don't want to bore you with my problems, but they seem to be getting the best of me. What was it you were saying about Carla?"

"Just that she and Johan miss seeing us. I told her that although we badly want to visit, it will have to wait until the case you're working on is finished. Did something happen today?"

Ekman told her about the meeting with Norlander and how frustrated it made him feel.

"They won't let me handle this investigation the way I need to. There's too much damn political interference. They all want me to solve these murders quickly, but at the same time, not step on anyone's toes." He threw up his hands in disgust. "Right now, we're at a standstill."

Ingbritt was quiet for a moment. "Walther, I don't know what would be best for you to do. But sometimes, when I'm writing a children's book and feel blocked, I've gone back to the beginning to look for a new approach."

Ekman considered this. "Maybe you're right. Thanks, I'll think about it."

He sat in his study wondering what that new approach might be as he went over the case from the moment the Dahlin woman fell. What weren't they seeing?

Then it came to him. It was so obvious he couldn't believe they'd missed it. Drugs.

Lynni Dahlin had been drugged to get her to that apartment. She'd dropped her boyfriend when she'd found out he was dealing drugs. They'd assumed that Jakobsson had been killed because he knew something about Dahlin's death and its connection to the women trafficking, but maybe his murder was really about drugs.

And Joumari, Chafik's uncle, was a major figure in drugs as well as prostitution in many Muslim countries.

All along they'd been too focused on the women trafficking to see that a drug operation could also be behind the multiple deaths.

Ekman felt energized. Tomorrow morning he'd ask Rystrom to talk with the CID section that handled national drug investigations.

64

DRUGS

Monday, February 13, 8 a.m. The team members and Kallenberg were standing around the sideboard drinking coffee and munching the pastries Ekman had ordered when he came into the conference room.

As they took their seats, he went over and grabbed a cup and a sweet roll before sitting down.

"The Grundström interview I told you about on Saturday was the last time we'll be speaking with him. Unless we come up with something that clearly ties him to the Haake killing, it's hands off. That's yesterday's order from above."

"But, Chief, we need to find out if it was a copycat murder, and Grundström is a more likely suspect than Hult," protested Holm.

"Yes, you're right, Enar. And I'm not happy about it." He glanced at Kallenberg as he said this. "It's what the commissioner wants and he's the boss, so we have to put that line of inquiry to one side for now."

"Politics," rumbled Rapp. "Fucking politics."

Kallenberg looked over at Rapp. "Let's not forget that Grundström's presumed to be an innocent man. There's nothing that proves otherwise."

"It looks like we'll never be able to get the evidence to do that Herr Kallenberg," said Vinter.

Kallenberg just shrugged in reply.

"Okay," said Ekman. "Moving on. What's happening with the Hult surveillance?"

"Alenius and I took it over, and nothing's happened, Chief," said Rosengren. "There haven't been any suspicious contacts that we could see."

"And his phone conversations have been the same," said Rapp.

"All right. That's also not going anywhere then," said Ekman.

"You've reached the end of the week's surveillance on Hult that I authorized," put in Kallenberg. "Close it down. We'll have to assume he wasn't involved in Haake's death."

Ekman frowned; he would have preferred to continue the surveillance for at least another week, but there was nothing he could do except say, "Agreed."

"I've been considering a new approach," Ekman said, and outlined his idea about the involvement of a drug operation.

"What do you think?" he asked them.

"You're onto something, Chief," said Rosengren enthusiastically.

"We should have thought of that before," said Rapp, shaking his head. "We zeroed in on the women trafficking right away and completely overlooked the drug angle."

"So are we all agreed this is worth pursuing?" asked Ekman, looking around the table, and ending at Kallenberg. The others nodded.

"It should be looked into," said Kallenberg. "But let's not do it the way the copycat murder idea was handled. We don't want to start surveillance of a lot of innocent people that leads nowhere."

Ekman stared at him. Kallenberg could be a stickler for legalities, but he was already sounding unnecessarily negative at the start of this new inquiry.

"Garth," said Ekman, "could you speak with the national drug squad and see if they have anything that looks like it might be connected to our case?"

"I'll do that right away, Walther."

"Alrik, before our team starts to check out the local drug scene, coordinate with Annborg Eliasson," Ekman said, referring to the head of Weltenborg's own drug squad.

"She may already be able to identify Jakobsson's supplier. And ask her to tomorrow's meeting,"

Ekman stood up. "See you all then."

Later that morning, Rystrom came into Ekman's office and sat down.

"Any luck?" asked Ekman.

"Yes and no. The head of the drug enforcement section is a chief superintendent named Holmger Gradin. He has a reputation as a tough guy, a heavy-duty enforcer of the national zero-tolerance policy. I've worked with him, off and on, for the last ten years with mixed results. I described our case over the phone and he agreed that the drug angle probably should be explored."

"So?"

"But he doesn't have the manpower to help us with it and he's not about to let us in on any of his current investigations. He plays everything close to the vest. I guess it's understandable because he's had some problems in the past with leaks screwing up drug busts. All he would say is that there's been an increase over the last few years in heroin being brought in," Rystrom said.

"When I mentioned that we've been looking at that spice company in Stockholm in connection with the women trafficking case, he immediately changed the subject, and said he had to get back to work."

"That's interesting. It sounds like there's something there we need to take a closer look at," Ekman said.

"I agree."

"Unfortunately when I'd suggested we start a surveillance operation on the company, Kallenberg refused."

"It can't hurt to ask again," said Rystrom.

65

SECOND REQUEST

Monday, February 13, 2:30 p.m. Arvid Kallenberg greeted Ekman in his usual friendly manner and led him over to a couple of armchairs near the windows overlooking the park. The morning rain had cleared, but dark, scudding clouds, driven by a strong wind, still raced across the sky.

"You sounded like it was important, Walther, so I moved another meeting. What can I do for you?"

Ekman described the conversation Rystrom had had with the head of drug enforcement.

"It's suggestive, but what would you like me to do?"

"I think it's time to reconsider my request for surveillance of the spice company."

"I see," said Kallenberg, and getting up, looked out the window.

"You said that Gradin didn't want to talk about the company?" Kallenberg asked.

"Yes, that's what Garth thought."

"It could indicate that he already has an investigation underway."

"It's possible, I suppose, or he's considering it."

"Well, in either case, I don't think we should get in his way. They're the experts when it comes to drug-related matters. Let them handle it."

"Gradin didn't tell Garth that we shouldn't interfere."

"Perhaps because it's highly confidential. All the more reason for us to just leave it alone. We don't want to mess up an ongoing operation. Stockholm wouldn't appreciate it."

"I think a multiple murder investigation should have priority."

"You're right, Walther. But let's compromise. Let's wait a couple of weeks and give Gradin a chance to complete any investigation. If nothing's happened by then, I'll reconsider the surveillance. How's that?"

"Frankly, Arvid, in view of the urgency of our own investigation, I don't think it's good enough." Ekman had difficulty keeping the anger out of his voice.

"Well, I'm sorry you feel that way, Walther, but it seems to me the best course."

Ekman had gotten up.

"We mustn't let this little disagreement spoil our good working relationship," Kallenberg said, and then walking ahead, opened the door for him.

66

LOCAL DRUGS

Tuesday, February 14, 8 a.m. When Ekman came into the conference room he saw that Chief Inspector Eliasson had joined them. She was a short, stout woman of fifty, with a brisk manner. Eliasson was extremely competent, and so effective that although she reported to Ekman, he let her work virtually on her own and submit periodic reports.

"Annborg, thanks for joining us. I'm sure Alrik has filled you in on the case we're working. We need your expertise."

"I'm glad to help, Walther. It sounds like you've got a complicated problem that's been getting an awful lot of public attention."

"Unfortunately. It's added to the urgency."

As everyone took their seats, Ekman looked around and saw that Kallenberg was missing. He was still upset with him and decided not to wait.

"As you know, this all started out with a woman's death due to trafficking," Ekman said, "and then expanded into a triple murder case. Different avenues we've explored have dead-ended, so now we want to see if a connection to drugs might open up the case. Is this a sound approach?"

"It's certainly a possible one, Walther. I've been thinking about it since Alrik briefed me yesterday. As I understand it, you want to find out who was Jakobsson's dealer and then trace the supply chain."

"That's right. We originally thought he was killed because he knew something about the woman's death, but it could have been a drug deal that went sour."

The others had been listening intently to this exchange.

"We now know that Chafik was killed before Jakobsson, and in the same way, with a garrote," said Vinter. "This could mean that Chafik was also involved in the same bad drug deal."

"But what about Haake?" asked Holm. "If it wasn't a copycat murder, was he dealing drugs too?"

Vinter was silent, considering this. "Could be. Just because he was a prominent banker, doesn't mean he couldn't also be a drug dealer."

"Jakobsson was a small-time pusher," said Eliasson. "I checked our file on him and mostly, he worked alone. He had one or two friends in the business. We'll need to squeeze them to see if a supplier's name comes up. For now, we don't know who it was. What we do know is that over the last couple of years there's been an increase in available drugs in Weltenborg, particularly heroin."

"Unlike illicit prescription drugs, it's got to be coming in from Asia," said Ekman. "Garth spoke yesterday with Holmger Gradin and from the conversation, or rather what he wouldn't talk about, we suspect that Stockholm's been looking at a spice importing company we're interested in. Have you heard anything about that?"

Eliasson shook her head. "Sorry, Holmger wouldn't share information like that with local drug enforcement. But I've got some contacts up there. I'll ask around."

"Thanks, Annborg. And I'd like you to join our team from now on."

Ekman glanced around the table. "Let's see what Annborg can find out about Jakobsson and the spice company and we'll take it from there," he said as he stood up, ending the meeting. They hadn't yet gotten the answers they needed, but he was hopeful Eliasson could discover something.

Back in his office, Ekman called Kallenberg to bring him up to date. His assistant said he wasn't in. He was at a conference in Stockholm and wasn't expected until tomorrow.

67

RETRIBUTION

Tuesday, February 14, 7:20 p.m. Ivar was running late for his own seven o'clock meeting. He'd set it at the farm to discuss the drug distribution operation and his plan to disregard the arrangement with Karim: they'd need to find new women and other buyers. As he pulled into the dark farmhouse yard, he saw that Marta already was there and he parked next to her car.

A light was on upstairs, but the ground floor was dark. That's strange, he thought, as he went up the porch steps.

The front door, usually kept locked, was partly open.

"Hello, Marta?" he called as he came in. His hand groped for the light switch, found it, flicked it a few times, but nothing happened. The damn bulb must be out.

He moved toward the stairs, dimly visible in light from the bedroom above.

Ivar heard a slight sound behind him and had started to turn as the killing wire noose came down over his head, rapidly tightening around his throat. A harsh voice whispered something in his ear, but he couldn't make out the words as he struggled to breathe.

His arms flailed about trying to find his attacker, but it was futile. As the wire cut more deeply into his throat, severing his windpipe, he collapsed.

Strong arms gripped Ivar's armpits, and dragged his body out of the hall and into the kitchen. The killer went back to his car to wait for other arrivals.

Ten minutes later, Thore Ostlund drove into the yard and parked next to the two other cars. The only light on was upstairs.

The door was wide open.

"Ivar, Marta, are you up there?" he called. "What's wrong with the lights?" He tried to turn them on, but nothing happened.

He could make out the stairs and moved toward them. They creaked as he climbed up.

Ostlund went down the small hall to the bedroom on the right where light shone through the partially open door.

He pushed it open.

Marta was sprawled across the bed, her face contorted in a horrifying grimace, her tongue protruding from her mouth.

He stared transfixed, his eyes drawn to the thin red line around her throat. There was no need to check, she was obviously dead. What the hell was going on? And where was Ivar?

Ostlund backed out of the room and ran down the stairs. Turning at the bottom, he went into the kitchen and groped for the light switch. It worked. Light flooded the room.

Ivar's body lay in the middle of the floor. His friend's protruding eyes and distorted features told Ostlund he was dead, with the same red line around his throat as Marta's.

He didn't know what to do. His mind refused to function. He heard a footstep behind him and he spun around quickly to see Gotz.

Gotz looked with an amazed expression at Ivar's body and then at Ostlund.

"When did this happen?"

"You should know. You did it. You're fucking insane," Ostlund said, as he pulled out a pistol from under his jacket, racked the slide, and aimed it at Gotz.

"Now wait a minute, wait a minute, I had nothing to do with this. I just got here."

"I don't believe you. And you killed Marta."

"Marta's dead too?" Gotz's voice and face registered his shock.

"Don't play innocent. She's upstairs, garroted like Ivar."

"I didn't do it. You've got to believe me." He sounded desperate.

"No one else uses a garrote. I told Ivar you were out of control when you killed Haake."

"I never did."

"Now you've gone completely mad. But you're not going to get a chance to kill me too," Ostlund said, and raised the gun.

In desperation Gotz lunged at him and Ostlund fired, hitting him in the chest. He staggered back and Ostlund fired two more times.

Gotz's dead body fell across Ivar's.

Ostlund looked around with a wild-eyed expression and then ran from the house to his car. He didn't know where he was going yet, he just knew he had to get away, far away.

From behind the barn where it had been hidden, the car that had followed Marta from Stockholm pulled out with its headlights off and followed him at a distance.

68

KALLENBERG'S REQUEST

Wednesday, February 15, 9:30 a.m. The team meeting that morning had been brief; Eliasson was still working on yesterday's assignment. Until she came up with a lead, they were stymied. Kallenberg hadn't been there again and Ekman decided not to call him. Maybe the prosecutor was losing interest. It was just as well.

Ekman was in his office trying to clean up some of the routine matters that had gotten pushed to one side during the investigation when the phone rang.

It was Kallenberg.

"Walther, I need to speak with you. Could you come by my office in half an hour?"

"Certainly, Arvid. I'll see you then."

Ekman was surprised. He wondered what Kallenberg wanted now. Was the case going to hit another roadblock?

It was chilly and damp from the morning's cold rain. Looking out the windows he could see that the wind had picked up. He decided to walk anyway. It's only a few blocks and God knows I need the exercise, he thought.

Bundled in his heavy overcoat and with a warm woollen cap pulled firmly down, he set out for the landmark Belle Époque courthouse.

The police guard on duty saluted him as he came into the foyer. He returned the salute with a wave of his hand and took the ancient, gilded elevator up. He'd had his exercise and taking the stairs would be overdoing it.

When he came into Kallenberg's office, he found him pacing by the windows.

Kallenberg turned when he heard him enter.

"Thank you for coming right away, Walther. Can I get you some coffee?"

"That sounds good. It's biting cold out there."

Kallenberg phoned his assistant and asked for two coffees that soon arrived.

Seated in armchairs near the windows, the two men sipped their coffee quietly for a moment.

Kallenberg broke the silence. "Walther, as you can probably tell, I'm having some difficulty starting."

Here it comes. Another problem with how I'm handling this investigation. Is he going to remove me?

"It's a private matter that I think requires police attention," he paused.

Ekman was relieved. It didn't sound like what he'd been afraid of.

"I don't believe you know about my personal situation. I've always tried to keep my private life private, but now I need your help." He looks increasingly uncomfortable, thought Ekman.

"My partner is a man called Ivar Skarin. We've been together for ten months. Yesterday he told me he had an evening meeting up north, but would be home by eleven o'clock.

He hasn't returned and his phone is turned off. I'm very concerned that something's happened to him."

Ekman was surprised. It had never occurred to him that the prosecutor was gay. He'd just supposed that he was a confirmed bachelor. Your old-fashioned mores are showing, Ekman, he thought. The last "confirmed bachelor" probably died in Queen Victoria's time.

"I can understand why you're worried, Arvid. I'll organize a search right away. Do you have his vehicle information and a photo of him?"

Kallenberg got up and went to his desk. "He drives a black Land Rover," he said, handing Ekman the vehicle's description that he'd copied from a paper on his desk. Opening a drawer, he took out a small, framed photograph of a handsome man's smiling face. He brought it over to Ekman, who'd gotten up.

"This is Ivar. Can I have it back when you're finished with it?"

"Certainly. We'll be careful," Ekman said, and going over to the coatrack, put it in a pocket.

"We'll also need his physical description."

"He's forty-six, tall and slender, about six feet two, 180 pounds."

Ekman had taken out a small notebook and wrote down the information. "Do you know exactly where he was going last night?"

"No, just that it was a few hours north and it was an important meeting."

"Did he mention who he was meeting with?"

"He only said they were business associates, people I didn't know."

"What sort of business was he involved in?"

"Ivar told me when we first met that he was an investor in import-export businesses. He didn't elaborate and I never

pressed him about it. My understanding was that he did quite
well financially. He bought the large house we're living in. I
could never have afforded it on my government salary. He
always said he liked to live well and wanted to share everything with me. He's a wonderful, generous person." Kallenberg's eyes grew moist as he said this, and he looked away.

Ekman had never before seen the urbane prosecutor
emotional.

"Please try not to worry, Arvid, I'm sure we'll find him
and he'll be fine." But Ekman already suspected that something very bad had happened to Ivar Skarin.

69

SEARCH

Wednesday, February 15, 1 p.m. Ekman had called a special meeting of his team, but had decided not to include Eliasson and let her continue her work. They were waiting for him when he came in and took his seat at the conference table.

"We've got a new problem," he said.

"As if we needed another one, Chief," put in Rosengren.

Ekman ignored him. "Prosecutor Kallenberg's partner, a man named Ivar Skarin, has gone missing since last night. We need to find him." Ekman repeated what Kallenberg had told him.

"Who'd have guessed Kallenberg is a fag?" Rosengren smirked.

Ekman glared at him. "You're way out of line, Rosengren. There's no place for homophobia on this team. One more remark and you're out."

"I'm sorry, Chief. I shouldn't have said that," he replied.

"You shouldn't even have thought it," Ekman said, and turned to the other team members.

"I want to know everything we can about Skarin, who his business associates are, where they were meeting, if he arrived, and when he left. We can track him from there.

"Alrik, have all our data bases checked for information about him and his business partners. And have copies made of this photo and distributed with an APB for his car." Ekman handed the photo and vehicle information across to Rapp. "Take good care of the photo. I promised Kallenberg he'd get it back."

"Gerdi and Enar, we probably would have heard something by now if there was an auto accident, but just in case, take a look at all of last night's accident reports between here and Stockholm.

"Rosengren and Alenius, check all the hospitals and morgues in the same area."

"That's a lot of territory, Chief," protested Rosengren.

"Yes, I agree it will be tedious, but it's necessary. I know you're good at tedious work," said a straight-faced Ekman. Holm suppressed a laugh.

"We're going to give Kallenberg's request everything we've got. He's our colleague and we owe it to him. It's now one fifteen," he said, checking his pocket watch. "We'll meet back here at four fifteen."

When the team reassembled three hours later, Ekman was hopeful they'd found Skarin, one way or another.

"Enar and Gerdi, anything?"

"We checked all the auto accident reports, Chief," Vinter said, "but there was nothing involving Skarin."

"Okay. Rosengren, anything from the hospitals and morgues?"

"We worked our butts off, Chief, to cover them all in three hours. There were two cases we thought might be Skarin.

They had no ID, so we faxed his photo, but they said there was no resemblance."

"Alrik, what can you tell us about him?"

"The APB went out right away, but his car hasn't been sighted. Skarin has no record, not even a parking ticket. While he claimed to have business interests, there's nothing to show what they are either. He was probably a silent partner. We need to look at his financial records to find out more."

"I'll ask Kallenberg to let us examine Skarin's papers at their home," said Ekman, standing and looking around at the team. "Plan on working into the night if we have to. I'll be back in a few minutes," and then headed to his office to make the call.

"Arvid, I have some partly good news for you. Herr Skarin has not had an accident, and isn't in a hospital, or anywhere else that we can discover." Ekman didn't mention that they'd also checked morgues.

"What we need to do now is take a look at his personal papers to find out who he was planning to meet. My team and I can be at your house in half an hour, if that's all right with you."

Kallenberg hesitated. "I hate to violate his privacy, Walther, but if it's going to help you find him, it has to be done. I guess I'll just have to apologize profusely, later," he said with a slight laugh.

"The address is Forehingsgatan 37. That's in the Arboga district," he said, naming the fashionable section of Weltenborg.

"We'll see you there at five o'clock," said Ekman and hung up.

The house was not just large, as Kallenberg had told him, it was a huge three-story, 600-square-meter building, set back from the quiet residential street on two acres of manicured grounds.

As their cars pulled into the brick-paved, circular drive behind Kallenberg's modest little Peugeot, he opened the front door.

"This way to his study," said Kallenberg, leading the six of them down a wide hallway to the rear of the house.

The room was beautifully furnished with antiques. An ornate Louis XVI desk faced out windows overlooking what in spring would be a flower garden, now turned brown and desolate.

Alrik immediately took charge, organizing the search of the room and Skarin's desk for papers. On one side of it was a new computer.

Glancing at it, Ekman asked, "Do you have the password for his computer, Arvid?"

"No, I don't, Walther. Is it really necessary to get into it?"

"Unless we find the information we need in his papers, I'm afraid so. He may have kept his calendar on the computer with details about that meeting."

"All right. Do whatever you have to."

"We're going to have to take it with us for our technicians to examine. Their equipment is back at headquarters."

"I understand," said Kallenberg. "I hope it won't slow you down."

"I'm going to assume that most of what we need is on his computer. I'll tell our techs to expect it this evening," he said, and taking out his phone, called the office.

"I'll get equipment and a cyber specialist from Stockholm who can help with that," said Rystrom, and walking away, placed a call.

Ekman, Rystrom, and Kallenberg left the others going through Skarin's papers and went back down the hall into the tall-ceilinged living room with comfortable, masculine furniture upholstered in a muted burgundy and green plaid.

"Can I get you anything, Walther, Garth?"

They both shook their heads.

"Tell us a little more about Ivar," Ekman said.

Kallenberg became thoughtful, remembering. "We met at a museum exhibition. I was admiring a sculpture, he struck up a conversation with me, we hit it off, and over a few weeks, one thing led to another," and he gestured at their surroundings.

"That was ten months ago?"

"Yes, although it seems like yesterday," said Kallenberg, becoming silent.

"What sort of person is he? Does he talk much about his past?"

"As I told you, he's kind, and generous to a fault. Also extremely intelligent and well-read. But he's reticent about his past. I think some of it must have been unpleasant and he doesn't want to be reminded of it."

Rapp came into the room. "We've gone through all the papers we could find, Walther. Mostly bills relating to this house, car repairs, and so on. There's no diary, nothing that tells us about his business interests or that meeting last night. No bank statements either, so his financial information must also be on the computer. We're ready to take it with us."

Going over to Kallenberg, Rapp handed him Skarin's framed photo. "We've finished with this. I know you wanted it back."

"Thanks, it was a gift."

Ekman got up. "Arvid, we're going to be working on this into the night. Let me know if you hear anything from him."

Kallenberg came over and shook hands with each of the three men. "Thank you, and your team. You don't know how much this means to me."

As the hours passed with no trace of Skarin, Ekman grew increasingly convinced that Kallenberg would never see him again.

70

BREAKTHROUGH

Thursday, February 16, 6:30 a.m. Ekman had gotten home last night after eleven, exhausted from the long day. Hours before, he'd grabbed a small sandwich for dinner at the police cafeteria and it hadn't been enough. He was famished.

Ingbritt had waited up, and warmed some soup and sausages for him. While he ate and sipped a beer, he told her about the search for Skarin.

"We'd hoped his computer would give us the information we need to find him, but our technical people couldn't break into it. So we had to wait for Garth's cyber specialist to come down from Stockholm. She didn't get in until after nine, and wasn't a happy woman about having her life disrupted on short notice. When I left at ten thirty, she was still at it. I sent everyone home to get some sleep. Until she cracks that computer, we have nothing to go on."

"What do you think has happened to him?"

"My guess is he's wrecked his car in some offbeat location and that's why our highway patrols haven't found it. He's probably badly injured, unconscious, or dead."

"But if you can find out where this meeting was, then you may be able to track him going to or from there?"

"That's our belief."

"I feel so sorry for Herr Kallenberg. He must be frantic with worry."

"I can well imagine what he's going through," said Ekman, and meant it.

The sun wouldn't be up for another two hours. Heavy snowflakes were swirling out of the dark onto the windshield as Ekman headed down Brunnvägen.

He wanted to get in early and find out whether work on the computer was getting anywhere. While the search for Skarin was taking immediate priority, he also needed to check with Eliasson to see if she'd come up with something that could move the murder investigation forward. There were just too many balls in the air now and he felt the frustration of not being able to field any of them.

Holm was already at his desk and absorbed in sorting through stacks of paper when Ekman arrived. His face was drawn from fatigue as he followed Ekman into his office.

Ekman took one look at him and said, "Don't tell me you didn't go home after I left?"

"I caught a couple of hours on the duty officer's cot. I'm okay. I've got great news for you."

"She got into the computer?"

"Two hours after you left, there was a breakthrough. Everything opened up and I've just finished printing it all out. Those are the papers I was working on when you came in."

"Do we know where Skarin's meeting was?"

"Yes, but there's much more than that, Chief. Skarin was running major drug- and women-trafficking operations. Everything he did is on the computer. Names of associates, dates and amounts of deliveries of drugs and women, money paid and received, client lists with dates, videos of them he probably used for blackmail, financial statements, real estate holdings, and a daily diary. He also put down his thoughts and future plans. It's all there." Enar was so excited by this recitation he could barely contain himself.

Ekman was stunned. It was a treasure trove. Now they'd be able to roll up the drug and trafficking rings. And with the information they had they should be able to solve the murders that must be linked to the rings.

"That's great work, Enar. Congratulations. Where's Carlin?" he asked, referring to Tyri Carlin, Rystrom's cyber specialist.

"She's exhausted and crashed after she broke through. I got her a room at the Thon."

"When she surfaces, make sure you bring her here. We owe her big time: flowers, champagne, whatever she wants." A weight had been lifted because the way ahead was now open.

The question was where to start, and how to break the startling news to Kallenberg. If indeed it was news. Ekman's frustrations with Kallenberg were now becoming serious doubts about Weltenborg's prosecutor.

At eight, the team, a little the worse for wear, assembled. Kallenberg didn't join them, and Ekman thought that was just as well. He needed to speak with him privately.

"It's a very good morning indeed, even with this snow-storm. As Enar may have told some of you," he said, smiling at Vinter, "we've had a breakthrough thanks to Tyri Carlin, Garth's brilliant specialist. Garth, getting her here has made all the difference. Thank you."

"You're very welcome," Rystrom said, grinning back at him. Carlin had reported to him what she'd found as soon as she had gotten into the computer.

"Enar, why don't you brief everyone on what we now know," Ekman said.

Holm repeated to the others what he'd told Ekman. Those for whom this was news were astonished.

"That's amazing stuff," said Rapp.

Rosengren said enthusiastically, "We're on a roll, Chief." Taciturn as usual, Alenius just nodded agreement.

Annborg Eliasson was smiling broadly. Her research hadn't turned up any good leads. This new information with details about the drug distribution network would keep her and her squad busy for weeks, probably months.

"Okay, everyone," Ekman said. "We now know where Skarin's meeting was held. It was at a farmhouse about two hours north. We don't know why Skarin hasn't contacted Kallenberg, but we'll assume the worst because there's no indication in his notes that he was planning to just drop everything and make a run for it."

Ekman turned to Rapp. "Alrik, you, Garth, and I will head there as soon as the snow stops and the roads are cleared. We don't know what we'll find so let's bring the Piketen SWAT team, forensics techs, and a pathologist with us.

"Enar and Gerdi, I want you to go through the reams of information Enar was organizing and map out some strategies for us to consider."

"Annborg, they'll give you copies of everything related to the drug business so you can decide how you want to proceed. Brief me on what you propose.

"I'll need to speak with Kallenberg when we get back from the farmhouse. Until then, no one should answer any calls from him."

71

CRIME SCENE

Thursday, February 16, 10:50 a.m. It was midmorning before the snow let up. They waited another half hour for the roads to be cleared and then set out in a convoy. Ekman led the way in a police car seated next to a constable who was driving, with Rapp and Rystrom in the back. Behind them was a lumbering SWAT van, then a bus with a dozen other officers, and a van with the forensics team and pathologist.

They'd found the location of the farmhouse and adjoining barn from a deed that had been scanned into the computer. Using a detailed topographical map, they'd been able to pinpoint the access road.

As they approached the farmhouse down the rutted, snow-covered dirt lane, Ekman called the commander of the Piketen team on the secure police car-to-car radio link.

"I'm going to have us pull over and slow down so you can take the lead and check out the farmhouse and barn."

"Roger, affirmative that," replied the commander, a grizzled army veteran who preferred jargon to a simple "Okay."

By the time Ekman and the others had pulled into the yard, the SWAT team had cautiously entered the house and barn. Everyone waited ten tense minutes until the SWAT commander came over to Ekman's car.

"It's all clear," he said. "You can go ahead in. I have to tell you there are bodies all over the place. There's nothing more for us here, so we're heading back."

"Thanks for your help, Janrik. Sorry to bring you all the way out here for nothing."

"No problem, you can never know. So it's what we do. You've got a real mess on your hands in there," he said, gesturing to the farmhouse. "Good luck," he said and went back toward the house, calling out to his six-man team to assemble outside for the ride back to Weltenborg.

Ekman, Rystrom, and Rapp headed up the steps into the farmhouse. The constable who'd driven them stayed outside and recorded who entered the crime scene and the time, while the police from the bus cordoned off the house and barn with crime scene tape and stood guard.

The five forensics technicians had begun photographing everything and dusting for fingerprints.

Roffe Bohlander, the pathologist, was kneeling beside Gotz's body, sprawled across Skarin's.

"Which bullet killed him?" asked Rapp, looking at the riddled corpse.

"I'd say it was this one," Bohlander said, putting a gloved finger on a hole near Gotz's heart. "I'll be able to tell you exactly after I get him on the table."

"Do you think he died Tuesday?" Ekman said.

"It's hard to say right now," he replied, looking at Skarin's body, "but it could well have been."

Rystrom was peering down at Skarin's corpse. His head and wounded neck were visible. "It looks like another garrote killing," he said to Ekman.

Ekman leaned over to see. "You're right. It's significant that they were killed, apparently one right after the other, using two very different methods."

"So you think there were two killers?" asked Rystrom.

"It looks that way."

"There's another one upstairs," said the forensics team leader.

The three policemen and the pathologist went up the stairs and into the bedroom where the woman's corpse lay across the bed.

"It's the same garrote MO," observed Rapp.

"What it looks like," said Ekman, "is that she was killed first, otherwise she would have heard the shots and either run downstairs or tried to hide."

"Or maybe Skarin was killed, then the woman, and last, a second killer shot Gotz," suggested Rystrom.

"That's a possibility," replied Ekman, looking thoughtful. "I suppose there's no way you can tell us which it was, Roffe?"

"Not if everything happened rapidly. If there was a time lag, maybe. But from the look of things it all went down very quickly."

The three men left Bohlander bending over the woman's body. After looking around upstairs, they went back down to check out the rest of the farmhouse.

"Let's head over to the barn," said Ekman when they were satisfied there was nothing more to see at the house.

The ground floor of the barn contained a small living room with a TV, a Spartan bedroom and bathroom, and a tiny kitchen.

Five bedrooms with adjoining bathrooms had been built on the barn's upper level.

They went upstairs and walked from one room to the next, looking at the outside bolts on the doors and the barred windows.

"They're prison cells," said Rapp.

"Yes," Rystrom said. "This must be where they kept the women."

"Those goddamn lousy bastards. May they burn in hell," Rapp said in a shaky voice, picturing Mia there. He turned away so they wouldn't see his anguish.

"If there's any justice in this world or the next, my friend, that's where they are now," said Ekman quietly, and put his hand on Rapp's shoulder.

In the car on the way back to Weltenborg, Ekman turned and said to Rapp and Rystrom, "From what I saw of the material on Skarin's computer, he had one more confederate, a man named Thore Ostlund, the spice company manager."

It had become clear to him from the information they'd found just how the spice company drug operation and women trafficking were interwoven.

"Do you think Ostlund was one of the killers?" asked Rystrom. They'd all agreed that two killers were the most plausible explanation for what they'd seen.

"He must have been at the meeting. Either he was a killer, or the only person who managed to escape."

"But if there was another killer, who was he?" asked Rapp.

"That's something we'll have to figure out. In any case we need to get our hands on Ostlund as quickly as possible," Ekman replied.

Taking out his phone, he called Holm asking him to get Ostlund's driver's license photo and car registration, put out an APB, and alert the border police.

"And Enar, warn them that he's dangerous and may be armed."

Turning to Rystrom, who'd been listening to his phone conversation, he said, "Garth, can you get a Stockholm prosecutor to issue arrest and search warrants for Ostlund and his apartment?"

Ekman's concerns about Kallenberg's possible involvement in his partner's crimes had solidified. He no longer trusted Weltenborg's prosecutor to authorize the necessary warrants.

"And then," he went on, "could you get some of your people to search Ostlund's apartment? He's not likely to be there, but they may find something that could give us an idea of where he's gone."

Rystrom said, "Consider it done," and took out his phone.

But Thore Ostlund had anticipated what the police would do, and he had a two-day lead.

72

Bad News

Thursday, February 16, 3:50 p.m. As he walked down Biblioteksgatan past the fine nineteenth-century stone library, Ekman debated how he'd break the news about Skarin. He'd have to tell Kallenberg not only that the man he obviously loved was dead, brutally murdered, but that he was a criminal of the worst kind, who'd preyed mercilessly on women and the weak.

But maybe Kallenberg already knew. Ekman would be watching him closely to see how really shocked he was.

Ekman hadn't resolved what he'd say as he turned into Fridhemsplan and saw the setting sun burnishing the copper roof of the ornate old courthouse across the square.

"You said on the phone that you had news, Walter. I hope it's good, but I'm afraid of what you're going to tell me," Kallenberg said, in an anxious voice, his face drawn with worry.

"Arvid, I wish that I had good news for you, but as you've already guessed, I don't."

"Let's sit down. I don't think I can take this standing."

When they were seated, Kallenberg said, his voice quivering, hoping against hope, "Was there a bad auto accident and Ivar's been seriously hurt?"

"I'm afraid it's worse than that: Ivar's been killed."

"In the accident?"

"He was murdered."

"My God, my God, I can't believe this," Kallenberg said, and put his face in his hands. Ekman was silent until Kallenberg raised a face wet with tears, and said, "Tell me everything. I have to know."

As gently as he could, Ekman described what they'd found on Skarin's computer and how it had led them to the scene at the farmhouse.

"I'm having a hard time grasping all this, Walther. If it weren't you telling me, I couldn't believe it. All I can say is that the man you've told me about is the exact opposite of the man I've known."

"Sometimes people have two contrasting sides. I'm sure the Ivar you knew was real too."

Kallenberg had recovered somewhat and straightened in his chair.

"It's kind of you to say that, but now I'm not so sure." His grief was turning to anger visible in his tight expression.

"The man you've told me about was a criminal psychopath, charming on the outside, and utterly cold on the inside. A person like that doesn't change." Kallenberg paused. "He used me."

"How was that?" asked Ekman, but he already knew the answer.

"He picked me out, pretended to love me, showered me with attention, gifts, and a house. He wanted my influence to protect himself, and when push came to shove, he'd have tried to blackmail me into becoming his accomplice."

Kallenberg was silent for a moment. "I've been a fool, 'a fool for love.'" He laughed harshly. "Isn't there a play with that title?"

"Did you discuss the cases I'm working on?"

"Oh, yes. He said it was important to share everything with each other. Of course he never told me what he was really doing. He suggested that I shouldn't approve surveillance of that spice company, that it would be an unwarranted infringement of their civil liberty."

Kallenberg paused and looked directly at Ekman. "Walther, I'm sorry. There can be no adequate apology."

He was quiet for a long moment as he thought. "I can't effectively serve as a public prosecutor anymore. I have to resign, effective immediately. And I can't go on living in a house bought with human suffering. I'm going to sell it and donate the money to a fund for trafficking victims."

"Arvid, a resignation is pretty drastic. I have every confidence in your integrity."

"That's good of you to say, but most others won't agree. There really isn't any alternative. Ivar brought on his own destruction, and now he's destroyed me too," he said, tears rolling down his cheek. He wiped them away with the back of his hand.

Ekman had no doubt Kallenberg was completely sincere. His earlier doubts about the prosecutor had vanished. Although he didn't say anything, his face showed his concern for this tormented man.

After a minute, Kallenberg pulled himself together. "Well, enough of the histrionics. The prosecutor-general will have my resignation 'for personal reasons' on his desk tomorrow morning." He stood up, and a remnant of his urbane persona reappeared.

"Walther, thank you for telling me all this in such a kind way. And thank you for putting up with my loss of self-control. It's been a privilege working with you. Try not to think of me too harshly."

Ekman stood facing him and grasped Kallenberg's hand. "Arvid, I would never think of you that way. You've been another of Skarin's victims. Give yourself time to get over all this, to forgive yourself. Good-bye, and the best of luck to you. Call me if I can ever be of help," he said, and turning, walked out of the office.

He doubted he would ever see Arvid Kallenberg again.

73

MASSACRE

Friday, February 17, 6:40 a.m. Yesterday had been physically and emotionally draining for Ekman. After his meeting
with Kallenberg, he'd just wanted to go home, have a drink
or two, and rest. But instead he'd dragged himself back to the
office and spent an hour drafting a report he sent to Norlander and Malmer. Then he gave in to those urges, although
there was a mountain of work remaining.

I'll deal with the guilt tomorrow, he'd thought, as he
pulled into his driveway.

Over dinner, he'd told Ingbritt everything that had happened. She was horrified by his brief description of the triple
murder scene.

After he'd related his meeting with Kallenberg, she was
quiet, and then said, "That poor man. My heart goes out to
him. First, his lover is killed, and then he discovers he's been
deceived and his career is ruined. It's too awful. But you were
kind to him, Walther, and that must have helped."

"I hope being sympathetic made things a little easier for
him. It must have been the roughest day of his life."

"What will happen now, Walther?"

"We'll get a new prosecutor, one I hope to God I'll be able to work with."

"And what will happen with your case?"

"A lot of the questions we had have been answered. The trafficking ring Skarin was running has been stopped, and his drug network will be rolled up. Now our most important tasks are to find this Ostlund, and search for one, or possibly two killers, and convict some rapists. That's all," he said with a sardonic smile.

"So you'll be busy for quite a while."

"Yes, very, unfortunately. What are you thinking about?"

"I've been hoping for a nice long visit with Carla and Johan before more time goes by."

"Look, Ingbritt, this case could drag on for who knows how long, although I'd love to wrap it up in the next few weeks. Why don't you go see them on your own?"

"Would you mind?"

"No, of course not. I'll just wish I were with you, but you go ahead. Give her a call and arrange something. She'll be delighted, and so will Johan."

"All right. I'll talk with her tomorrow."

"Okay, that's settled then."

Instead of going to his study after dinner to read, he'd gone to bed early and immediately fallen into a deep sleep.

The next morning, as he always did, he retrieved the morning *Sydsvenska Nyheter* from the front stoop, and standing in the front hall, took it out of its protective plastic wrap.

The bold print, front-page headline jumped out at him: **Farmhouse Massacre.** The story carried Bruno Haeggman's byline.

Goddamnit, he thought, another leak. With so many police and technicians at the crime scene it was probably unavoidable.

Going into the kitchen, he held up the paper so Ingbritt could see it as she stood at the range stirring a pot of oatmeal.

"Look at this. He's done it again!" he exclaimed, and slapped the paper.

She turned, and said in a mild voice, "Walther, you know I can't see that without my reading glasses. What does it say?"

Ekman adjusted his own glasses and quickly ran through the story of how three more people had been horrifically murdered and their bodies left to rot in a remote, abandoned farmhouse. The police, led (the story implied) by the perpetually bumbling Chief Superintendent Ekman, were again totally baffled.

"What Haeggman says is that people are being murdered left and right, and I don't know my head from my ass." His face had turned an apoplectic red.

Ingbritt came over and took the paper from him.

"Walther, you're upsetting yourself. Please don't let Haeggman do this to you."

He took a deep breath trying to calm down. "You're right. I'm not going to give the bastard the satisfaction of me dropping dead from a heart attack. I can just imagine the obit he'd take great pleasure in writing."

Ekman expected that a summons from Norlander would soon be waiting for him at the office. He wasn't looking forward to that or what the rest of the day held in store.

His fears were confirmed a half hour later when he got a call from TV8 asking for his reactions to Haeggman's story. He restrained himself with difficulty from using the first expletive that came to mind, and said in a calm voice, "Please understand, this is an ongoing investigation. I can't comment at this time." The reporter wasn't pleased, and tried to press him for details.

Ekman hung up the phone with a soul-satisfying thunk.

74

A NEW LEADER

Friday, February 17, 5 p.m. Karim sat facing the old man and Askari Harrak. They'd all read Haeggman's story, which was on the Internet.

Joumari had been praising Karim effusively.

"You've done well, extraordinarily well, Karim, Allahu akbar. *Don't you agree, Askari?"*

"He did what he was told to do," replied Harrak.

"Yes, and returned without anyone knowing he did it and trying to stop him. It was cleverly done. You can feel proud of what you've accomplished for our family, Karim."

Karim bowed his head silently. He'd never heard such praise from the old man for anyone.

Harrak was becoming visibly annoyed. He changed the focus of the conversation.

"Eliminating these people who killed Ahmed tells our enemies how far we'll go to protect our honor. They've now been warned not to try anything."

"That's true. And we owe this to Karim."

"I disagree. We owe this to my insistence, Uncle, that we avenge Ahmed's death."

"Do not presume to correct me," said Joumari, raising his voice. "You will remember your place."

"I'm tired of 'remembering my place,' as you put it. And I'm not alone. Most of the family agree with me. They want fresh leadership."

"I can't believe you have the gall to say that to my face," the old man said, getting to his feet. "This family's success is my doing, not yours, or the other fools."

"You shouldn't call me a fool. It's you who have grown foolish, old man. Your time is past," said Harrak, standing.

Joumari's normally tan complexion had reddened and he raised his cane as he moved toward Harrak.

The younger man grabbed it and pulled it away from him.

Joumari screamed, "How dare you?" and suddenly fell to the floor clutching his chest.

He lay there at Harrak's feet gasping for breath. A harsh, rattling sound came from his throat.

Karim had watched their exchange in silence. Now he bent down to loosen the old man's collar, as Harrak said, "That's useless. He's dead."

Karim put a finger on Joumari's throat. "I'm not so sure. I think there's a faint pulse. We need to call an ambulance."

"I said it's useless. He's gone, or very soon will be."

Karim straightened and looked at him.

"The family has already chosen me to succeed the old man. You work for me now. Do you understand?"

"Perfectly," Karim replied. "I will serve you, *insh'Allah*, as I served your uncle."

But Karim was extremely unhappy with this sudden turn of events. His hope of becoming the old man's successor had abruptly vanished.

75

DISCOVERIES

Friday, February 17, 8 a.m. When Ekman came into the conference room, he saw that Tyri Carlin had joined them and was sitting next to Alenius.

Ekman got up from his place at the head of the table, and as the others' conversations died down, he looked at Carlin and without a word, began to applaud. Rystrom got to his feet and began to clap too, and soon everyone was standing and applauding loudly.

Carlin, a pretty brunette in her early thirties, sat blushing. "Please, please," she protested, "I only did my job." The clapping gradually subsided and people resumed their seats.

"And what a great job you did," said Ekman. "We just wanted to show you how much you're appreciated. Your expertise has helped us uncover three new murders and may resolve three other deaths."

"Thank you, everyone," she said, looking around the table.

"Now," said Ekman, "let's see what we've learned from Tyri's efforts. Annborg, you've been sorting through the drug-related material, what have you found?"

"I've prepared chronological lists of all the drug sales, with the most recent first, the amounts, the money paid, and to whom. Skarin had an extensive distribution network throughout Sweden, Norway, and Denmark, and what we now have will enable us, and our colleagues there, to put these people away."

"What about the spice company's involvement?" Ekman asked.

"As you know, it was controlled from Morocco, but the drugs were shipped through India, concealed among the spices, on two ships owned by the Moroccans. Drugs came in and the trafficked women were shipped out. It was a reciprocal deal. The price Skarin received for selling the women, and the money he got by providing them to his clients here, helped offset the cost of the drugs.

"But lately, there'd been a change of plan. The three deaths, particularly Haake's, had increased police pressure on the trafficking side of the business. The Moroccans wanted him to close that down because it had become too risky and discovery would threaten the drug operation. They'd offered a 10 percent price cut on the drugs to sweeten the change. Skarin accepted, but his notes show he'd already reneged and was negotiating with other buyers to sell the women."

"Then it's possible the Moroccans learned about it and decided to intervene," said Rystrom.

"Yes," Ekman said, "and the discovery that Chafik had been murdered, probably by Skarin or his people, would have given them another reason to kill him."

"In his notes," Annborg said, "Skarin described meetings with a Moroccan named Karim to negotiate a new drug arrangement."

"Is it possible this man is the second killer we're looking for?" Rapp asked Ekman.

"It's something to go on," he replied. "Better than any-thing else we've got. Alrik, let's find out whether anyone with that name recently flew to Stockholm from Morocco and whether he's returned there."

Rapp got up and left the room to make the necessary calls.

"Enar and Gerdi, what have you got for us?"

"We have lists of the women Skarin trafficked," Enar said. "He wrote down when he procured them, the dates they were sold to his drug supplier for auction in Marrakech, and how much he got for them. He'd had them kidnapped, mostly from Eastern European countries, by Thore Ostlund, the guy we're searching for, who brought them to that farm. Skarin wrote how they broke them in: they were abused and raped repeatedly, first by Ostlund, then the woman, Marta, and the man, Gotz, and afterward by Skarin's customers."

Vinter continued. "We've also got the customers' names, the dates they assaulted the women, and how much they paid. It seems they were only interested in terrified victims, not prostitutes. They paid heavily to rape women who were forced sex slaves."

"My God," said Carlin, her face turning pale. She hadn't had time to read all the information she'd extracted from the computer.

"There's more," said Enar. "I think you're going to have some trouble with this, Chief."

"What's the problem?"

"It's who Skarin's clients were: eight wealthy men, actu-ally nine when you include Haake, from all sorts of occupa-tions. They're three senior business executives, a physician, a lawyer, a clergyman, an army colonel, and two bankers. And you'll really appreciate this: Håkan Grundström was one of the bankers."

"The dates show that Grundström must have been the person who introduced Haake to the ring," said Vinter. "We were right to suspect him all along. Because he was the contact man, after Haake's picture was published, he had even more reason to kill Haake to make sure he didn't expose him as another rapist."

"What a can of worms," said Rosengren.

"For once, you've got it exactly right," Ekman said to him. "Enar, order surveillance on Grundström and Skarin's other customers. We want to make sure they're around when we come for them."

"There's something we discovered that you'll be interested in, Chief," said the usually taciturn Alenius. "Rosengren and I looked over Skarin's notes about his final shipment of women to Morocco and we got curious about where the ship was now. We called the port captain's office in Casablanca to see if it was there and it hadn't arrived yet. So we asked our Coast Guard to check the AIS, automated intelligence system stations tracking ships along the freighter's likely route. They found it had docked in Rotterdam. It had engine trouble that's just been repaired, and only left today. The ship won't put into Casablanca for five more days."

"That's terrific work, both of you. We're going to get those women off that ship."

76

BUILDING CASES

Friday, February 17, 10:30 a.m. Ekman was sitting in the commissioner's office, updating the report he'd sent yesterday with new information from the morning meeting.

Norlander and Malmer sat listening without interrupting, stunned looks on their faces.

When he'd finished, Norlander said, "Congratulations, Walther. In just two days you've broken these cases wide open."

"Thanks, Commissioner, but the credit really goes to my team, and Garth Rystrom's cyber whiz, Tyri Carlin."

"Nonsense. Don't be so modest. This morning's paper suggested you were getting nowhere and you've proven them completely wrong. You were improperly blamed, and now you shouldn't hesitate to publicly take well-earned credit."

"I think we need to be extremely careful with the next steps, sir," said Ekman, reaching into his jacket pocket and handing him a sheet of paper.

"These men were Skarin's customers."

As Norlander read the list of nine names, his eyebrows shot up. "My God," he said. "You're sure these men are all rapists? I know some of them personally, it's unbelievable. Accusing people this prominent is going to cause a national media storm. We'd better be right about this." He handed the paper to Malmer, who read it with growing amazement on his face.

"There's absolutely no doubt, Commissioner. We have dates and amounts paid by each of the men to rape these women. Besides that, Skarin made secret videos of them doing it. His notes show he was planning future blackmail."

"Maybe the women were really willing prostitutes," Malmer said hopefully.

"Not a chance. We know where they were kidnapped from and when. We also have DNA evidence that one of them, the late, unlamented Herr Haake, was a rapist."

"I saw Grundström's name on the list," Norlander added. "Frankly, I'm beyond shocked."

"We now think he may have killed Haake to protect himself from disclosure. There are also videos of him raping women. I want to interview him again, and then arrest him."

"With this new information we're now on solid ground. Bring him in. These men may have known about each other," Norlander went on. "If we can leverage the videos, they may become witnesses in return for reduced sentences. It could cascade. We might be able to get them to turn against each other.

"But they may claim the women were willing participants or prostitutes, despite the information from Skarin's computer. We could build airtight cases if we had victims who'd testify against them. Are there any women who can do this?"

"I've just found out that Skarin's last shipment of women has been delayed en route to Casablanca. They won't get there for another five days. We have to make sure these women are rescued. They may be willing to testify.

"Commissioner, there's one other thing. We've been trying to get our hands on a Moroccan whose full name we've discovered is Karim Serhane, who may be involved in the new murders. We know he was in Sweden during the time they happened and he's now back in Morocco. He had several reasons to kill Skarin and the others. We badly need to question him and I've asked CID to have an Interpol 'red notice' sent out.

"I'd like your permission to go to Morocco and be there when that ship comes in to make sure the women are safe and speak with them. Then I'll try to locate this man, Serhane.

"I have a strong gut feeling, call it an old police officer's intuition, that he's the other killer we're looking for. If we can find Thore Ostlund, it may be possible to wrap up all the murders."

"Traveling all the way to Morocco is ridiculous," exclaimed Malmer. "It's too expensive and you've plenty to do right here. Leave it to the Moroccan police."

Norlander ignored Malmer's outburst and was quiet as he considered Ekman's request. "You can't go alone, Walther, and you've no contacts there."

"I was thinking that Garth Rystrom, and Valdis Granholm, from CID's international relations unit, would be willing to come with me. She's already been in touch with the Moroccan police about Chafik and Joumari, the head of the ring."

"If you think it's necessary, I'll agree, but only if they can go with you. Please make it a quick trip; Olav's right about us needing you here."

"Thank you, Commissioner. I appreciate your support.

"As I mentioned in my report, Kallenberg is resigning this morning. I don't believe that he knew about his partner's activities. But he felt certain that others' doubts about his integrity couldn't be overcome. He's probably right to resign. So we won't have a prosecutor until another one's appointed."

"That could slow us down, Walther. Is there anyone you'd prefer?"

"The best choice would be Malin Edvardsson, if she can be transferred back here from Malmö on a temporary basis, perhaps as special prosecutor to handle all these cases."

"That's a good idea. I'll speak with the prosecutor-general today. Also we need to get his agreement that the farmhouse murders are part of our case, even though they happened outside our jurisdiction."

The commissioner and Malmer stood, as did Ekman. "Good luck, Walther. And be careful over there," Norlander said, shaking his hand. A frowning Malmer said nothing.

Ekman went directly from the commissioner's office to Rystrom's to tell him about the meeting.

He described the reasons behind the Moroccan trip he'd gotten approved.

"Garth, Norlander made it dependent on you and Valdis coming with me."

"I've never been there, and although this won't exactly be a pleasure trip, I'll be happy to go along. Why don't you let me call her and ask?"

Ekman quickly agreed. He thought Rystrom would be much more persuasive, considering their relationship.

That evening, Ekman described the day's events to Ingbritt over dinner, and then he brought up his trip to Morocco.

"When will you be leaving?" she asked.

"In the next few days. I'll probably be gone less than a week. If this weren't for work, I wish you could come with me. Maybe after this is all over we can take a vacation there. It's supposed to be an interesting country."

"I'll miss you when you're away," Ingbritt said. They'd seldom been apart in all their years together. "Maybe I'll arrange to be at Carla's while you're gone."

"That's a great idea. I won't have to worry about you being alone."

77

New Prosecutor

Saturday, February 18, 9:30 a.m. At that morning's meeting, Ekman had brought everyone up to date on his conference with Norlander, and the trip he'd be making to Morocco. He'd been glad to hear Rystrom announce that his CID superiors had agreed to let him and Granholm go along.

They'd spent the rest of the time reviewing efforts to roll up the drug distribution network and find Ostlund. It had been decided that Holm and Vinter would bring Grundström in that afternoon, and he'd be arrested. At the same time, the seven other men being watched would also be arrested.

There had been a few smiles around the table when they'd heard that Kallenberg, whom most of them had disliked, had resigned and that Edvardsson, someone they all respected, would be handling the slew of new cases. And Rapp was particularly pleased when he learned he'd be in charge while the chief was away.

Ekman glanced at the clock on his bookcase, and saw it was almost time for his meeting with Malin Edvardsson. He was looking forward to seeing the formidable prosecutor again.

There was a knock at the door, and Edvardsson came in. Ekman went over to greet her and to his surprise, she reached up to hug him.

"It's been too long since I last saw you, Walther," she said, and then shook her finger at him. "You and Ingbritt never came to visit me in Malmö as you promised."

"Malin, believe me we wanted to, but I've just been swamped."

"Yes," she said playfully, "I did hear something to that effect."

When they were seated, he said, "Malin, thank you for agreeing to take on these cases. I know it's a terrible imposition to ask you to leave the home you've just made down there."

"You're right, it's very inconvenient, but I'll manage. Now tell me all about it."

Ekman spent the next half hour describing how the interlocking cases had evolved and what lay ahead. Edvardsson listened intently without interrupting.

When he'd finished, she said, "What an awful business. These men deserve to be made an example of and I'm determined to see that it happens. They'll all be charged today when you arrest them." She was now the consummate professional prosecutor.

"Walther, before you leave for Morocco, I'm going to need a full written report detailing what you've just summarized."

"I'll try to get it to you by tomorrow."

"I'll also need crime-scene, forensic, and autopsy reports, together with the complete printout from Skarin's computer, your inspectors' investigation notes, and transcripts of all interviews."

"Alrik Rapp will be working with you while I'm gone. I'll ask him to pull all that together for you right away."

"You said a major reason you're going to Morocco is to make sure those poor women are rescued and brought back to Sweden. They're important witnesses in building the strongest possible cases against these rapists."

"The other reason is to find this man Karim Serhane who may be the other killer we're looking for."

"I understand that's important for resolving the murders. But from my point of view, your first priority should be to secure those witnesses."

"You're right. I'll keep that in mind."

Ekman heard the clock chime and said, "Malin, Norlander wanted to see you when we'd finished. Let's head up there."

When they entered his office, Norlander came over to shake Edvardsson's hand. "It's good to see you, Malin. Thanks for coming back to handle these cases." Malmer, who everyone knew couldn't stand Edvardsson, hadn't been invited to the meeting.

"The drug distribution network is being rolled up, and the men involved in the women trafficking ring are being arrested and charged today," she said. "From the evidence Walther has gathered, it looks like they're all guilty of terrible crimes. I'll do my best to see they're convicted, Commissioner."

"And I know you'll be successful," he said, leading the way to some comfortable armchairs.

"If there's anything I can do to help you, please let me know."

"Thanks, I appreciate that, but right now, I think I'm fine. Walther and I have gone over all the information I'll need to get started."

"Since the stories about the murders at the farmhouse, the men have been watched," said Ekman. "Some of them may have considered making a run for it, and probably would when news of Grundström's arrest comes out. To prevent that, as Malin said, they're all being brought in today."

"I think it would be best to preempt hysterical media reports by holding a conference," said Norlander. "The public has the right to know what's happening and it's better they hear it from us, rather than distorted media accounts."

"I agree that the public has a right to know," Edvardsson said. "With these arrests it's unavoidable. But we have to be careful not to prejudice our cases until they're completely built. A lot may depend on the women Walther hopes to bring back and their willingness to testify about their ordeals. Some may not want to."

"Malin's right, Commissioner. And I've got six murder investigations underway that can't be discussed."

"You're both correct, of course. However, with all these arrests, we need to throw some red meat to the media," Norlander said, "even if, as usual, they won't find it a completely satisfying meal."

"Public relations," said Ekman wryly.

"Yes, it's 'public relations,' but it's vital to maintain the public's confidence, and their support for the police," said Norlander, and turning to Edvardsson, added, "And the prosecutor."

"When do you want to do it, Commissioner?" asked Ekman.

"The sooner, the better. How about tomorrow, Sunday afternoon, when coverage may be thinner? Will you be able to be there, Malin?"

"Yes, certainly."

"It will be a good time to reintroduce you," Norlander said.

"Haeggman will have a field day with us," said Ekman, grousing, as he and Edvardsson got up.

Norlander shrugged. "So what else is new?"

78

CHARGES

Saturday, February 18, 3 p.m. Advokat Edgren was indignant, or at least pretended to be.

"I thought it was clearly understood that Herr Grundström was not to be harassed. You can be sure that Commissioner Norlander will learn of this outrage."

Ekman's and Edvardsson's faces were expressionless as they sat facing Edgren and Grundström.

"What is my client accused of now? Not that ridiculous charge of murder again?"

"Herr Grundström was never charged, as you know, Herr Edgren," said Edvardsson.

"All right, 'suspected of' then, to be exact."

"We still have that suspicion," said Ekman. "But that's not why Grundström is here today." He'd purposely dropped the polite "Herr."

"Well, what is it now?" asked Edgren in an exasperated voice.

"The principal charges are aggravated rape, unlawful deprivation of liberty, gross violation of integrity, unlawful coercion, and accessory to kidnapping," said Edvardsson quietly. Grundström's face turned pale as she said this and moisture began to form on his forehead.

"This is beyond bizarre. You said 'charges.' Surely you don't actually intend to bring these insane accusations against a man like Herr Grundström."

"They're well-founded accusations, as you'll see, Herr Edgren," Edvardsson replied, turning to Ekman.

He reached under the table for his briefcase and taking out a computer, opened it so the two men could also see the screen. Then he played Skarin's video of a man whose face was turned away, having sex with a woman gagged and tied to a bed.

They all watched, mesmerized, for several minutes.

"We didn't come here to see pornography," said Edgren dismissively.

"Wait a bit," said Ekman.

The man turned toward the hidden camera. It was Grundström.

Edgren was silent for a long moment. His face registered shock as he glanced over at Grundström, who was now perspiring profusely. His client obviously hadn't prepared him for this. Edgren attempted to recover.

"Herr Grundström is now a single man. He's free to have sexual relations with whomever he chooses."

"But not forcible relations with an enslaved woman, Herr Edgren," said Edvardsson. Her voice was cold.

"That isn't clear from this video. The woman could simply have been playacting."

"We have other evidence that makes it quite clear."

"I'd like to see this evidence."

"You will, as we both prepare for trial."

"So you're really going to charge Herr Grundström?" He sounded incredulous.

"Yes," said Ekman. "And we also know that he was the person who introduced Haake to this rape and slavery ring. We have even more reason now to believe that he may have killed him to prevent disclosure after Haake's picture was publicized."

"But you're not going to charge him with murder too, I hope?"

"Not yet," said Ekman, standing, and walking over to the interview room door to open it. He gestured to the two constables waiting outside.

Turning to Grundström, he said. "You're under arrest. You've heard the charges."

The officers went to Grundström, pulled his arms behind his back, and handcuffed his wrists. He didn't protest and offered no resistance. His normally erect posture had collapsed, and his pallid face sagged.

Edgren had gotten up. "Håkan, don't worry. I'll see what can be done about this," he said, as the officers led Grundström from the room.

The attorney turned to Edvardsson. "Surely, confinement isn't necessary for a man of Herr Grundström's stature?"

She looked at him with a puzzled expression. "Just how much stature can a snake have, Herr Edgren?"

79

ANOTHER CONFERENCE

Sunday, February 19, 2 p.m. It was a dismal afternoon, with a cold rain falling in sheets. Despite this, media representatives packed the large assembly room.

At the team meeting that morning, Ekman had told them about the conference Norlander had scheduled. From his seat on the platform, he could see them standing along the back of the room.

"Ladies and gentlemen, we need to start the conference. Please take your seats," said Lena Sahlin, the tall, fortyish, media-relations officer.

There was some shuffling about and everyone found a chair as talk gradually subsided. The TV cameras on each side of the room scanned the speakers' platform and then focused on Sahlin.

"Thank you all for coming on such a gloomy Sunday," she said. "I'll give the microphone now to Commissioner Norlander."

Norlander, impeccably dressed as usual in a dark, custom-made suit, walked to the podium and looked around the room.

"I see we have a full house today. Let me add my thanks to Fru Sahlin's for coming here on short notice. I'd like to introduce you again to our new prosecutor, Fröken Malin Edvardsson. I said 'again' because, as most of you know, she previously served with distinction as Weltenborg's prosecutor before moving on to Malmö. She's graciously agreed to return on a temporary basis," he said, turning to Edvardsson as she came forward.

She stood beside him for a moment and smiled at the crowd, waving to a few reporters she knew, before going back to her seat.

"Now I'll turn the meeting over to Chief Superintendent Ekman who heads the investigation you've all been covering."

Ekman came forward and leaned on the lectern.

"My thanks too to everyone for coming out on such a bitter day. I'll make a brief statement, Prosecutor Edvardsson will speak, and then we'll try to answer your questions.

"I'm glad to be able to tell you that our investigation of the multiple murders is moving ahead aggressively. We've been making what I believe is exceptional progress lately, although because it's an ongoing investigation I can't as yet share details, as I'm sure you can understand.

"I can say, however, that in the course of these murder investigations we've uncovered evidence of a widespread drug-distribution network. We've also found very disturbing evidence of a ring of individuals who rape kidnapped and enslaved women."

The reporters, who'd been listening intently, started talking excitedly among themselves. Ekman held up a hand for silence.

"Fröken Edvardsson will tell you more about this ring in just a moment. Before she does, I want to ask your help publicizing the search for a man we'd like to question in connection with these crimes. His name is Thore Ostlund," Ekman said, holding up a large photo taken from his driver's license.

"Fru Sahlin will distribute copies of this photo and his physical description to you as you leave. We believe he's dangerous and may be armed, so please emphasize to the public that he's not to be approached. Anyone seeing him should contact the nearest police headquarters or phone us at the large red number at the bottom of the photo.

"I know Prosecutor Edvardsson will give you as much information as she can, but again, I want to remind you that we're in the middle of an intensive investigation and can't share details." Ekman turned to Edvardsson who got up and came to the lectern.

She reached up and adjusted the microphone to her diminutive stature. The talking that had sprung up again died down and she waited until the room was completely quiet.

"As Herr Ekman has said, multiple other crimes have been uncovered during his murder investigations. A major, international drug-distribution network was discovered and is being broken up as we speak.

"A gang of rapists has also been uncovered. These men brutalized women who were made sex slaves after being kidnapped from all over Europe. Their victims were later sold into a life of slavery in the Middle East. We know who these rapists are and they now have been arrested.

"I regret to tell you that they are all prominent Swedish men. Some of their names will be familiar to you and the public. Yesterday we charged them with the major crimes each of these men are accused of: aggravated rape, unlawful deprivation of liberty, gross violation of integrity, unlawful coercion, and accessory to kidnapping. One of these men I'm speaking of is well known in financial circles: his name is Håkan Grundström."

The room again exploded with loud talk. Edvardsson stood quietly until the noise subsided.

"Fru Sahlin is handing out a list of all the men's names, ages, and occupations. They will be formally arraigned tomorrow on the charges I've mentioned.

"Now Herr Ekman and I will be glad to try and answer any questions you have," Edvardsson concluded, as Ekman joined her at the microphone.

She pointed to a heavyset reporter in the front row.

"It's nice to see you again, Fröken Edvardsson, but what happened to Herr Kallenberg?" he asked.

"I understand he resigned for personal reasons."

"Would they have anything to do with these cases?"

"I have no information about why he resigned."

The man persisted. "How about you, Herr Ekman, do you know why he left?"

"I really couldn't say," Ekman replied. It was a subject he wouldn't talk about, ever. In his mind, Kallenberg was another of Skarin's many victims and deserved privacy. He knew, however, that once reporters found out Kallenberg had been his partner, some would suggest that he was implicated in Skarin's crimes. But there was nothing Ekman could do about that.

He gestured to a woman two rows back, who was waving her hand wildly.

"You said that these drug and rape gangs were discovered during your murder investigations. Are they the reasons for the killings?"

"We believe the deaths are related to these crimes."

"Can you tell us how they're connected?"

"I'm sorry, but that has to remain confidential while the investigations are ongoing."

Edvardsson motioned to a well-dressed man farther back.

"I represent *Göteborgs Industri*," he said, naming a widely circulated financial paper. "It will come as a great shock to our readers, and to major financial institutions throughout Scandinavia, to learn about Herr Grundström's arrest on these appalling charges. Are you sure you're not mistaken?"

"Please believe me, I thought very carefully before bringing such charges against a prominent banker. There's not the slightest doubt in my mind that he committed these crimes."

A woman from one of the TV networks stood up and Edvardsson gestured to her as the cameras zoomed in.

"I've been looking at the list of the other men you've charged with the same crimes as Herr Grundström. I think our viewers will find the names very distressing. These are all well-known people. If you're wrong, these accusations alone can destroy their lives and their families."

"Let me reiterate that I have no doubt whatsoever that these men have committed the terrible crimes with which they've been charged. I don't know how much more unequivocal I can be, even though I understand that some people may have a hard time accepting this."

"How come you're so certain?" said Bruno Haeggman, as he stood up.

"As you know only too well, Herr Haeggman," Ekman answered for her, "Prosecutor Edvardsson can't fully reveal her reasons yet because they're tied to my ongoing investigations. When they're completed and all the facts come out, I think everyone will agree with her."

"At least tell us what you're going to do at the arraignment."

"What I will do tomorrow, Herr Haeggman, is present the full charges against these defendants, and they'll be able to enter pleas of guilty or not guilty. Then I'll ask the court to continue their detention since they're all flight risks."

Haeggman responded in an angry tone. "I, and probably everybody else here," he looked around as he said this, "will be there to see what happens. But you're holding back information from us and the public that we have a right to know, aren't you?"

"I can't say more now," she said mildly, and turning, walked back to her seat.

"Ladies and gentlemen, you have all the information we're able to share with you at this time," said Ekman. There was an audible groan from the media people.

"Thank you again for coming, and for your help. Please remember to pick up the photo of Ostlund as you leave."

"They weren't particularly happy, were they?" said Norlander. "But then, they never are."

"I think Malin and I gave them some meat to chew on."

"Yes," she said, smiling, "They may act frustrated, but they actually love to keep their audiences on the edges of their seats waiting for another episode so they'll buy the next issue and stay tuned to the TV."

80

ARRAIGNMENT

Monday, February 20, 1:30 p. m. Ekman and Rapp were having lunch again in the small restaurant across Stortorget Square from headquarters. It had been a long morning in court for both of them. Ekman was feeling tired and still had a full day's work ahead preparing for his trip tomorrow to Morocco.

The courtroom had become so crowded with defendants, their attorneys, some family members, media representatives, and police that the district judge had moved the hearing to a larger room down the hall. The officers who'd escorted the defendants from their cells, and Ekman, Rapp, and Rystrom, sat to one side of the room.

When order was again established, at the judge's request, Edvardsson stepped to the microphone.

"Madam President, each and every defendant is accused of the following crimes," she said, and read the lengthy list.

As the judge called their names, each of the eight men came forward and was asked how he pleaded.

"Not guilty to all charges," was the uniform response.

"Fröken Edvardsson," the judge said, "you've requested extended detention for these defendants."

"Yes, considering the gravity of the charges, the lengthy prison sentence they face if convicted, and their financial ability, these defendants are serious flight risks."

The judge looked at the defense attorneys. "Do you want to oppose the prosecutor's request?"

An attorney came forward. "My name is Birghir Edgren, Madam President, and I represent Herr Håkan Grundström. By agreement with other counsel, I'm authorized to speak for all the defendants. Each of these men is a prominent member of his community and profession. They have spotless reputations and have never been accused of any offense, let alone the grave crimes Fröken Edvardsson has charged them with.

"These accusations have forever damaged their professional standing and created terrible turmoil in their families. Prolonged detention will only serve to magnify the hardships they already have undergone. Their strong ties to their families and communities argue against them being flight risks. We ask that detention not be extended and that you allow these men to return to their homes and families until the trial."

The judge turned to Edvardsson. "Do you have any further comments?"

"These charges of horrendous crimes against helpless women would never have been brought without a thorough examination of the evidence, which is indisputable. If you would like to see the videos that provide part of the basis for these charges, Madam President, I ask that it be done *in camera* because of their sexual nature."

"The court will recess for an hour," said the judge. "The prosecutor and attorneys for the defendants will accompany me to my chambers to view the prosecutor's evidence."

When the court reconvened, it was obvious from the shaken appearance of the attorneys and the judge's grim expression that Edvardsson's offer had had quite an impact.

The judge looked for a long moment at each of the men as though she were seeing them for the first time.

"The defendants are remanded to custody for two weeks," she said.

The courtroom burst into loud noise as the despondent-looking men were led away and the media people made a dash for the exit.

81

DEPARTURE

Tuesday, February 21, 2:45 p.m. Ekman and Rystrom were waiting at the gate to board Royal Air Maroc's direct three thirty flight from Arlanda to Casablanca's Mohammed V Airport. They kept looking around for Valdis Granholm who was supposed to meet them there.

"I can't imagine what's keeping her," said Rystrom. "Maybe I'd better try calling."

Just as he took out his phone, she appeared and hurried over, breathless.

"Sorry to be late. The damn traffic held me up. I was afraid I'd miss the plane."

Rystrom went over, hugged her, and gave her a kiss on the cheek. "We're just glad you made it."

Watching the two of them confirmed again for Ekman that they were much more than colleagues. "It's good to see you," he said, as they heard the first boarding announcement.

In the police car driving them up to Arlanda, Ekman and Rystrom had talked about what they would do once they got to Casablanca.

"That ship will be arriving sometime tomorrow," Ekman said. "And we need to be there when it docks to get those women off."

"Valdis has been in touch with her Interpol contact in Rabat," Rystrom said. "He'll meet us at the airport and take us to the Moroccan police handling the operation. He's explained the situation to them and they've agreed to arrange a suitable reception committee for the ship."

"Besides police, we should have ambulances ready for the women," Ekman said. "God knows what shape they'll be in."

"You're right. I'll be sure to mention that to Valdis so she can alert her contact. The women will need to recover before we can put them on a plane to Sweden."

"Skarin indicated they're from all over Eastern Europe. They may want to go home instead."

"We'll have to persuade them to come back to Sweden and testify against the men who raped them."

"It could be a hard sell. It's the sort of experience they won't want to relive in a courtroom."

"Yes, but they need to realize that testifying is the best way to make sure those bastards pay for what they did to them."

"I agree; however, I'd understand it if they don't care, and simply want to try and forget."

"I guess all we can do is be as persuasive as possible. But after we get the women sorted out, what about this guy, Serhane?" asked Rystrom.

"There's a good chance he's one of the farmhouse killers. Let's hope the Moroccan police know more about him than we do and can put their hands on him."

That morning, as Ekman had packed for his trip, Ingbritt had been getting ready for her visit to Carla.

"I wish I were going with you," he said.

"Well, hurry back and maybe you can join me. I know Carla and Johan will miss seeing you."

"After this case is over, we'll both have a good visit with them. And then you and I are going to take a long vacation together, just the two of us. I've got weeks of leave coming to me."

"We're not heading back to Morocco?" Ingbritt said, laughing.

"No, not there. In my mind it'll always be too involved with this case. I'm thinking of a place that's completely relaxing, somewhere in the Caribbean, like Barbados. There'll be plenty of warm sun, and we'll just lie on the beach under a palm tree, listen to the surf, and sip piña coladas."

"It sounds idyllic, but don't get my hopes up. Something always seems to happen at your work that prevents us from doing things like that."

"I know. But this time I mean it. Just as soon as this case is finished, we're going to do it. That's a promise."

"This time, Walther Ekman, I'll hold you to it," she said, and kissed him hard on the lips. "Just come home safely."

Whenever he travelled, Ekman knew that Ingbritt's pervasive anxiety level soared and that she'd worry constantly until he was home again.

82

ARRIVAL

Tuesday, February 21, 8:15 p.m. As the three Swedish police officers, carrying heavy coats, wheeled their luggage out of the Casablanca airport's immigration and customs area, they saw a man standing just outside the exit holding a large cardboard sign that read, GRANHOLM.

"That's got to be my Interpol contact," Granholm said, as she led the way over to him.

"Hello," she said in English, smiling at him, "I'm Valdis Granholm, and you must be Girgis Akhrif. Thanks for coming down from Rabat. It's good to finally meet the voice at the other end of the line." The short, thirtyish man, dressed in a light, beige jacket and open-collared shirt, smiled.

"It's good to see you too, Valdis," he said, in English with a mixed Moroccan-French accent.

She turned, and introduced Ekman and Rystrom to him.

"Glad to meet you," Akhrif said, shaking hands with them. "My car is just outside and I'll take you to your hotel."

"I'm sure Valdis told you about the ship we need to meet" Ekman said. "We don't know when it will dock, but we have to be waiting for it. So although we'd like to get to the hotel and relax, it might be better if we checked in at police headquarters to help organize the reception."

"That's not a problem," Akhrif said, with a wide smile. "It's all been taken care of."

"We think the five women we'll be taking off that ship might require medical attention, so several ambulances may be needed," said Granholm.

"It's already been arranged. We've tried to think of everything, *insh'Allah,* even though this is only Morocco and not Sweden."

"I'm sorry, Girgis," she said. "I didn't mean to be offensive."

"It's all right. Now I'll drive you to your hotel."

Outside the large international terminal, indistinguishable from any other, it was twelve degrees Celsius and tall, straight palm trees lined the exterior. The three Swedes smiled and took deep breaths of the warm air.

It was a sixteen-mile drive, mostly on the busy A7 highway, to Morocco's largest city of over four million. As he drove carefully through heavy traffic, Akhrif chatted with them about how different the climate and scenery were from Sweden.

Forty-five minutes later, he pulled up at a huge hotel complex, the five-star Four Seasons on the corniche waterfront.

Looking around, Granholm said, "This is much grander than we're accustomed to, Girgis. I'm afraid it's going to break our budget."

He grinned again. "Like everything else, it's all been taken care of."

She began to protest, but he raised a hand, "Please, you are our guests as long as you are in our country. It's our custom," he said. "And you have to become used to it, or we really will be offended."

"Thank you," she said. "I guess we'll just have to accept it."

As porters hurried over to unload the luggage, Akhrif told them about the plans that had been made. Police would be waiting at the ship's berth when it docked late tomorrow morning. First thing tomorrow they'd go see Hamza Barrada, the divisional commissaire from national headquarters in Rabat, who was in charge of the operation.

"I know he's looking forward to meeting you," Akhrif said.

They shook hands, and then followed the porters into the ultramodern lobby. They'd eaten on the plane, and weren't hungry, just tired. They agreed to meet for breakfast at six thirty.

The next morning, seated in Mint, the Moroccan-themed restaurant in the hotel's lobby, Ekman asked Rystrom and Granholm how they liked their rooms, and then, realizing he shouldn't have asked, turned red with embarrassment.

"It's okay, Walther," Rystrom said with a grin. "We've known for a long time that you realized we're together."

"It's impossible to conceal anything from you two," said Ekman, recovering with a laugh.

"I only asked because they gave me an oceanfront suite and I wondered whether your rooms were the same."

"No, but they're very nice ones with ocean views," said Granholm.

"I guess rank has its privileges," Rystrom said, shaking his head in mock envy.

They each ordered french pastries, fresh orange juice, and coffee, leaving the heavier Moroccan specialties for a later meal. Over breakfast, they talked about how the case's convoluted path had led them there, far from Sweden.

"This is something of a silver lining," said Granholm, as she looked around at their luxurious surroundings.

"Yes, for us," said Ekman, "but it's the bright lining of a very dark cloud."

83

BARRADA

Wednesday, February 22, 7:30 a.m. It was already a brilliant, sunny day with a temperature in the midteens, as the car headed into the city center along roads crowded with morning traffic.

"We'll be meeting Commissaire Barrada at the Waliya, the regional governor's office," Akhrif said, "instead of the local police station."

Ekman wondered why. Probably it was because Barrada was from national headquarters.

They drove into the wide Mohammed V Plaza and pulled up in front of what was an obviously historic tan stucco building with a tall, imposing tower.

Akhrif showed his identification and spoke briefly with one of the guards out front about leaving the car where it was. Then he gestured to the others to follow him.

In the cool, dim interior, he led the way up a broad central staircase and down a tiled corridor to a large wooden door.

Knocking first, he entered, and they followed him into a huge, ornately plastered, high-ceilinged room with tall windows looking out on the plaza, its floor covered with bright Berber rugs.

Divisional Commissaire Hamza Barrada appeared to be in his midfifties. He was a powerfully built man, almost as big as Ekman, dressed in a dark business suit that seemed barely able to contain him.

He came around the wide, elaborately carved desk.

"I'm delighted to meet you, Chief Superintendent," he said in perfect Oxford English, without the trace of an accent. He'd obviously been briefed on his guests and what they looked like.

"It's a pleasure to meet you too, Commissaire," Ekman said. "Let me introduce my colleagues, Superintendents Valdis Granholm and Garth Rystrom of our National CID."

"Please," Barrada said, gesturing to armchairs around a low table set with a coffee service, rather than traditional Moroccan mint tea.

As they sipped their thick, too sweet Turkish-style coffee, Barrada explained what was happening at the port.

"My officers have been there since last night, waiting for the ship you're interested in. The port captain has now told us it's expected to dock around ten o'clock this morning. Customs officers will board immediately and the ship will be searched. Then the crew will be arrested by my men and the women you're looking for will be taken off, placed in ambulances, and driven to the new Sheikh Khalifa Hospital, where you can interview them."

"We'd like to be there when the ship docks," said Ekman.

"Certainly, that won't be a problem, but you understand you'll only be observers. I'm sure you can appreciate that all interactions with the crew, and the transfer of the women, have to be handled by us."

"That's understood," said Ekman. "It would be done that way in our country."

"Excellent, then we're on the same track. Human trafficking is not tolerated in Morocco. We're delighted to see this ring broken up here and in Sweden."

Ekman thought he was being disingenuous. Joumari had been active for a long time in Morocco and the police had to have known about his operation, but hadn't done anything to stop it. The question was, why?

"Girgis has told me you have another objective besides rescuing these women: you're looking for a man named Karim Serhane you believe has fled to our country, probably to Marrakech."

"That's right," said Granholm. "Do you have a file on him?"

"His name is known to us. He's been working for Joumari."

"We suspect he may have committed multiple murders in Sweden," said Rystrom. "Does he have that kind of record, or reputation, here?"

"Not to my knowledge."

Ekman had been listening carefully to Barrada's replies. They seemed vague and cautious to him.

"Besides assisting police from other countries, which we very much appreciate, Commissaire, could you tell us a little about your other areas of responsibility?" Ekman asked.

He wanted Barrada to become more relaxed and expansive with them. He'd found this happened most easily when people had a chance to speak about themselves and their work.

"I'm the odd jobs man around here. Special assignments of all kinds, that sort of thing. I don't want to bore you with the details," he said, standing and looking at his watch.

Now he's being openly evasive, thought Ekman.

"I think it's about time for us to head to the port," Barrada said. "We need to be there in case the ship comes in early."

84

MISSING

Wednesday, February 22, 9:35 a.m. Barrada's car led the way to the docks, with his Swedish visitors following in Akhrif's auto. Behind them was a police bus with more officers.

Casablanca, in addition to being Morocco's biggest city, is also its major port. Their convoy moved slowly through the dense warehouse district surrounding the port. They threaded their way cautiously among a logjam of lumbering tractor trailers, loaded with steel cargo containers. As they got nearer, Ekman and the others could see enormous cranes towering over the large container freighters that lined the rows of docks.

Ten minutes later they were at the far end of the port and came to a berth that had been reserved for the *Kharon*. Several cars, some filled with customs officers and others with police, were parked nearby. Barrada's car pulled up close to these vehicles, and Akhrif did the same.

Barrada got out and went over to a car in front, speaking through the rolled-down window to an officer Ekman assumed must be in charge.

Akhrif and the Swedes had also gotten out of their car and Barrada now came over to them.

"We got here just in time," he said. "I've been told the ship will be arriving shortly, and as a matter of fact, we may be able to see it already," he said, pointing to a distant black dot on the blue line of the horizon.

The five of them stood watching silently as the dot gradually grew larger and became a ship.

The rusted freighter slowly turned and carefully backed into its berth. A few crew members could be seen gazing down over the rails at them.

The engine shuddered to a halt and after a few minutes, a gangplank was lowered onto the dock. Immediately a group of customs officers hurried up it and boarded.

Ekman and the others stood on the dock beside the ship, waiting impatiently for the officers to reappear with the women.

After twenty minutes, Ekman turned to Barrada and said, "The ship's not that big. I wonder what's keeping them."

"They've been told to be thorough, and I imagine that's what they're doing."

The customs officer in charge came down the gangplank alone. He went over to Barrada, saluted, and spoke to him in Moroccan Arabic. Barrada asked abrupt questions to which he got rapid responses, then the officer saluted again and reboarded the freighter.

Ekman and the other Swedes had stood listening to this unintelligible exchange with growing impatience.

Barrada turned to them and said, "I'm sorry to tell you that it appears there are no women on board."

"How can that be?" asked Granholm.

"Yet we know they were put on that ship," said Rystrom, pointing to the freighter. "They can't have just vanished."

"They haven't," said Ekman, "They must have been taken off somewhere between Stockholm and Casablanca."

"So it would seem," said Barrada. His voice told them he wasn't overly concerned.

The customs officers had left the ship and Barrada's police had boarded in force. They now reappeared leading the crew down the gangway in handcuffs.

They watched as a man wearing a jacket with captain's stripes on his sleeves was led away, protesting in a loud voice until one of the officers slapped him in the face and then smacked him so hard on the back of his head that he staggered and almost fell.

Barrada observed this without changing expression and without comment, while his visitors stood there shocked. This wasn't the way people arrested in Sweden were treated.

"Why don't we go back to my office, and plan the next steps? Besides, I'm sure we could all do with some refreshments after this unfortunate disappointment," Barrada said blandly.

85

LUNCH WITH BARRADA

Wednesday, February 22, 1:15 p.m. Lunch at Barrada's office turned out to be an elaborate affair. A circular folding table had been placed in the middle of the room, covered with a white tablecloth, and set with heavy linen napkins, silverware, and glasses. Five dining chairs had been placed around the table.

Three white-coated servers moved about, setting out hot and cold salads, and filling glasses with mint tea. It was going to be a typical Moroccan meal.

When they'd arrived back at Barrada's office, Ekman and his friends had wanted to speak with Barrada immediately about their next steps, but he'd insisted they should first have lunch and hold off any discussion until afterward.

His visitors had tried to make small talk with him as one dish after another was served, but it was hopeless; they were too preoccupied with what had happened. Conversation faded as they lapsed into silence and concentrated on their food.

The variety of appetizers seemed endless, but eventually they reached the main course: chicken with preserved lemons and green olives. It was followed by a fig and sesame tart dessert.

After the table had been cleared and removed, Barrada and his visitors gathered in the comfortable seating area.

"Well," said Barrada, "how did you like lunch?"

"Everything was delicious," said Granholm, and the others seconded this.

"Thank you for going to all that trouble," said Ekman.

"No trouble at all. It was my great pleasure."

"As you could no doubt tell during lunch, we can't get the situation of the disappearing women out of our minds," Ekman said.

"We have to find them," said Rystrom. "The cases against the rapists need their testimony."

"I understand," Barrada replied, as his phone rang. Going over to his desk, he picked it up, said "Barrada," and listened for a moment. Then he smiled and put the phone down.

Resuming his seat, he said, "The mystery has been solved. I've just been informed that the ship's captain has confessed everything."

Ekman wondered what methods might have been used to extract such a quick confession.

"He got a phone call from the freighter's owner," Barrada continued, "directing him to anchor outside the harbor last night. He put the women, who were drugged, into a fishing boat that had come out to meet the ship."

"How did they know we were waiting?" asked Granholm.

Barrada shrugged. "Who can say?"

"It may have been the call Alenius made to the port captain's office to find out if the ship had arrived," said Ekman.

"Someone there must have tipped off the traffickers that we were looking for the ship," Rystrom said.

"That's probably it," said Ekman.

Turning to Barrada, Rystrom asked, "Can you discover who the leak is in that office?"

"Yes, but I don't think that's our primary concern now."

"You're right," said Ekman. "We need to find out where they've taken the women."

"Exactly," Barrada said. "Let me work on it today. I may have some news for you tomorrow morning."

"You have informants?" asked Ekman.

"Always," Barrada replied with a predatory grin.

86

TRANSFER

Wednesday, February 22, 6:30 a.m. In the predawn darkness, the fishing boat headed across the sheltered bay, with only its running lights on. The captain, a grizzled man of sixty, kept his eyes fixed on where he knew the shore would soon appear and spoke clipped directions to his brawny mate.

They both ignored the two other men and the cargo that they carried. They'd been well paid to do exactly that.

In the cramped cabin below, five barefooted women dressed in soiled sweat suits lay in a drugged sleep, sprawled on piles of burlap sacks that stank of fish.

The shoreline loomed out of the dark marked by a few scattered lights. The captain sighted the jetty he'd been looking for and pointed the boat's prow toward it. He slowed the engine to a crawl as they carefully pulled alongside the dock. It was suddenly bathed in the headlights of the large truck that had been parked there waiting for them.

Askari Harrak, and the other man, a cousin named Youssef Daoud, a muscled thirty-year-old, carried each woman from the boat to the enclosed truck, whose tailgate was open. A

third man, Karim Serhane, the driver, stood in the back under
a hanging light bulb and helped deposit the women on the
torn padding spread across the truck bed.

When the last woman had been carried ashore, the captain
started the engine and slowly pulled away from the jetty. He
wanted nothing more to do with that night's work. If anyone
should ever ask, he and the mate would say it had been a
disappointing trip, they hadn't caught a thing.

Harrak and Daoud crowded into the truck's cab, as Serhane got back behind the wheel. It had been a long night and
it would be three more hours before they got to Marrakech.
They were tired and hungry, and sat silent, too worn out for
small talk.

Harrak, always a bitter, angry man, was in a particularly
foul mood.

"*Insh'Allah*, they'll pay for making us go through this," he
finally muttered.

"Who's that?" asked Serhane.

"Those Swedish bastards. They messed up our business in
Europe and now they're fucking with us here. They're waiting
for the ship in Casablanca. Just look what we've had to do to
hang on to women we paid good money for."

Serhane didn't think now was the best time to remind
Harrak it had been his idea to disrupt their Swedish drug
and women-trafficking operations in order to avenge Ahmed's
death.

"Screwing with us is going to cost them," Harrak said as
an idea began to take shape in his mind. "More than they'd
ever expect."

87

LEAVING CASABLANCA

Thursday, February 23, 8:15 a.m. The three Swedish officers and Girgis Akhrif sat in Barrada's office waiting for him to appear. Akhrif had joined them for a quick breakfast at their hotel, but they were still hungry enough to sample the coffee and tray of honey-soaked pastries they'd found set out for them.

"Sorry, I was held up," Barrada said as he came in, sat down with them, and poured a cup of coffee.

Ekman was bursting with impatience and was tempted to ask right away if there was any news about the women, but managed to restrain himself. He didn't want to risk offending Barrada by being pushy.

After making polite inquiries about how they were enjoying their stay in Casablanca and whether they'd slept well, Barrada at last said, "I have some information for you."

He paused, looking around at them. "We've found out what's happened to the women. They've been taken to Marrakech."

"Do you know where they are in Marrakech?" Rystrom inquired.

"Not yet, but we expect to have that information soon."

"When you do, you'll rescue them immediately, won't you?" Granholm asked.

"We may have to wait a bit."

"What will you be waiting for?" Ekman asked.

"We know that sometime in the next week the women are to be auctioned to a group of bidders from the Middle East. We want to arrest them, as well as the traffickers."

"Think about what those poor women may be going through in that time," said Granholm.

"I expect they'll be well-treated before the auction."

"Maybe physically, but psychologically they'll be suffering terribly."

Barrada shrugged. "We need to put a stop to foreigners who use our country as a source of sex slaves. Jailing these men will be a major step in that direction."

"I think we can appreciate your reasons for wanting to arrest everyone involved, Commissaire," said Ekman. He was uncertain how he would handle it, but he hoped he'd opt to rescue the women as soon as he knew where they were being held, and deal with the buyers later.

"What should we do now?"

"I imagine you'll want to be there when we retrieve the women, so why don't you plan on driving to Marrakech this afternoon."

"When should we meet you?" asked Rystrom.

"It will take me a little more time to get the information we need and to organize. Why don't you leave and I'll follow in the next day or so? That way you'll have a chance to look around Marrakech. It's a fascinating city and I've already reserved hotel rooms for you. I know Girgis will be happy to take you," he said turning to him.

"It will be my pleasure," Akhrif said.

"All right," Ekman said. "We'll head there today."

But he had no interest in playing the tourist. He just wanted this trip to be over so he could get back home.

As much as he wanted to return quickly though, Ekman realized that rescuing the women would only accomplish one of the tasks that had brought him to Morocco. He'd still have to get his hands on Karim Serhane.

88

ILINCA

Thursday, February 23, 12:40 p.m. She came awake gradually from her drugged sleep and slowly opened encrusted eyelids. Lifting her head too quickly from the pillow, she immediately became dizzy and fell back. Her eyes blinked against the glare of fluorescents fixed to the dirty white ceiling. It was the only light in the grey, concrete-walled room.

The air was humid despite the cooling flow from several overhead vents. Turning her head carefully to the right she could see part of the room.

There was a cot a few feet from hers, with another just beyond it. A sleeping woman in a stained sweat suit identical to hers lay on each. At the end of the room was a partially open door.

Moving her head to the left, she saw two more cots with sleeping women. At that end of the room was a heavy door with a small window.

A steel clothes rack, filled with garments she couldn't make out, lined part of the cinder-block wall facing the beds.

A wooden dressing table with a mirror and chair stood next to it against the wall.

Ilinca moved cautiously, trying again to sit up without becoming ill. She sat still for several minutes waiting for a lingering nausea to pass. She had an overwhelming need for water, but there was nothing to be seen nearby. Even before that she needed to relieve herself.

She tried sitting on the edge of the cot and waited a moment. Then she stood, her bare feet feeling the hard cement of the floor, steadying herself with one hand on the cot. When she felt she wouldn't fall, she took a few tentative steps and then walked cautiously to the open door. Peering in she was glad to see a small bathroom.

She used the toilet and then went to the sink and turned the faucet. Cold water gushed out and she splashed some on her face, rubbing her eyes clean. Scooping some water in her hand she drank greedily, over and over again. A toothbrush and a tube of toothpaste lay on the sink and she used it. Afterward she felt a little more human.

Ilinca knew she had to be somewhere in Morocco. The ship's captain had taken a fancy to one of the women and brought her to his cabin. She'd spent three days there before being returned to the large compartment holding the others.

"He told me they're going to sell us in Morocco," the woman, a pretty Hungarian brunette named Gizela had said in English, bursting into tears. "What can we do?"

"There's nothing to do now, we have to wait. There may be a chance to escape later," Ilinca had replied. "They might get careless and we'll have an opportunity."

She badly wanted to use the small shower now and change clothes, but first she had to find something to eat: she was famished.

As though in response to her thought, she heard the door at the other end of the room open and then close with a thud.

Coming out of the bathroom she saw that two small, elderly women in traditional ankle-length black robes had come in wheeling a cart that held covered dishes on top, and on a bottom shelf, bottles of water.

She went toward them and they stopped.

"Can you help us?" she asked in English.

Both women responded with gap-toothed smiles, and rapid Moroccan Arabic.

Ilinca saw it was hopeless trying to communicate with them; besides they obviously were working for their captors, whoever they might be.

The women wheeled the cart to the dressing table and began putting paper plates and small plastic forks on it. Lifting the lids from several dishes they pointed first to her, then to the food. She didn't need a second invitation, but grabbed a plate and began loading it with pita bread, couscous, and sliced chicken.

Taking the plate and a bottle of water to her cot she sat on its side and hungrily used the pita to scoop up the food. She stopped between mouthfuls, still extremely thirsty, and gulped down the entire bottle of water.

As she finished, she noticed that two of the other sleeping women had begun to stir.

The elderly servers had knocked on the door to be let out. A face in the door's window looked them over and the door was opened.

A short time afterward, a man entered. She stood, as he looked around and then approached her.

"Feeling better?" Harrak asked in English.

"Yes," she responded. "Thank you for the food." Ilinca had decided that being pleasant would be more useful than showing how she really felt: she had a quick mental image of herself plunging a knife into his chest.

"You and the others will be my guests for a little while. I want you to relax, eat, get cleaned up, and try on new clothes," he said, pointing to the garment rack filled with different sizes and colors of lingerie and thin robes.

"Soon the women will bring you toiletries so you can put on makeup." He reached over and lifted her chin. "Although you're pretty enough as it is."

Ilinca flinched at his touch.

"What's the matter? Don't you like me to touch you? Plenty of men have already done much more than that."

"Only because I couldn't stop them," she said, defiant despite herself.

"I bet you liked it well enough, you little slut."

"I hated it."

"I think you fuck like a rabbit," he said, wriggling his hips in an obscene pantomime. "You're nothing but a filthy whore, aren't you?"

Ilinca fell silent and lowered her head. This man could do what he wanted with her, she mustn't antagonize him.

He smiled at her apparent submissiveness. "I'll let you and the other whores get presentable so you'll bring a better price. You'll have a new owner very soon. Think about how much you'll enjoy pleasing him," he said. He walked toward the door where a face at the window watched him approach. It was opened for him, then closed with a clang as the bolt slid home.

89

MARRAKECH

Thursday, February 23, 7:30 p.m. When Akhrif had dropped them off at their hotel that afternoon, he'd apologized for not being able to be with them any longer. He'd be spending the night at a small hotel elsewhere, and would be returning early in the morning to Rabat and another Interpol assignment. Barrada would handle their transportation needs from now on.

"Thank you for all you've done for us," said Ekman.

"It was my pleasure," Akhrif said. "Can I have a selfie as a souvenir?"

"Of course," said Ekman, thinking that young people are alike in every country these days. The three Swedes and Girgis got together and smiled for his cell phone's camera.

"Thanks, and good luck finding the women," Akhrif said, as he headed back to his car.

They all agreed that their rooms at the fashionably remodeled, 1923 La Mamounia, the grande dame of Moroccan hotels, were the most luxurious they'd ever stayed in.

"If this was good enough for Churchill, I guess it's good enough for us," Rystrom said with a laugh, as they sat in the traditionally decorated Churchill Bar before heading in to dinner. Granholm smiled back at him and placed her hand on his.

Ekman said nothing. He was uncomfortable with the VIP treatment they were receiving from Barrada and would rather they paid their own way at more modest establishments. But as Akhrif had told them when they first arrived in Morocco, they were guests of the country, and had to accept the hospitality or risk offending their hosts.

As they sipped their cocktails, Ekman was restless. There was nothing he could do right now, but found it impossible to relax knowing that the captive women were somewhere in the city and going through God knows what.

They'd decided that although they liked Moroccan food, tonight they'd try L'Italien, the hotel's two-star Michelin-rated restaurant. Dinner more than lived up to expectations, and it was almost ten o'clock before they said good night.

That evening a call was made to Askari Harrak.

"The Swedes are here in Marrakech, staying at the La Mamounia," his caller said. They spoke briefly and hung up.

Harrak was pleased. His tentative idea about how to pay these foreigners back in a way they'd never forget had become a definite plan. Soon he'd put it into action.

90

TOURIST TRAP

Friday, February 24, 8:40 a.m. It was already fourteen degrees Celsius on a brilliant, sun-filled day that promised to reach twenty-one by noon. They decided to have breakfast at the poolside restaurant that offered a sumptuous buffet, and sat down at one of the round, umbrella-shaded tables beside the shimmering, Olympic-size pool.

Looking at the long, heavily laden tables lined up nearby under colorful tents, Granholm said, "If we go on eating like this, I'll have to let out all my clothes."

"Nonsense," said Rystrom, casting an admiring glance at her figure. "There'll just be a little more of you to love," and taking her hand, kissed her palm.

"I don't know if Ingbritt would say the same about me," Ekman said, looking down at his expanded waist, ill-concealed beneath a straining vest. Worried about his health, she'd been urging him for years to slim down.

"Why don't we just enjoy ourselves for once," said Rystrom. "We need some distraction. There's nothing else to do, right now."

"Yes," Ekman said. "Until Barrada finds out exactly where the women are being held and gets here with his men, we might as well." But he was a reluctant tourist. The need to rescue the women was always on his mind, making it impossible for him to relax.

It was close to ten o'clock by the time they'd finished breakfast. Going to the hotel's reception area they asked the concierge what sights to see in Marrakech. He hesitated, then suggested they might want to hire a car and guide.

After looking at the others, who shook their heads, Ekman said, "No, thanks. It will be more fun to find our own way."

"As you think best, sir," the cosmopolitan, grey-haired man said, and handed each of them a small, colorful booklet with descriptions of attractions in several languages, and a street map in English showing the hotel's location in red.

"If you change your mind, please call the hotel and we'll send a car for you," the concierge added, handing Ekman his card.

As they headed for the entrance, Rystrom said, "Now that's service for you. We could learn something in Stockholm from them."

After consulting the list of sights, they decided to first see the architecturally significant Ali Ben Youssef Madrasa, a sixteenth-century building, now a museum that had originally been a religious school founded in the fourteenth century.

From the map, it looked like it was almost three kilometers away, so they decided to take one of the cabs lined up in front of the hotel.

"Ali Ben Youssef Madrasa," Ekman said. The driver nodded and headed away from the hotel down Avenue Hommane Al Fatouaki.

They didn't notice the panel truck that pulled out of a nearby side street and kept several car lengths behind the taxi.

The traffic was light and in less than ten minutes the cab stopped in front of an imposing, ancient building. Ekman bought the three tickets to the museum, fifty dirhams each, which after a moment's mental arithmetic, he converted to about forty-four Swedish krona apiece.

Inside they stood in silent admiration in a huge courtyard with a shallow, central pool. It was surrounded by colonnaded arabesque arches covered with intricate, bright tiled patterns.

"It's all quite beautiful," said Granholm, as they wandered from one ornate room to another.

"Well worth seeing," said Rystrom, and Ekman nodded agreement.

After an hour, they decided to leave. Standing outside, they consulted the booklet again. They decided to forego the Almoravid Kouba El Ba´adiyin shrine, even though it stood just across the square.

"Whatever other historic sites we see, it's going to be downhill after this one," said Rystrom.

"You're right," said Granholm. "So let's go shopping."

Ekman agreed. He needed to buy presents for Ingbritt and Carla.

They walked to a nearby taxi stand and Rystrom told the driver, "Carre Eden," naming a major shopping mall mentioned in the guidebook. He figured if he couldn't see what he wanted, there would be other shops lining the nearby streets where he could find the special present for Valdis that he had in mind.

Serhane was driving the panel truck that followed their cab down crowded Avenue Mohammed V. Harrak and Daoud were crammed into the front seat beside him.

"This is a mistake," said Serhane. "We should just forget about the Swedes."

"Shut up, Karim," said Harrak, "and don't lose their taxi."

"I still say it's not worth the risk."

"I decide what's worth it, not you. If anyone messes with me, they have to pay the price," Harrak said, glowering at Serhane, who lapsed into silence. "Besides, I have a plan. You'll see."

The cab stopped in front of the sprawling Carre Eden Shopping Centre, housed in an ultramodern five-story building on a wide boulevard, Rue Tariq Bnou Ziad.

Going into the busy, enclosed mall, they strolled among the crowd, some dressed in Moroccan robes and others in jeans and colorful tee shirts. They peered into store windows, many displaying the same brands they were familiar with in Sweden. Global commerce definitely had reached Morocco. This up-to-date mall, which could have been almost anywhere in the world, contrasted sharply with the medieval splendor of the ancient Madrasa.

"I don't see what I'm looking for," said Rystrom.

"What's that?" asked Granholm.

"I'll know it when I see it," he said, smiling at her.

"Why don't we look around outside?" Ekman said, and they headed to an exit.

Daoud had followed them into the shopping center and walked behind them as they left. He jumped into the panel truck that had pulled up beside him, and that slowly trailed after the three visitors.

They wandered away from the busy thoroughfare into less crowded side streets, looking at different shops.

Rystrom paused to examine the window of a jewelry store. "I'm going in here," he said. "I'll be a little while. Why don't you keep on down this street and I'll catch up shortly."

"Okay," said Ekman. He guessed what Rystrom had in mind, and so did she: an unusual engagement ring.

Rystrom went in the store and the two of them continued slowly on for half a block down the street, which had only a few pedestrians and vehicles.

The panel truck pulled ahead of them and stopped halfway up on the sidewalk. Harrak and Daoud got out quickly, and coming around the truck, blocked the way preventing Ekman and Granholm from going by. There was no one else on the street ahead or behind them, and the truck concealed what was happening from some people across the way. The Moroccans pulled out pistols, and Daoud jerked open the truck's side door.

"Get in," said Harrak in English in a harsh voice, aiming his gun at them.

Ekman and Granholm stood frozen, exchanging shocked looks.

"Get in now or I'll kill you right here," said Harrak, in a voice that told them he meant it.

Ekman didn't understand why this was happening, but they had no choice. He climbed into the truck and helped Granholm in.

The door slid shut and locked, as Harrak and Daoud got back in front and Serhane gunned the engine.

Ekman and Granholm sat on the corrugated metal floor. As the truck accelerated and swayed, he put his arm around her shoulder to steady her.

"Try not to worry. We'll sort this out," he said. But he knew they were in dire trouble.

When Rystrom came out of the jewelry store a short time later with a small, gift-wrapped package in his pocket, he was elated. He'd found exactly what he'd wanted. He looked up the road where his friends should be, but there was no sign of them. Perhaps they'd gone into a store.

He started along the street, peering into store fronts, and kept this up for half an hour. Eventually he decided they must have become tired and headed back, although it was strange they'd do that without telling him. Rystrom had become increasingly annoyed with them when he finally gave up and got a cab to the hotel.

He found that Ekman and Granholm weren't in their rooms or anywhere else in the hotel. Now he became really worried and decided to call Barrada.

The handwritten number on the back of Barrada's card was his personal cell phone, so he tried that first.

"Barrada here."

"It's Garth Rystrom, Commissaire," he said, and quickly explained the situation.

There was a long silence. For a moment Rystrom thought the call had been dropped.

"Stay at your hotel, Herr Rystrom. I'm already on my way to Marrakech and will be with you in an hour." The line went dead.

91

HOSTAGES

Friday, February 24, 1:15 p.m. The truck had been driven into a garage and Ekman and Granholm had been ordered to get out. They were marched at gunpoint into a connected building that appeared to be a warehouse, and then down a dimly lit back corridor to the room they were now in. Its heavy wooden door had slammed shut behind their captors and they were left alone.

It was a stifling, windowless cement box with a single air vent. Florescent lights glared down on three wooden chairs and a table. Three folding cots were stacked against a wall and on Ekman's right was a small alcove with a toilet and tiny sink. The room had apparently been set up for three captives, but Rystrom had gotten lucky.

"What are we going to do, Walther?" asked Granholm in a voice she was struggling to control.

It was apparent to Ekman that she was scared, but trying hard not to show it.

"There's nothing we can do right now, Valdis. We'll just have to wait and see what they want," he said and sat down on one of the chairs which creaked under his weight.

She took another chair. "Who are these men and why have they done this?"

"They're probably part of the trafficking ring. Why they've kidnapped us isn't clear. I don't know what they hope to gain," Ekman replied.

As though in answer to their questions, the door opened and the three men came back in, two with guns in their hands. Ekman and Granholm got to their feet.

"Sit back down," ordered Harrak, as Serhane handed them cold bottles of water. They were terribly thirsty and quickly opened them and took long swallows.

"What do you want from us?" asked Ekman, wiping his mouth with his sleeve.

"Just cooperation. If I get it, and all goes well, you'll be free to leave in a few days," Harrak replied.

"What sort of cooperation?"

"First, you need to call your friend. I expect he's back at your hotel by now," Harrak said, taking out a cell phone.

"No doubt he's worried about you and you should reassure him."

"What else do you want me to say?"

"He's to give a message to Barrada telling him to back off. Coming from one of you, rather than me, it should be more persuasive. I know he's planning to stop my auction, but he must agree not to interfere and to let the buyers leave Morocco with their purchases."

"And if he won't agree?" It was an outrageous demand. Ekman thought Barrada would never consent.

"Then things will go very badly for you, your lovely companion, and all the women," Harrak replied.

"So we're the leverage?"

"If you want to put it that way, yes, all of you are my leverage."

"I don't think Barrada can afford to accept your offer. He'd lose every bit of credibility and be fired."

"Perhaps. But would the government be willing to admit they'd caused the deaths of two Swedish police officers and five European women? It would become an international scandal they don't want. Will you give him my message?"

"Yes, but I think you're making a terrible mistake. Barrada can't agree to your terms, and if you harm us and the women, he'll come after you and your organization with everything he's got."

"We'll worry about that later," Harrak said. The prospect didn't seem to faze him. Ekman wondered why.

"For now, just pass on the message." He punched in some numbers and handed the phone to Ekman. "It's ringing at the hotel."

Rystrom was in his room, pacing restlessly as he waited for Barrada to get there, when the phone rang. He rushed over to it.

"Rystrom," he said.

"Garth, it's Walther."

"Thank God. I was going crazy with worry. Are you and Valdis all right?"

"We're okay. For now. We're being held by the traffickers. I don't know where we are. They want me to give you a message for Barrada."

"I spoke with him a little while ago. He should be at the hotel in the next half hour."

"Well, here's the message: they want him to let the auction go through and let the buyers take the women out of the country. If he doesn't agree, they're threatening to kill us and the women."

"But Barrada will never agree."

"I've already told the kidnappers that. They think he'll give in to avoid an international incident."

"Say good-bye," Harrak said.

"I have to go now. Good-bye, Garth. Help us if you can." He handed the phone to Harrak who shut it off.

"I did what you asked," Ekman said.

"We'll see what the results are fairly soon I think."

He and the two other men turned and left the room.

Granholm had been listening intently to the conversation.

"Is Garth all right?" she asked.

"He's fine. He's waiting for Barrada, who should be at the hotel soon."

"Will Barrada do what they want?"

"I don't see how he can."

"Do you think this man is bluffing?"

"Maybe. If he goes ahead with his threat, there's no way out for him, even though he acts like somehow there is. I can't imagine what it could be."

"Walther, tell me straight: are we going to die?"

"Don't give up hope, Valdis. Everything is too uncertain now to give way to despair." He went over and hugged her tightly for a moment. "We have to be strong."

Rystrom had gone down to the lobby to wait for Barrada. When he saw him enter, he was surprised. Barrada's usual conservative business suit had been replaced by a green and brown field uniform with the shoulder boards of a brigadier general.

Barrada saw him, and noticed Rystrom's drawn face.

"How are you, my friend?" he asked.

"Not well. We need to talk," Rystrom replied, quickly leading the way to a secluded seating area just off the lobby.

"There isn't much time," Barrada said.

"This won't take long," said Rystrom, as he gave him Harrak's message.

Barrada was silent for a moment. "It can't be done. I have my orders and they won't be changed."

"So my friends and those women will be killed? There's no alternative? Can't we negotiate with this guy?"

"I know all about him. He never negotiates. We just have to go in. I know where your friends are and I have a busload of heavily armed men with me."

"But that won't help them."

"We'll see," said Barrada, standing. "Are you coming with me?"

"I need to be there," Rystrom said, as he got up. His heart was sinking as he thought about Valdis and Walther. Somehow he had to help save them.

92

Deaths

Friday, February 24, 4:40 p.m. The three men burst into the room with their guns out, startling Ekman and Granholm.

"Get up," screamed Harrak, and shoved them both out the door ahead of him.

His two men led the way, running rapidly down several twisting corridors. "Faster," he yelled, pushing his captives in the back. Somewhere behind them, Ekman heard barked orders and the sound of many running feet.

The two men suddenly turned into a room with Ekman, Granholm, and Harrak just behind them. They all stopped as Harrak slammed shut a steel door and slid home two bolts.

The medium-size room contained a metal desk, three chairs, and two tall filing cabinets. A large safe stood against the rear wall. Harrak's office was also his safe room, a place he could retreat to.

"Sit down," he ordered. Granholm and Ekman pulled over two of the chairs and sat facing the door.

"Your friend wasn't convincing enough. Barrada and his men are here now. Don't expect to be rescued. He's signed your death warrant."

"Let me talk to him," said Ekman in desperation. "We can work something out that you can accept."

"I don't negotiate. He had my offer and turned it down by coming here. I won't have a chance now to kill the women, but you two will die as they come through that door. You're lucky, it will be a quick death," he said, and stepping behind Ekman leveled his pistol at the back of his head. He gestured to Daoud, who did the same to Granholm.

Serhane stood behind all of them in the rear of the room with his gun at his side.

They waited in silence for several minutes and then heard a pounding on the door.

"Give up, Harrak, and let them go," yelled Barrada in Moroccan.

"Fuck you. I'm going to kill them in the next ten seconds," Harrak yelled back. "One, two . . ."

Barrada had six of his men in SWAT gear with him and motioned to four others holding a heavy metal battering ram. They swung it at the door, which gave a little. Rystrom stood next to Barrada, horrified by what was happening.

"Five, six . . ." They swung it again and the door gave some more but still held. They wouldn't be in time.

"Eight, nine . . ." Two shots rang out.

93

DISCOVERY

Friday, February 24, 4:46 p.m. Rystrom and Barrada and his men paused, shocked by the sound of the gunshots. Barrada gestured again at the men with the battering ram. With a huge swing, they crashed it into the door as it finally buckled and sprang open.

Rystrom had tried to steel himself, picturing his friends lying dead, but was astounded to see them standing, huddled in a corner of the room. Lying crumpled on the floor were the bodies of Harrak and Daoud with bullets in their heads.

Serhane stood over them, his gun now shoved into his pocket, as Barrada ran up to him and his men rushed into the room.

Serhane saluted and said, "I know you wanted to take him alive, but I had no choice, sir."

"You did what had to be done," Barrada said, and clapped him on the shoulder.

Rystrom had shoved his way in after Barrada. Going to Ekman and Granholm he gave her a tight hug, before turning to Ekman and asking, "Are you okay?"

"More than okay," said Ekman. "That's as close to death as either of us ever want to be for a long time."

Serhane and Barrada had come over to them as Barrada's men dragged the two bodies into the corridor.

"I'd like to introduce Senior Inspector Karim Serhane," Barrada said.

The three Swedish officers' amazement was written on their faces.

"We owe you our lives, Inspector," said Ekman, recovering from his surprise. His feelings had been on a roller coaster from peaks of anxiety and fear to resignation at imminent death, and then profound relief. Now he felt emotionally drained, as well as physically exhausted.

Granholm wanted to hug Serhane, but remembered that wouldn't do in Morocco, and just shook his hand, adding her thanks over and over, as Rystrom did the same.

"I only did what had to be done," Serhane said, embarrassed.

"No false modesty, Karim," Barrada said. "He's the most brilliant undercover officer we have. But there will be time for explanations. Now let's find those women."

The five women had heard the commotion and the shots, and stood petrified in the middle of their prison room as they watched the door swing open.

They didn't know what would happen to them next, but the tall, red-haired woman who came toward them was totally unexpected.

"My name is Valdis Granholm," she said in English. "I'm a Swedish police officer. You're safe and free at last. Do you understand me?"

At first they just stared at her, uncomprehending. Then they began to cry, with long, sobbing sounds. As tears streamed down their faces, Granholm went up to Ilinca, who stood in front, and held her close for several minutes.

When Granholm turned to Ekman and Rystrom standing in the doorway, they saw her face was streaked with tears, and these two, hardened officers found their own eyes had become moist.

94

EXPLANATIONS

Friday, February 24, 8 p.m. Ekman, Granholm, and Rystrom sat on one side of the small hotel conference table sipping the champagne and hungrily consuming the appetizers Barrada had ordered, while he and Serhane sat facing them drinking orange juice.

As soon as they'd gotten to the hotel, Ekman and Granholm had excused themselves to shower and change into fresh clothes. Now they and Rystrom were anxiously waiting to hear what Barrada had to say, but first he'd insisted on observing the amenities by having drinks and food served.

After a series of mutual toasts, Ekman finally said, "Commissaire, or should I call you General, don't keep us in suspense any longer, I don't think we can stand it."

Barrada smiled. "All right," he said. "I know you're concerned about the women. They've been taken in ambulances to Marrakech's Ibn Tofail University Hospital. I've ordered guards placed outside their rooms as a precaution against members of Harrak's family attempting to retrieve or silence them.

"Let me start at the beginning. As you know, I'm a divisional commissaire in the Sûreté Nationale, and as you see, a brigadier general in the army reserves. I report only to the minister of the interior, a cousin of His Majesty Mohammed VI. In actuality I work directly for our king, the source of all real authority in Morocco, on projects that are particularly sensitive.

"My country is modernizing rapidly, although customs and traditions still play a major role. But drug and women trafficking rings will no longer operate with impunity. They undermine His Majesty's efforts to make Morocco a modern country.

"The Joumari family's activities have been well known to us in the police for a long time, but they were protected by the *makhzen,* the elite who have traditionally run Morocco. Through bribery, and favors for people high up in the government, Joumari's operations had become untouchable. But with the king's new policy, and the old man's death that ended the personal immunity he enjoyed, everything changed.

"Harrak was oblivious to this, and still thought he was protected. That's why he believed he could kidnap you," Barrada said, looking at Ekman and Granholm, "or even kill you, and get away with it.

"Karim had been selected to penetrate their operation and had become a favorite of old Joumari."

"I even had some hope of becoming his successor and discovering everything about their activities, until Harrak took over," Serhane added. "I kept the commissaire up to date on exactly where the women were being taken and all that was going on, but I have to apologize to you," he said to Ekman and Granholm. "Harrak didn't share his plan to kidnap you and use you as leverage until it was actually put into operation and too late to warn you."

"It wasn't your fault," Ekman said. "You should know, however, that we suspected you of killing Ivar Skarin and the others in Sweden." He watched Serhane closely. Could he have gone that far to protect his undercover role?

"I was actually ordered to avenge Ahmed's death and was sent to Sweden to kill the people who'd murdered him, but of course, as a police officer, I couldn't. I was going to tell Joumari and Harrak that I'd become too sick to do it, and was heading back, when I learned the traffickers had been killed. It was easy to take credit for it. From my point of view, it was a stroke of luck that gave me increased credibility, even though Harrak still disliked me."

"Karim wasn't the only hidden operative," said Barrada. "Girgis Akhrif has been arrested. He was working for Harrak and told him where you were and what you looked like. We'd been watching him for some time because his bank account had become suspiciously bloated over the last year."

"I'm afraid rescuing us has ruined your plan to get hold of the auction buyers," Ekman said.

"Not at all. We've just altered our plans. The buyers are due to arrive in two days. When they show up at the warehouse, they'll be greeted by our friend here," Barrada said, turning to Serhane. "Once they're seated in the auction room, my men will close in. After we arrest the other members of Joumari's family, it will be a clean sweep."

"Will you need to keep the women as witnesses?" asked Granholm, obviously concerned for them.

"No," Barrada replied. "With the information we have and what we'll learn from Harrak's files, we'll have more than enough to convict all the traffickers, and the buyers. The women will be free to leave. I'll arrange for the necessary travel documents for them, and for transportation for all of you to Sweden, and wherever else the women choose to go."

Ekman stood up and looked at Barrada. "On behalf of all of us," he said formally, "we owe you our profound thanks, and Valdis and I owe you and Inspector Serhane everything. We'll never forget you."

Coming around the table, the usually reserved Ekman went over to Barrada and Serhane, who'd both gotten up and, to their astonishment, he wrapped each of them in a bear hug.

95

WITNESSES

Saturday, February 25, 8:30 a.m. Valdis Granholm listened intently to the white-coated woman doctor, grey-haired and stocky, who had completed examining the five rescued women.

"So there's nothing wrong with them?" Granholm asked. They were speaking in English, their only common language.

"I didn't say that," the doctor replied. "Their physical injuries will heal with time and rest. But their mental state is something else. They're very fragile after having been held captive and sexually abused. They've gone through a horrible ordeal and will probably bear the psychic scars for the rest of their lives."

"But they're well enough to travel?"

"Yes, they can leave whenever they want."

Granholm had led the five women to a conference room. They were wearing the new, Moroccan-style robes and slippers she'd brought for them and sat regarding her anxiously.

"The doctor has told me you're ready to be released from the hospital," Granholm said. "Air reservations and temporary travel document arrangements will be made today, and you'll be able to go wherever you wish.

"I know you've all suffered terribly, and want nothing more than to go home. But I have to ask a great favor of you.

"The men who raped you have been arrested in Sweden and will be brought to trial. Your testimony is certain to have a tremendous impact on the court and ensure their conviction. Are you willing to return to Sweden as the guests of the government and testify?"

There was silence, broken when Ilinca spoke.

"I'll do it," she said. "I want to do anything I can to put those bastards behind bars." She looked around the table at the others. "What about it? Don't you want to make sure they're punished?"

No one else spoke until the Hungarian woman, Gizela, sitting next to Ilinca, said, "I'll testify too," and put her hand on Ilinca's.

"Is there anyone else?" asked Granholm. Two witnesses would be helpful, but it would be better if they all agreed to do it. She was intensely sympathetic to those who declined and understood very well why they were reluctant to relive what they'd gone through.

"Yes, include me," said a blonde Ukrainian woman named Ionna.

Granholm didn't attempt to persuade the other two women, both from Slovakia, who'd remained silent. They'd been through more than they could bear.

"All right, I understand," she said to the women who wouldn't be returning with them to Sweden. "Let me know where you want to go, and I'll arrange tickets, and travel documents and money for you. All of you spend the rest of the day recuperating. I'll be back tomorrow morning and we'll go to the airport."

That night, Ekman called Ingbritt at Carla's to tell her he was coming home.

"I should get in tomorrow afternoon," he said.

"I'll be there. I can hardly wait. It seems much longer than five days."

"Longer than you can imagine. I'll tell you all about it tomorrow, my love."

96

HOME AGAIN

Sunday, February 26, 9 a.m. Barrada was saying a final good-bye to his Swedish visitors in the Marrakech airport's huge modern lobby. The three women who were traveling with them stood a little way apart. The other two already had left on a connecting flight to Bratislava.

"Please come back to Morocco for a vacation, as my guests," Barrada said to them. "It's a wonderful country and it will be my pleasure to show it to you under more pleasant circumstances."

"We'd be delighted," said Ekman as they shook hands all around. But it would be awhile before what they'd gone through faded enough for him to consider accepting the offer.

With Barrada's help, the six of them passed quickly through customs and immigration, and only had a short wait at their gate before boarding the flight to Stockholm.

"It will be good to get home," said Rystrom as they settled in the business-class seats Barrada had obtained for them. "It's been quite a trip."

"More exciting than I ever expected," exclaimed Granholm, sitting next to him.

From just across the aisle, Ekman added, "If it were any more exciting I'd have had a heart attack." They all laughed, but he was only half joking.

Ekman had phoned ahead yesterday to Edvardsson, who'd contacted the necessary Swedish officials to explain the unusual circumstances. The officers, and the three women with them, were able to pass through immigration and customs without problems.

Two police cars were waiting for them as they came out of Arlanda's terminal for the drive to Weltenborg. Granholm sat next to the driver of one car, while the three women sat together in the back. They'd come to depend on her. She wanted to reassure them that she would look after them as long as they were in Sweden.

After Rystrom, Granholm, and the women were dropped off at the Thon Hotel, Ekman was driven home.

When he came through the front door, Ingbritt was waiting in the hall. He dropped his bag and took her in his arms. They kissed and held each other for a long time.

"How I've missed you," he said.

"No more than I've missed you," she replied. "Take off your things and come into the kitchen."

Seated at the kitchen table with a glass of Dugges ale in his hand and slices of cheese and ham on a plate in front of him, Ekman heaved a deep sigh of relief. He had a hard time believing that just two days ago he'd been moments away from death.

"Now, tell me all about your trip," said Ingbritt.

"Well, we rescued the women we'd gone to find and three of the five have come back with us to testify against their rapists." And then he decided to tell her everything.

When he'd finished, she'd turned pale and reached across the table to hold his hand. All her pervasive fears for his safety had nearly become reality.

"If I'd even suspected that something like that could happen, that you'd be in such terrible danger, I'd never have let you go."

"I'll tell you honestly, if I'd had the same suspicion, I wouldn't have gone," a laughing Ekman said. He could laugh now, but wondered what he'd actually have done if he'd had an inkling of the extreme risk he'd face in Morocco.

97

BRIEFINGS

Monday, February 27, 8 a.m. When Ekman, Rystrom, and Granholm came into the conference room from his office, they found the team members standing around drinking coffee and sampling the pastries he'd had sent up from the cafeteria.

Ekman went over to get a cup and a sweet roll before sitting down in his usual place at the head of the table.

He looked around and smiled at everyone, while Rystrom and Granholm took seats next to Rapp, who was facing him.

"It's good to see all of you," he said, and meant it, remembering how close he'd come to never seeing them again. Then he introduced Granholm to those who hadn't met her.

"I know you're anxious to hear what happened to us in Morocco and I won't keep you in suspense." He told them everything in more detail than he'd described to Ingbritt.

"My God, Chief, that was a close call," said Rapp. "If it hadn't been for that Inspector Serhane . . ." he let the words trail off.

"We're so glad to see you and Superintendent Granholm back, safe and sound," said Gerdi Vinter, as Holm nodded agreement.

"That goes for us too, Chief," said Rosengren for himself and Alenius.

"Alrik, why don't you bring us up to date on what's been happening here while we were away," Ekman said.

"The drug distribution network is still being rolled up," Rapp said. "It will probably be a month or so before trials start, but we're sure to get a slew of convictions here, and elsewhere in Scandinavia."

"Where do we stand with the search for Ostlund?"

"There's been no trace of him in Sweden or anywhere else. He's just vanished."

"Then we've still got six murders on our plate and no solutions. Ostlund looks good as a candidate for some of the three farmhouse killings, if we can lay our hands on him, but with Serhane out of the picture, we're still left hunting for the other killer we think was involved.

"Do we have anything more on Grundström?" For some-time now, Ekman had felt he was the most likely person to be Haake's murderer, since he had multiple reasons to kill him and no alibi for the time.

"Unfortunately not, Chief," Rapp replied.

With no tangible evidence, they couldn't charge him, let alone hope for a conviction. At least they'd be able to convict him of rape and the other charges, which should put him away for a long time.

"It's likely that one of the people who died at the farm-house, or Ostlund, killed Chafik, because he was a risk, and then Jakobsson, to silence him. Assuming that's so, we don't need to find who murdered them," said Holm. "But there's still an unknown, farmhouse killer out there."

"You're exactly right, Enar. And if Grundström didn't kill Haake, then it may also have been Ostlund, or one of the others who died," said Ekman.

"The only way I see to discover what actually happened in all these deaths, is to find Ostlund and get him to talk," said Rystrom.

"You're right, Garth, that's where we need to focus our efforts. Valdis, can you try to get Europol and Interpol to make the search a priority?" Ekman asked.

"I'll contact them again today and emphasize how important this is," she said.

"Thanks, Valdis," Ekman said. He had noticed an unusually large diamond engagement ring glittering on her right hand. He guessed it was the special gift Rystrom had bought in Marrakech. Rystrom was also now wearing a plain gold men's engagement band. Ekman looked around the table as he got up. "I'm very glad to be back and with all of you again, but now I'd better see the commissioner and explain how I got this tan when I was supposed to be working." Everyone laughed as he headed for the door.

Elias Norlander, Olav Malmer, and Malin Edvardsson were waiting for Ekman when he came into the commissioner's office at nine o'clock.

They all stood.

"We're happy to see you back, Walther," Norlander said. "Now sit down over here and tell us all about your trip."

For the second time that morning, Ekman described what had happened in Morocco.

There was a long moment's silence when he finished. Then Edvardsson came over and took his hand in both of hers. "Walther, I think God was looking out for you."

Norlander said, "I don't know how we'd have managed if we lost you."

"You were damn lucky," said Malmer.

"Yes, thank you all. You're right, Olav, I was lucky," Ekman replied. "And so was Valdis Granholm. I hated to see her in such danger. The threat of death would have been easier to bear if she hadn't been there too."

"So where do we stand now?" asked Norlander.

"Valdis was able to persuade three of the women to return with us. Their testimony should ensure that the rapists are convicted."

"I'll want to start taking their testimony tomorrow," said Edvardsson. "Do you think they're well enough for me to do that?"

"They seem like strong individuals," Ekman said. "And they're determined to see these men punished. They should be fine."

"Good," Edvardsson said. "Their testimony will make a critical difference. I'll ask the judge to continue the men's detention and set a trial date. It should take place in about a month to give their attorneys time to prepare, although I can't imagine what sort of defense they can come up with. I'm going to try to get the maximum penalty possible, fourteen years. I wish it could be even more."

"Are you sure you can get convictions?" asked Malmer, with apparent skepticism, always adversarial where Edvardsson was concerned.

"As sure of that as it's possible to be," replied Edvardsson. "The evidence is overwhelming, even without the women's testimony. With their testimony, it seems certain."

"The reason Olav is concerned, Malin," said Norlander, "is that he and I have been getting a lot of pressure in the form of calls and letters from very highly placed, politically influential individuals in support of these men, who are all prominent and well-connected." He paused. "It still seems to me incredible that they could have committed these crimes."

"Blind arrogance convinces some people that laws don't apply to them, Commissioner," Ekman said.

"Have you made any progress on those unsolved murders?" asked Norlander.

"I was just saying to my team that maybe Chafik, Jakobsson, and Haake were killed by the traffickers who died, or by the fugitive, Ostlund. That would leave us with the three traffickers' deaths to resolve."

"Do you have any answers yet?" Malmer asked.

"No, not yet. We suspect Ostlund probably killed one or two of the other traffickers, but the different methods used suggest that there may have been another killer as well. Theoretically it could be one of the traffickers who was later killed, but we can't dismiss the possibility that there's still another, unknown killer somewhere out there."

"Do you have any idea who that person is?" asked Norlander.

"We thought it might be Karim Serhane, but that turned out to be wrong. So no, at the moment, we don't know who it could be. But when we find Ostlund, we think he can tell us."

98

THE BALTIC

Wednesday, February 15, 10:40 p.m. *Thore Ostlund, wrapped in a heavy coat, a woollen watch cap pulled down tightly against the bitterly cold salt air, stared out across the Baltic Sea's dark water. He could feel the vibration of the huge ferry's engines six floors below where he stood leaning on the railing, alone on the deck. Sweden was far behind him.*

He'd parked his car yesterday in a space he'd already rented for three months in an underground garage four blocks from his apartment. By the time it was discovered he'd have been in Brazil for months with a different identity, and thanks to plastic surgery, a totally different appearance. The police will have a hell of a time trying to find me, he thought.

After going to his apartment and grabbing the already packed emergency suitcase, he'd spent the night in an obscure hotel. In the morning, he'd taken a cab to his bank and closed out his accounts, in cash. Another taxi had dropped him that afternoon in front of an office building two kilometers from the ferry landing. He'd walked the rest of the way pulling his small suitcase.

A forged Danish passport under a different name was in his breast pocket. He'd bought it for just this sort of situation right after the Dahlin woman escaped.

An hour before departure, he'd boarded the Tallink Silja line's five thirty p.m. ferry for the seventeen-hour voyage from Stockholm to Tallinn, Estonia. From there, he'd planned a route that would take him to three other countries over the next week before the nonstop TAP flight from Lisbon to São Paulo.

God, he was glad to be out of that mess. Killing that maniac Gotz had been self-defense. He had no qualms about it. His thoughts lingered for a moment on the dozens of women he'd enjoyed as Tomas when he collected them. It had been a satisfying operation in every respect that also had made him very rich. Too bad it had come to such a disastrous end. Maybe he could replicate it in Brazil. The thought pleased him.

He heard a soft footstep behind him and was about to turn when the killing wire noose slid over his head and was pulled tight around his neck. He raised his hands trying to get a grip on it to pull it away, but it cut into his throat, choking off his air. He couldn't breathe as he thrashed about and a rough voice whispered something in his ear.

Ostlund felt powerful arms lifting him up and over the railing as he plummeted down the side of the ship and into the heaving waves. He was dimly conscious as the icy waters closed over him.

"Give me a double vodka," the burly man in the navy pea coat said to the young woman working the ship's bar, and slapped some bills on the counter. There were just a few late-night drinkers in the room as he sat down at a corner table.

The man raised his glass in a toast, and murmured the same words he'd spoken into the ears of his four victims, "For Lynni," he said with tears in his eyes, and swallowed the vodka.

After a few minutes, Nils Dahlin got up and left the bar. Out on the deck he walked to the railing, not feeling the freezing wind. For a long moment, he stood looking across the Baltic's black water toward a distant shore visible only to him.

ACKNOWLEDGMENTS

Many people's kindnesses and efforts have come together to make this book a reality. My sincere gratitude and thanks are owed: To my friend, Howard Owen, for taking time from his own prize-winning fiction, to read the manuscript, suggest changes, and recommend it to his publishers; to Martin and Judith Shepard, copublishers of The Permanent Press, who enthusiastically endorsed this second novel of a late career effort and improved it with their thoughtful suggestions; to Chris Knopf, their associate publisher, for his perceptive comments; to Barbara Anderson, the most understanding of copy editors, for gently pointing out where improvements were needed; to Lon Kirschner, for his striking cover that conveys with graphic immediacy the sense of isolation and abandonment experienced by the victims of human trafficking; to all the others at The Permanent Press, and its literary agents, who have worked diligently to bring the book before the public; with affection, to my sister, Barbara, and my daughter, Alicia, who read the book in early drafts and offered many helpful